GOING DARK

KATHRYN M. HEARST

Published by
Wyndham House, Inc.

Going Dark © 2017 Wyndham House, Inc.

Editors
TIM MARQUITZ
DEBORAH OSMENT
CHRISTINE HUGHES

Cover Artist
DEAN SAMED

For Deborah

Acknowledgements

Special thanks to my friend and editor Deborah Osment. Thank you. I couldn't have done it without you. I pick up the phone a million times a day before I remember you're gone. Drop me a line when they get cell service in heaven.

To Dean Samed for the beautiful cover. Who says a horror artist can't do romance?

Also by
Kathryn M. Hearst

Tessa Lamar Novels

The Spirit Tree

Twelve Spirits of Christmas

Sinistra Dei Series

Feast of the Epiphany

Feast of Mercy

ONE

CRYSTAL BEACH, FLORIDA HAD A LOT IN COMMON with decomposition. It was slow, tedious, and systematically sucked the life out of a person. They say you can't go home again, but until recently, it had never occurred to Trip Peyton to test the theory. Nonetheless, she now stood outside the local bar waiting for the brother she hadn't seen in fourteen years.

"There she is." A man strode across the patio and pulled her into a bear hug.

Trip expected Ryan. Instead, she stood crushed against his best friend's chest. Nate had crossed her mind many times over the years. He may not have thought about her, but a girl never forgets the first boy she fell in love with.

Trip grinned as she dropped and turned, taking his arm with her and twisting it behind his back. He leaned forward to alleviate the pressure on his shoulder, and she pushed his face against the wall.

He half-groaned and half-laughed when she shoved his elbow toward his spine. "Ease up, Trix. It's me, Nate."

She laughed and released his arm. "You can't go around hugging random women like some drunk asshole."

"I *am* an asshole, but I'm stone-cold sober." Nate chuckled. "Should I be hurt you didn't recognize me?"

"Who says I didn't recognize you?" Her gaze wandered from his head to his boots. *My God, he's even better looking now.*

"Then why the assault and battery?"

The way his gaze moved over her body made her want to crawl back into his embrace. "Payback for all those times you tossed me in the river. I was too small to defend myself before I left."

Nate squeezed her bicep. "You're not small anymore."

"Job requirement."

"I'm not complaining." He slid his hands into his back pockets. His hips rocked forward a fraction of an inch, but the movement drew her attention.

Her stomach did a backflip, and her mouth went dry. She had to get a grip before she embarrassed herself. "Where's Ryan"

"He's in with the boss. It's going to be a while, so he asked me to take you back to my place and keep you entertained."

"Excuse me?" She'd spoken to Ryan earlier in the day on her drive from Camp Lejeune. They'd planned for her to meet him after work for a drink. Although, Nate entertaining her had its merits.

"That came out wrong." He massaged his elbow. "Ryan is meeting us at my place when he's finished. He didn't want you waiting out here alone, not that you need protecting."

She couldn't help but grin. "I didn't mean to dent your man-card."

"My man card's just fine, Trix."

"I go by Trip now, or Peyton." She offered her hand.

He canted his head as if he didn't know whether to shake it or kiss it. He did both. "I can't get over how much you've grown up. What's it been? Ten years?"

"Fourteen."

"Long time. What have you been up to?"

"Work mostly." Trip hadn't had an actual conversation with a guy in ages. She'd forgotten how much she hated small talk.

"No man to keep you warm?" He rubbed his chin as if considering applying for the position.

"Nate Benz, are you flirting with me?" She wondered how Ryan would feel about Nate hitting on her.

"That depends. Are you going to dislocate my other arm if I am?" He rotated his shoulder as if to remind her she'd wounded him.

Trip groaned. "Don't tell me you've turned into one of those sensitive guys who can't handle a little rough and tumble?"

"You caught me off guard. It won't happen again." Nate laughed as he grabbed her and tossed her over his shoulder.

He'd moved so fast, she didn't have time to dodge. Trip hung upside down, admiring the view of his backside. *Heaven help me. I'm in serious trouble.* "Isn't this against the bro-code?"

"I haven't broken any rules." His hand came down on her butt hard enough to elicit a yelp. "There isn't anything in the bro-code about sisters."

"I'm surrounded by men twenty-four/seven. I know the code." Trip giggled as she struggled against his grip. "Ex-wives, sisters, and moms are sacred. Aunts and cousins are negotiable."

"Get a fucking room," someone said from behind her.

Nate sighed and set her down. His face hardened as he turned to the other man. "Hey, Boss. I thought your appointment was at one-thirty?"

Trip understood the change in his demeanor. In the service, they called it military bearing. She walked to the other side of the patio and pulled out her phone. She hadn't liked Carson James before she left, and doubted she'd like him now.

Carson chuckled and made a show of glancing at his watch. "I thought you left an hour ago? Did you lose track of time trying to get that one in the sack?"

Trip bit back her words and scrolled through her email. Anything she said would likely come back and bite Nate and Ryan in the ass.

Carson whistled. "She's built like a brick shit house. Not enough tits, though."

Nate shook his head. "That's Ryan Peyton's little sister."

Carson glanced over and caught her staring. "Seriously?"

Trip didn't care for the look in Carson's eyes, any more than she cared for his attitude.

Nate nodded as a group of men walked into the bar. "Looks like your meetings about to start."

"I'll go see what's taking Ryan so long. He best not be sampling the product again." Carson took a step toward the door and turned back. "Take little sister home and fuck her silly."

"I'll think about it."

Trip waited until Carson went inside to join Nate. JJ's had a bad reputation before she left for boot camp, from the looks of things, it hadn't improved. "Carson hasn't changed."

"He's older and has more money." Nate frowned.

"You're working or him, too?" She figured Carson had a reason for wanting her gone. If things went south with whatever deal they were working inside, family tended to get in the way. Trip didn't mind spending more time with Nate, but the situation made her hesitant to leave.

He set his hand on the small of her back. "Let's get out of here."

She turned her face toward his and whispered, "Are you planning to take me home and *fuck me silly?*"

"You should know all about following orders." His smile didn't reach his eyes. "Something tells me you're going to give me a run for my money."

"I intend to try." She slid her hand up his chest. "Is Ryan okay in there?"

"He's fine, but we should go."

Trip looked him in the eye, all joking aside. "Is he using?"

"That is a question for your brother, but no, he isn't using. Growing up watching your mother get high was enough to keep him straight."

Trip released a breath she hadn't realized she held.

Nate walked behind the patio bar and retrieved a helmet. "Carson likes to push people's buttons. Don't let him rattle you."

Easier said than done. She smirked and followed him to a Harley parked beside the walkway.

He pulled his dark hair into a low ponytail. It had been a long time since Trip had her fingers in hair like that. The thought made her blush, something she hadn't done in years. Ten minutes with Nathaniel Benz had her nervous as a cat in a dog yard.

"Put this on." He tossed her the helmet.

Trip pulled it over her head and fastened the strap. "Let me guess, you keep this behind the bar for the lucky girl who gets to go home with you?"

He cracked a grin. "Nope. I don't usually take them home. I like my personal space."

She rolled her eyes behind the face shield. "I'm honored."

He threw his leg over the seat and balanced the bike before hitting the kickstand with his heel. "You should be. Usually, I fuck them in the bathroom or back of the parking lot."

The mental images caused her brain to stutter. "Such a gentleman."

He fired the bike up and walked it to the edge of the patio. "Hop on, sweetheart."

Trip set her hand on his shoulder and climbed on. "Don't you need to rev it up?"

He spoke over his shoulder. "Not unless you want me to make it vibrate for you. Only douche bags rev properly tuned bikes. This one's a cold-hearted bitch, but she'll warm up. Ready?"

Trip wrapped her arms around his waist and gripped his hips with her knees. "Yes, sir."

They turned out of the parking lot and took the entrance ramp to the freeway. Her arms tightened around him, and she rested her head gainst his back. She wished she had refused the helmet, missing the wind on her face. Considering her clothing was out of regulation for riding a motorcycle, she didn't want to risk going without the helmet, too. A Marine is a Marine, on duty or off.

Nate and Ryan had been best friends since grade school. He'd gone out of his way to make her feel included when she was a kid. Seeing him again brought back old emotions, but she wasn't that scared little girl anymore.

Nate turned onto a gravel road and eased the bike forward. Pine and oak trees surrounded the gravel drive. The street lamp marking the turn provided the only light until they reached a large gate. He pulled up and punched a number into the box.

"You okay back there?" Nate ran his hand over her thigh.

"Yeah, I'm good."

"I thought you were trying to give me the Heimlich maneuver, you were holding on so tight."

"You're so full of shit." Maybe she had held on tighter than strictly necessary, but she'd never admit it. The Corps took care of her basic needs, but neglected to provide physical contact with another human being Maybe taking leave would do her good. For the first time in years, she had nowhere to be, and nothing to do, *except Nate.*

He pulled through the gate, onto a paved drive. Two hundred yards past the entrance sat a building that resembled a hanger. Nate eased the bike to the garage and cut the ignition.

She slid off the back and removed the helmet. Between the security and the landscaping, the place had to cost a fortune. "You live here?"

"I do." He pressed a code into an alarm panel before placing a key fob onto a second box.

"Jesus, that's some security system. What are you keeping in there? Or is this to keep people out?"

"Both. This is nothing, wait until you meet the girls." He chuckled and pushed the door open.

"Girls?"

He opened the smaller of two garage doors and rolled the bike inside. Dogs barked in the distance. "I suggest you come in."

Trip crossed the threshold as two Mastiffs hit the concrete. She froze as four hundred pounds of pissed-off, drooling dog bounded for her. "Nate?"

"Paris, Nicole, *platz.*" Nate raised his fist waist high. "*Platz.*"

The dogs sat, tongues lolling from one side to the other. A third dog came barking up the drive. Her six-inch-long legs worked hard to carry her rounded body.

Trip grinned. "A Bassett and two Mastiffs, trained in German?"

"Shhh. Mabelle thinks she's a Mastiff." He squatted and snapped his fingers. Mabelle approached and rolled to her back, exposing her belly. "She's mine. The other two belong to Carson."

"Carson lives here?"

"This is his property. He lives in the main house up the drive. I'm in the apartment behind the garage." Nate stood and clapped twice fast and twice slow. The two canine killers trotted off while the Bassett stayed close to his heels.

"Is he married?"

Nate chuckled at the thought. "Carson? No."

She grinned, curious to see if Nate saw Carson as competition. "He's the type most of the women in Crystal Beach go for."

"He's your type?" Nate turned toward her.

"No. I like my men tall, dark, and handsome. Not rich, hot, and douchey." Sure, Carson could turn heads with his blond hair and dimples, but he struck her as the type who loved himself too much to care about another human being.

Nate ran a hand over the back of his neck, clearly uncomfortable with the subject. "Can I get you a drink?"

"Sure."

He led her down a hall and into a living space. "Make yourself at home."

Trip removed her boots and wandered around the room. Had she entered through a different door, she'd never believe the homey apartment shared a roof with a garage. It screamed man cave even without posters of half-naked women and beer bottle sculptures. She picked up a photo of a little girl. "Who's this?"

"Sophia, my niece." He offered her a glass.

"Pretty girl." Trip returned the photo and sipped her whiskey.

"Thanks. She lives up north." He plopped down on the couch and grabbed the remote control.

Trip tilted her head. Had he brought her here to watch tv? Where had the smooth-talking guy from the bar gone? She could practically see the wheels turning in his head. Was he nervous? "What's wrong?"

"Nothing." He clicked through the channels. "Come sit for a while."

"I thought you were ordered to have sex with me?"

He laughed. "I was thinking about it, but I'm having second thoughts about sleeping with my best friend's sister."

Two

NATE SEARCHED FOR A MOVIE AS TRIP PACED the living room. The woman needed to relax. She kicked off enough nervous energy to power half of Crystal Beach. Ryan warned him she'd changed, but he didn't mention how. Nate remembered her as a shy, lanky, kid who'd gotten knocked up her junior year of high school. The woman standing in front of him could stun the ticks off a dog.

"You like the military?" He found an action movie and set the remote to the side.

"I love it. I'm the youngest female Gunnery Sergeant in my division."

"That's impressive." Nate couldn't help but stare. Bits of the girl he'd known remained, like the way her lips curled on one side when she looked at him. *Those eyes.* They'd always reminded him of a winter sky. *Damn, she's beautiful.*

"What do you do for Carson?" Trip sat beside him. Close enough that her scent invaded his space, but not close enough to feel her tight body against his.

"A little of this and a little of that. Officially, I manage the bar and the restaurant."

Trip tilted her head. The look in her eye told him she caught on quick. Considering her line of work, it'd be best if he kept her at a distance from the business. Marines were one step away from cops, but a little fun wouldn't hurt. He slid his arm around her shoulder and turned her to face him. "How long are you in town?"

"A couple of months." Her gaze dropped to his mouth and returned to his eyes.

Who taught her how to flirt like that? He hooked his arm around her neck and pulled her closer, brushing his lips across her temple.

"We could have a lot of fun in a couple of months." She pointed to the loft. "Is your bed up there?"

"Yeah." *Damn it, I can't do this.* He couldn't sleep with Trip. Growing up, she was like a sister. He moved his arm and eased away from her. "Relax, babe. Ryan will be here soon."

Trip glanced at the television, stood, and walked to the stairs. Her hips swayed back and forth, hypnotizing him. His breath caught as she pulled her tank top over her head and tossed it to the side.

She turned and grinned, bare-chested and eyes down. "Are you coming?"

"Right behind you." *To hell with it.* He stood, finished his drink, and followed.

Nate caught up with her in the bedroom. He moved behind her and ran his hands over her hips. The woman had him captivated from the moment he'd laid eyes on her that night.

Trip turned in his arms and unbuttoned his shirt while he fumbled with her belt. He hoped she hadn't noticed how his hands shook when he lowered her zipper.

Trip pulled his shirt from his shoulder and nuzzled into his chest.

Her hair smelled like vanilla and spice. The warm press of her body brought out his protective instincts. Somehow, she didn't seem so tough when she sighed in his arms. "Are you okay?"

"More than okay." Trip nodded and drew his nipple between her teeth.

"Ouch. That's how this is gonna go?" He ran his hands down her back and gripped her ass.

"Uh huh." She turned her face toward his and bit her lip.

The look in her eyes tightened his gut and sent his blood surging south. In a couple of months, she'd go back to Lejeune. How much damage could they do in such a short period of time?

Trip pulled his head to hers and kissed him. Her fingers tangled in his hair, holding him in place as her tongue invaded his mouth. The woman knew what she wanted and how to get it.

Nate's cell phone rang. "Damn it."

"Ignore it." She wrapped her arms tighter around him.

"I can't." He pulled away and grabbed the phone.

Her cell rang, too. She patted her back pockets. "Shit, where is it?"

Nate frowned. This is a God-smack. I have no business sleeping with Trip. Cursing under his breath, Nate went into the bathroom and closed the door. "Yeah?"

Carson shouted, "We have a problem. Ryan killed Domino and took off."

"Nate?" Trip called him from the hall.

He ignored her. Carson wouldn't appreciate the interruption. The less his boss thought about Trip, the better. "Where is Ryan now?"

"How the fuck do I know? He tore out of here about fifteen minutes ago."

Nate banged his head against the wall. "Are you sure Domino's dead?"

"Yeah, he's dead. I found him after the meeting with the Trevinos, right after Ryan left."

Nate's motorcycle revved below. He moved to the window as Trip shot down the drive. Nate ran to his desk to check the security feed. She knew how to handle a bike, even he didn't take the gravel that fast. *Where are you going, sweetheart?*

Carson continued speaking, "Three bricks missing. My guess is Ryan got squirrely, killed Domino, and ran. Marcy is with him."

Nate changed the feed to the secondary cameras near the road. *Which way did you go? She's heading for the highway.* "Ryan's sister just blew out of here. Something's up."

"I don't give a fuck what she did—"

"She got a call and tore out." He grabbed his shirt and pulled on his boots.

"Find little sister and get Ryan and Marcy to the marina, we have things to discuss." Carson disconnected.

Nate sprinted downstairs to his truck and snatched the keys from the visor. Someone had called. It had to be Ryan. Who else could it be? Nate didn't believe in coincidences, not when it came to business.

He pulled out his phone and headed toward the highway. Why hadn't he asked for Trip's number? Because his dick had done the thinking since she'd pinned him to the wall. He dialed Ryan. The call went straight to voicemail. "Hey, bro, we need to talk. I'm looking for Trip. Have her give me a call."

Not wanting to miss her, he held the phone while driving. *Where is she? What the hell is going on with Ry? Are the two of them in on something? No, Ryan wouldn't use his sister as a distraction.*

His phone rang. A female sobbed through the connection—not Trip. "Hello? Who is this?"

"Nate, it's Marcy. Ryan had an accident."

"Where is he?"

"On Oceanside. His sister just got here. She wants me to call 9-1-1."

"Trip's there now? Put her on the phone." *Damn, damn, damn.* A rustling sound filled his ear, followed by women arguing. Ryan must have told Marcy to call Trip. *If he can talk, he isn't dead. He can't die.*

Trip came on the line. "Nate, Ryan is seriously injured. He's nearly bled out. I lost my phone, and this bitch won't call 9-1-1. I'm gonna take her down if she doesn't call."

"I'll call, but I need you to do something for me." Nate prayed she hadn't forgotten the rules in Crystal Beach. Do as you're told, and deny everything if anyone with a badge asks. Trip had grown up with an addict for a mother. She could do what he needed done, but would she?

"God, damn it, he's going to die. I can't stop the bleeding."

"Babe, he's carrying three bricks. Do you know what that is?"

"I do." Her voice hollowed.

Nate hated himself for what he had to do. He wanted to be by her side to comfort her, but Carson would kill them both. "Good. Get them off him and get out of there. Meet me at the bar first thing in the morning for a drop. I'm calling 9-1-1 right now."

"How do you know what he's carrying?"

"Trip, the longer we argue, the longer it'll be before help arrives."

"I can't believe he's this stupid." She choked on her emotions. "I can't believe you *let* him be this stupid."

"I'm sorry, babe. Did you find them?"

More rustling filled the connection. "I got them. Tell EMS we're next to the bait shop. Call now. I'm out."

Nate pulled to the side of the road and reported the accident. He rested his head on the steering wheel and closed his eyes. "Lord, I have no right to ask anything of you. Please look after Ryan. He's the only real friend I have, Lord. He's a good guy, just stupid. Don't take him, Lord. He just got his sister back. She's a good woman. Look after her, too."

A motorcycle flew by with a trail of dark hair blowing behind the driver. "Slow down, girl."

Ryan had started the ball in motion, but Nate sent it into orbit. He'd involved Trip in things he shouldn't have. *She has a life outside this shit-hole of a town. I have to keep her away from me, Carson, all of it.*

Nate dialed his phone. "Marcy, get out of there. Meet me at the marina. Help is on the way."

"Are you sure?" She whined. "His sister just left with his backpack. She took it, she took the package. Maybe I should call Carson? I doubt she'll hand it over. She's probably going to the cops."

"Let me worry about Ryan's sister."

"I don't want to get in trouble with Carson."

Nate gripped the steering wheel harder. "You won't, hon."

"Forget it, I am calling Carson. No way this shit is gonna blow back on me."

Nate closed his eyes. "Marcy, Carson already knows about Trip. Meet me at the boat right now. You're in danger, sugar. Come now so I can protect you."

"Carson knows I don't have his stuff?" Her voice cracked.

"Yes, now please hurry."

"I…I'm on my way."

Nate made a U-turn and headed toward the marina. Two patrol cars and an ambulance barreled by in the opposite direction. He had to protect Trip. If she ran to the police, and Carson found out, he'd take his pound of flesh. Nate forced himself to calm and dialed his cell.

Carson answered on the first ring. "Did you find my stuff?"

"They're with a courier. EMS has Ryan, sounds like he's busted up pretty bad. I sent Marcy to the marina before the cops showed up. She's freaking out about the package. She's afraid you'll blame her for this." Nate bent the truth as far as he dared. "Why is Marcy involved?"

"Fucking Ryan, always thinking with his dick. I'll meet you there. Take care of the baby and don't let her leave."

"Baby?"

"Stupid bitch has the kid with her tonight."

Nate struggled to understand when Marcy had time to get her daughter from the sitter. "You mean she picked up the baby after they left the bar?"

"No, I mean she left the baby in the car while she partied *inside* the bar."

"Damn. Are you sure you want to handle this tonight? I can talk Marcy down and take her and the baby home with me." Nate's hands shook. If Carson got involved, it wouldn't end well for Marcy.

"Yeah, I'm sure."

The air left his lungs as if he'd taken a punch to the stomach. What kind of mother left her infant in the car of a bar parking lot? Marcy's emotions ran hot when sober. On the call, she'd sounded half-in-the-bag, hysterical, and thanks to him, behind the wheel with her child in the backseat. "I'll make sure Marcy and Izzy are okay."

"Get her on the boat and make sure she doesn't call anyone." Carson disconnected.

Nate hit the gas and hurried to the marina. If he got to her first, perhaps he could sober her up before Carson arrived. He sighed in relief when he pulled into the lot, Marcy's car sat crooked between two spaces.

He spotted Marcy on the dock. Her makeup had smeared down her face. She had dried blood on her clothes and in her hair. When she crumpled in his arms, the smell of stale cigarettes and beer made him recoil.

"Where's Izzy?" Nate glanced back toward her car, praying Carson was mistaken and the child slept safe and sound someplace far from here.

"Izzy?" Marcy furrowed her brow.

Nate snatched the keys from her hand and sprinted back to the parking lot. As he approached the car, the shrill cries of an infant pierced his eardrums. His hands shook as he unlocked the back door. *Damn, damn, damn.*

The smell inside the car knocked him back a step. The little thing reeked of piss. He bit back a slew of curses as he grabbed a clean diaper from the bag, then unbuckled the screaming baby. She'd soaked through her diaper, pajamas, and the car seat.

"It's all right, little one. I'll get you cleaned up." Nate opened her diaper and winced. He'd seen diaper rash before, but never like this. Angry red ulcers covered her from waist to thigh. This wasn't the first time Marcy had neglected her child.

Nate slung the bag over his shoulder and cradled the baby in his arms. A dent in the hood of the car caught his attention. He walked to the front of the car, and his knees went weak. The front bumper was dented with streaks of canary yellow paint—the same color as Ryan's bike.

Nate drew a breath and forced himself to calm on the walk back to Marcy.

"Where did you get her?" She scratched a spot on her cheek. Drugs had taken more from her than the ability to care for Izzy. A shell remained of the once beautiful woman.

"She was in the car, hon." He brought the baby to his shoulder and patted her bottom until she settled. "What happened to Ryan?"

Marcy's mouth opened, but no words came, though her tears returned. "I don't know."

She knew.

"Let's get you on the boat." He forced a smile and guided her toward Carson's pocket yacht.

Marcy stumbled as she stepped aboard. She glanced around, as if unsure what to do.

He motioned to a bench along the aft deck. "Sit there."

"I want to go lie down. I feel sick."

"Carson will have both our asses if you puke on his boat. You'll feel better with some wind on your face. If you have to, hang your head over the side. Okay?"

"Got that right, no puke on the boat." Carson unfastened the lines securing the yacht to the dock and hopped aboard. "Let's get this bitch movin'."

Marcy turned a pale shade of green at the sight of him but kept her mouth shut.

Nate took the baby to the cockpit and nestled her on the bench beside him. With one hand on Izzy and the other on the controls, he inched the boat forward without lights.

Carson joined him. "How's the kid?"

"She'll be okay." Nate sighed. "Let me talk to Marcy. She needs rehab."

"I can't risk her spouting off in front of the wrong people."

"Marcy won't talk. She's afraid of you. Give her a chance to clean up."

Carson smirked. "It's because of the kid, isn't it?"

"Marcy's a mess, but she's a mother."

"Marcy is a coke whore. That kid would be better off without her."

Nate hung his head. His throat constricted as he moved his hand over the sleeping baby's back. "Give her one more shot, for Izzy."

"I'll think about it. Head south."

Once Nate passed the wake-free zone, he opened the throttle and sped toward the Gulf of Mexico. His attention remained split between steering the boat, the baby, and her mother. Marcy rested her head on a cushion, smiling as the wind blew through her hair. Carson stood near her, staring out over the water.

Nate lost himself in thought. He wanted to check on Ryan's condition and make sure Trip knew she didn't have to go through this alone.

"Hey, Nate." Marcy smiled.

"Feeling better?"

"Yeah, thanks."

"I need to get Marcy to Sarasota tonight." Carson flopped down in the chair beside Nate. "Maybe I'll hang around, for old time sake."

"Sara-freaking-sota with Carson-freaking-James." She grinned.

Carson pulled her to his chest. "I'm going to grab a drink, want something?"

Marcy nodded. "Sure."

Nate opened the throttle and headed south. Carson counted on him to fix things. He paid him well and gave him a place to stay. Nate rarely asked questions, but he'd stood by Carson long enough to know the man's moods, and tonight Carson bordered on psychotic. Sometimes the best way to clean up a mess was to prevent it, and but he hoped Carson would show mercy.

Marcy motioned to the baby. "You're good with her."

"I don't mind babies."

"I'm not cut out for parenthood. Thank goodness for Ryan's momma. She helps me out, treats her really well considering she might not be Ryan's."

"I told you I'd have a paternity test, and I can snatch a piece of Carson's hair. We can put an end to the mystery."

Marcy's face crumpled. "I can't take the chance. If she's Carson's, he'll take her from me."

Nate shook his head. "What are you going to tell her when she's old enough to ask?"

"That Ryan is her daddy."

"Has he claimed her?"

"No, but he will. His momma says she looks just like him."

Nate knew Ryan well enough to know he'd never claim that child without proof she was his. "What happened at the bar tonight?"

Marcy shrugged.

"Where were you two headed?"

"A party at USF. Ryan said something about a buyer."

Nate ran a hand over the back of his neck. Ryan selling what didn't belong to him explained the heroin. "Marcy, did you know Ryan shot Domino tonight?"

Her eyes went wide. "Ryan wouldn't…"

"Tell me everything you know."

"I was waiting for him to finish up. We had plans to go to Tampa."

"To the party, to sell the drugs?"

She hesitated then nodded. "After you left, Ryan and I had a drink with Domino. They were waiting for someone to come in."

"Who?"

"I don't know. They were shooting pool. Then that asshole cop, Daugherty, came in. He was drunk, wouldn't take no for an answer. I went looking for Ryan, but he and Domino must have gone into the office. I hid out in the lady's room until Ryan called. He told me to meet him outside. Then we left."

Nate frowned. He and Carson had debated putting video surveillance in the bar but decided against it. Too many illegal things happened at JJ's, no sense in handing the cops evidence on a silver platter. "You're sure they were waiting for someone?"

"Yes, but I don't know who or why." She shrugged. "How long do I need to stay away? I didn't bring any clothes. I have work tomorrow. I…I need to check on Ryan."

Nate folded his arms. "You can't work tomorrow. It isn't safe. Can you call in tonight? Leave a message for your boss?"

She nodded.

"Tell them you have food poisoning."

"Good one. What about Izzy?"

Damn, what about Izzy? He couldn't leave her with Ryan's mother. "Call your sister. Tell her about the accident. She'll take care of her until it's safe."

He hung close while Marcy called in sick for the next day and called her sister. His hand closed over hers when she started to dial another number. "No more calls. No one can know where you are."

"I need to make sure Ryan's okay."

"Carson will let us know as soon as he knows something." Nate smiled and slid the phone from her hand, tucking it into his pocket.

Carson joined them. He handed Nate a beer and Marcy a cocktail.

"Jeez, took you long enough." Marcy slid the glass from his hand and downed it.

"Slow down, or you'll puke it back up," Carson smirked.

She wrinkled her nose. "What was in that?"

"Margarita mix, tequila, and a half cap of G." He slid his arm around her.

Nate sipped the beer and set it to the side. "When's the last time Izzy had a bottle?"

Marcy stared as if she didn't understand the question. Her eyes rolled back, and her knees buckled.

Carson eased her to the floor. "Take us due west."

Nate's voice rose before. "What the hell?"

"Two caps of *'liquid G.'* It knocks them out but keeps them breathing. Need water in her lungs when she washes ashore…if she washes ashore." Carson kissed her cheek and stood.

Nate bit back his words. He should have seen it coming, should have never brought her here. Killing a woman well on her way to an early grave was one thing, but orphaning a child was another. Nate had to break free from Carson James before the blood on his hands grew too thick to wash.

"Five minutes west should be long enough. We have to get back to the bar."

"Aye, aye, Captain." Nate swallowed bile as he opened the throttle. *Forgive me, Izzy.*

THREE

THE CHAPLAIN MET TRIP AT THE EMERGENCY ROOM doors. She'd been around enough hospitals to know that ministers didn't work at this hour. Someone had told him to come.

"Ms. Peyton?" He had a kind smile.

"I'm Gunnery Sergeant Trip Peyton." She went into work mode, shoving her emotions into a box, locking them down. Her uniform would have provided a layer of armor, but she could fake it with rigid posture and a stiff jaw.

"Thank you for your service." He motioned to a small waiting room. "Please."

She hoisted Ryan's backpack higher on her shoulder. "If it's all the same to you, tell me what you need to say. I have somewhere I need to be."

"Is there any other family we can call?"

Other family? Shit. "Is my brother dead?"

"No, no, he's not. He's in critical condition. He nearly bled out, his spine and pelvis are broken. He'll need surgery as soon as they can stabilize him. The doctors have asked me to offer prayers and support."

"Can I see him?"

The priest bowed his head. To an onlooker, he appeared more concerned about Ryan than she did. Inside, she crumpled into a bucket of tears. Years in the Corps had taught her to maintain tight control over her emotions, or people died. If she lost it in the hall, Ryan would die. Keeping her shit together meant he had hope. She would provide the strength Ryan needed to fight. Not to mention, she couldn't allow the cops to find the drugs he'd carried.

The priest wiped his eyes. "I'll go ask. Wait here please."

Trip wandered down the sterile corridor. The gleaming terrazzo floors reminded her of her barracks, gray and white, polished to create a sense of order and control. Only people who spent a lot of time here knew the truth. Control was an illusion.

She knew which cubicle held her brother before anyone told her. People ran into the space, while others ran out with mountains of bloody linens and paper. Had they forgotten to put a biohazard container in the room or had they filled it? She sidestepped a nurse rushing from the cube and peeked inside.

The gurney sat at an angle. Ryan's feet at the high end, while his head hung at the bottom. Orange foam pads blocked her view of his profile. The blood drained from her face, leaving her clammy and trembling.

"Ma'am, you can't be here." A nurse grabbed her arm, but Trip refused to move.

Blood dripped down the gurney and pooled on the floor. Why hadn't they stopped the bleeding? A bag of someone else's blood flowed into his arm, through his body, and onto the floor. *What the fuck?*

"Ma'am. You have to leave." The nurse pulled her again.

Trip snatched her arm away and stepped forward. Ryan's normally tanned skin had no color. His skin blended into the white sheet beneath him. The purpose of the angle of the gurney clicked. They'd lowered his head to allow gravity to help blood flow to his brain. She followed the path of the crimson tube from the nearly empty bag on the pole to his arm.

"Ma'am."

"I'm his sister. You need to back off and let me say goodbye to my brother."

"We're trying to save your brother."

She rounded on the nurse. Now, wasn't the time for lies. She wouldn't allow anyone to pen her in the waiting room while they pretended to work on Ryan. "Then show me which one of these nurses is a doctor? Where are the monitors? He doesn't have enough blood in him to keep his heart pumping."

The nurse gave up and stepped out of the room.

These fuckers left Ryan here to die. They didn't plan to take him to surgery, or he wouldn't still be here. They'd given her brother up for dead. "I want to speak with a doctor, now."

"Miss…"

"I'm a combat-trained Special Operations Gunnery Sergeant in the United States Marine Corps. Get a physician in here now, or I will find one myself."

All except one nurse left the cubicle. He tended to the IV in Ryan's arm as Trip took Ryan's other hand. His skin reminded her of a corpse. Even her brother had given up the fight. *God, I can't do this. I can't do this, please.*

"Hang in there, Ry. Just for a few more minutes." She met the nurse's eyes. "Can you call our mother? She needs to see him before he dies."

The nurse jotted down the number and left the cube as a physician entered the room.

Trip dropped Ryan's hand and stood. "Why aren't you doing anything to help him?"

"Miss…"

"Peyton."

"We aren't a trauma center. We are waiting for transport. I called Medevac, but they're grounded due to fog."

"I understand. So, the plan is to let him die?"

"The plan is to get some blood in him and move him to a facility that can help."

"Give me the odds. I want the percentages."

He stared at Ryan. "If this were my brother, I'd start making arrangements."

She smirked. "If this were your brother, you'd have ordered three times the amount of blood you have flowing into him and rolled him onto his side to pack the wound and stop the blood loss. Immobilizing his spine doesn't mean shit if he doesn't have oxygen getting to his brain."

The doctor looked her over, noting the blood on her jeans. "Nurse, get the trauma team back in here, and get Sergeant Peyton out of here."

Trip turned and left the emergency room. She needed to get rid of the drugs in the backpack. Maybe they would try to help Ryan, but they could just as easily let him bleed out waiting for an ambulance. She had no control here, but Trip could save his name. Ryan didn't deserve to be labeled a drug dealer, even if that's exactly how he made his money.

To get through this, she focused on what needed to be done, keeping her emotions in a small, black corner of her brain. She needed to call Nate but didn't have a phone or his number. She hadn't thought to ask for Ryan's personal effects. His phone would have Nate's number in memory. That blonde twit, Marcy, had Nate's info. She'd called half a dozen people before she called 9-1-1.

The parking lot outside the Emergency Room had emptied in the time she'd spent inside. The doctor had told the truth about one thing, a helicopter couldn't fly in this fog. It clung to her skin, chilling her to the core. Three people emerged from the haze. Trip would have known her mother anywhere but prayed the woman didn't recognize her.

Keep on walking. Head down eyes low. Keep moving.

"Trixie Rae Peyton," her mother called.

Son of a bitch. "Mom?"

"You know damned well who I am. You just walk by and not say a word? After fourteen years, you show up and pretend like you don't know me?"

"I just got into town. I was planning to call tomorrow."

"What-the-hell-ever. Some things never change, do they, little girl?"

A man, Trip assumed to be her fifth step-father, tugged her mother's arm. "Come on, honey. We need to go see to Ryan."

"Why aren't you in there?" Dixie narrowed her eyes.

"I was just inside. I need to run back to Ryan's and get my car."

"Whose bike is—Is that Nate's bike? Why are you on Nate's bike?"

"I met Ryan and Nate at the bar. Nate let me borrow it to come here." Trip pulled the backpack up her shoulder. "I'll be back in twenty minutes."

"That's Ryan's backpack. Give it to me." Dixie snatched the bag.

Trip pulled it back with enough force to rip the strap.

"I said give it to me." Dixie glared at her with such venom that it took everything in Trip to keep a hold on the backpack.

"Are you seriously going to stand out here harassing me while your son is in there fighting for his life?"

Dixie slapped her face. Once again, she was seventeen years old, standing in their filthy kitchen. Trip, mourning for her child, had shouted at her mother. Dixie, high on God knows what had delivered the same sort of slap. That was the last time she'd seen the woman, until now. Funny how things came full circle.

Trip rubbed her cheek. "That's the last time you hit me. You so much as raise your hand to me, and I will lay you flat."

"Oh, listen to her. Big bad soldier girl."

"I'm a Marine. Now get your skinny ass in the hospital and say goodbye to your son before it's too late." Trip stalked to the bike, ignoring her mother.

Four

NATE HAD LEFT MARCY'S SISTER'S HOUSE before the sun rose. He could barely look the woman in the eye when she asked about her sister. News of Ryan's accident hadn't done much to improve her mood. Not that he could blame her, no one liked being woken in the early morning to find a baby on their doorstep.

Nate pulled into the parking lot. Only a black SUV and Carson's BMW remained outside the empty bar. He hoped someone had the good sense to get rid of Domino's body, but he didn't hold his breath. The SUV belonged to Lurch, the mortician's son. Likely, they had waited for him before anyone made a move.

Carson climbed from the vehicle. "Took you long enough."

"You haven't gone inside?" Nate pushed down his fury over Marcy. Spouting off to Carson on a night like tonight would be like throwing gasoline on a fire.

"I had to make a call." His cell rang. He glanced at the screen and motioned for Nate to go inside.

Nate walked into the empty bar and straight into the barrel of a gun. "Jesus, Mack."

"What took you so damned long?"

"Put the gun down." Carson strode in. "We had to take care of a hysterical female."

Mack reeked of alcohol and looked like he'd had one hell of a night. "Marcy?"

Nate nodded.

Carson turned his head, frowning. "How did it go with Marcy's sister?"

The question surprised Nate. Carson had shown no interest in the baby. "She's pissed, but she'll look after the baby."

"Permanently?"

Nate shrugged. "I don't know what will happen now. The baby stays with Dixie most of the time."

Carson shook his head. "The coke whore handed her baby over to the ex-junkie?"

"We could put an end to this and have the test. If she's yours—"

"She's not."

The look in Carson's eyes said the discussion of paternity had ended. Nate motioned to the office door. "Is he still in there?"

"He didn't get up and walk away." Carson laughed. "Where's the chick with my inventory?"

"She'll be here." Nate moved to the office and opened the door. Domino sat slumped in the corner with a hole in his chest big enough to fit a fist through. *How had no one heard the shot? Better question, why hadn't anyone cleaned up?* Nate turned to Lurch and Mack. "You two couldn't have started cleaning up before I got here?"

They shared a glance and shrugged. "Carson said to keep people out of the office."

Nate wanted to smack them. Days like this, he hated his life. "I'm gonna need a hand in here."

Carson followed the two men into the room and rested his shoulder against the wall. "I'm going home, been a long night."

"You okay to drive? Careful or you'll end up sharing a room with Ryan," Nate said.

"Yes, wifey." Carson turned and strode out of the bar.

Nate's mother used to say that death came in threes. He had two down today, what did that mean for Ryan? Even if he survived the accident, the Trevinos would claim their pound of flesh. Nate needed to get to the bottom of what had happened here, but with Marcy dead and Ryan in critical care, answers would have to wait.

"You two, move the desk off the rug." Nate arranged Domino's body on the carpet. Rigor mortis had already stiffened the muscles in his neck, causing his head to remain lifted off the floor.

"Dude, that's sick." Mack gagged. He worked as muscle for Carson but had a notoriously weak stomach when it came to dead bodies.

"You puke, you're dead." Nate rolled Domino onto his side, tucking the rug around the body.

"Carson had me stick around to help, said I needed to toughen up." Mack covered the lower half of his face with a bandana and helped move the desk.

"How's that working out for you?" Nate continued to roll Domino in the carpet, cursing under his breath at the blood pooled on the terrazzo floor.

"Go behind the bar and get the first aid bag." Nate moved to the storage cabinet and retrieved duct tape. He secured the rug around the body with several loops of tape. Then mopped up the blood with a stack of bar rags.

Adult men had about a gallon and a half of blood. From the looks of it, half of Domino's covered the floor. Nate tossed the bloody rags into a trash bag. He wrapped the remaining bags around the rug and secured them with the more tape.

Mack returned with the first aid kit.

"Get the hydrogen peroxide out and set it on the desk."

Mack stepped further into the office.

"Stop," Nate said. "Did you two morons walk in here earlier?"

"Yeah."

"Lurch, load him up and toast him." Nate thought about telling them to toss their shoes into the trash bag but decided against it. If the cops investigated, it wouldn't be his bloody shoe prints they found in the bar.

Nate poured the peroxide on the remaining stains. When the bubbling stopped, he wiped the rest of the blood from the floor and threw the rags into the bag, along with the roll of duct tape, a box of trash bags, and his shoes. He followed the guys out and tossed the trash bag in the back of the SUV with Domino. By tomorrow, the reaming evidence would consist of ashes and chunks of bone.

Trip pulled into the lot as Lurch climbed into the driver's seat. She glanced at the license plate, the driver, and the guys. The way her brain worked impressed and scared Nate. She seemed to take in every detail as she marched over to Mack. "Hey, Nate, I need to talk to you."

Mack turned and grinned. "Wrong guy. He's over there."

Nate chuckled at her confused expression. Most everyone said he and Mack looked like brothers, but Nate never saw the resemblance.

"Over here, darlin'." He turned and walked inside, expecting her to follow.

"That guy looks just like you." She handed him Ryan's backpack. "Cleaning crew?"

"Something like that." He unzipped the bag and inspected the contents. "How's Ryan?"

"He's in critical condition. They're trying to stabilize him to move him to Tampa. I've got to get back to the hospital."

"Damn. I'm sorry, Trip. Hell of a way to spend your first night in town."

She shrugged but turned her head and set her jaw.

"Thanks for bringing this to me."

"Why did my brother have three bricks of heroin?"

"That's a good question."

"Cut the shit, Nate. I'm not stupid."

"I didn't say you were. Ryan shouldn't have had that on him. It looks like he took the goods and ran."

"What about the girl? Why did he have her follow him? She knew he was carrying because she refused to call for help. She might have cost him his life."

Nate ran his hand through his hair. "Babe."

"I need to go." She turned for the door.

"Come home with me, take a shower, and I'll drive you to your car or the hospital."

She rounded on him. "I'll walk. You have other things to take care of. It's what you do, right? Take care of things?"

He took a step back. "Trip, you need to be careful. Forget whatever you think you know."

"Are you threatening me?"

"No, but shooting off your mouth is a good way to catch a case of dead. Let me take you home."

"I need some air." She walked outside.

He followed her out and locked the door behind him.

"Where are your shoes?"

He could all but see the wheels turning in her head. She'd figured it out the moment she pulled in. The cleaning crew, the looks on their faces—she was too smart for her own good. "I stepped in puke in the parking lot. Had to throw them out."

"Why not rinse them?"

He cringed. "I don't do vomit. Did you find your phone?"

"No."

He slid his arm around her shoulder, ignoring the way she tensed when he touched her. "I have a disposable in the car. Come on."

"Take me to Ryan's." She slid into his car and tossed the keys to his bike on the console.

Nate reached across and opened the glove compartment. He powered up the phone and punched his number into the contacts. "All right, but keep this on you until you get a new phone."

"Thanks." She sighed and rested her head against the window.

"Do you remember how to get to my place?"

"I don't need to know how to get to your place because I'm through. Thanks for the kiss and all, but I don't hang with drug dealers."

He grinned, knowing full well she'd come to him. She had too many unanswered questions. Questions, he couldn't answer.

FIVE

TRIP SLAMMED THE CAR DOOR BEFORE NATE could say anything else. She prided herself on her ability to judge character but had made a mistake with Nate. How did Ryan get mixed up with this? How deep was he involved?

She slipped in the front door and stopped in her tracks. Someone had wrecked the house. Out of habit, she reached for her weapon. Finding nothing but Nate's disposable cell phone, she listened and crept into the living room. A bomb exploding would have caused less damage. The contents of the shelves lay on the floor. Couch cushions were cut and tossed around.

Whoever had done this trashed the kitchen, too. Trip slid a butcher knife off the counter and eased into the hall. Her back pressed against the wall, she peeked around the corner. A man walked out of Ryan's room with a gun in his hand.

Hispanic, a little over six feet, two hundred pounds or so, Trip weighed her options. She could stay put and wait for him to leave or could go on the offensive. The stress of the previous night had her on edge. Beating the hell out of someone would help blow off some steam, but he had a gun.

No random break in, this guy had come for the drugs, which meant he had answers. She drew a breath and went to the quiet place in her subconscious, the place where clarity reigned. Trip waited until he came close and lunged at him. She sank the knife into his shoulder and knocked the gun from his hand.

He turned and slammed her into the wall, hard enough to force the air from her lungs. She shoved her fingers into his stab wound and pulled. He pushed her aside, but Trip managed to grab his arm. The guy lost his footing, causing them to tumble. Trip rolled into the fall and came to her feet, as his fist to slammed into her gut. Once again, the air left her lungs, and she doubled over. *Gun, I need the fucking gun.*

"Where is it?" He pressed his hand to his shoulder, frowning at the blood on his fingers.

"Where's what?"

He came at her again, a staggering wounded wall of a man. This time she had time to assume a defensive stance. Knees bent and wrist straight, she shoved the knife up into his gut. Trip used their size difference to slip between him and the wall as he staggered and fell to the floor. She'd lost her weapon in the attack. If he recovered, he could turn the knife on her. She jumped and allowed gravity to do the work as she drove her elbow into the base of his skull, rendering him unconscious.

The adrenaline rush ebbed, leaving her with a pounding headache and tightness in her chest she couldn't ignore. She rolled him to his side and retrieved the knife; messy business that did nothing to ease her anxiety.

Trip stepped around him, picked up his discarded gun, removed the clip, and checked the slide. Tightness changed to pain and spots danced before her eyes. *Of all the fucking times for a God damned panic attack.*

Racing against time and her body, Trip went into the guest bedroom and retrieved her personal weapon from her bag. The people looking for the drugs would send someone else unless, of course, Nate or his boss had sent the guy to look for the drugs. They hadn't had much time to call off the search, but why would Nate bring her here knowing someone was in the house? *This isn't his doing.*

She clutched her chest as if she could squeeze her heart through her sternum and force it to cooperate. Trip went to the kitchen and used the house phone to dial her team's secure line. A pattern of three tones rang in her ear, and she punched her code into the phone. When the operator answered, Trip relayed a series of letters and numbers unique to her team. All the while, she maintained a visual on the guy's boots. He hadn't moved.

"McGuire here. Peyton, what's going on?"

"I need to give report, sir." Her lungs forced her breath out in quick huffs.

"Report? You're on medical leave."

"I find myself in the middle of a situation involving organized crime and narcotics, sir."

"Proceed."

She had to tread carefully. Say too much, and incriminate Ryan; say too little, and risk McGuire refusing to allow her to poke around. "I came into possession of approximately three kilos of heroin at zero two hundred, at the scene of a motor vehicle accident. The driver, Ryan Peyton, left Jessie James' bar in Crystal Beach for an unknown destination, followed by a female, first name Marcy. The civilian carried the narcotics in a backpack. Mr. Peyton was in critical condition when last seen."

"Jesus, Peyton. Are you all right? Is this your brother?"

"Yes, sir. I handed the package to a Nathaniel Benz at zero four hundred. Following protocol and delivering the narcotics to local law enforcement was not an option. Mr. Benz knew I was in possession of the package…" She leaned against the counter and focused on slowing her breathing as she continued to relay events up to and including those at Ryan's place. "End."

"Contact local law enforcement and report the break-in. Follow up with the case number and any further activity." He sighed. "Why are you panting?"

"There was a struggle. I'm catching my breath."

"Call EMS."

"Not necessary, I'm fine."

His voice rose. "Do I need to issue an order?"

"No, sir. My heart rate is already slowing."

"What's your gut saying about the break in, off the record?"

"I believe Nathaniel Benz, or Nate, is working for Carson James. James is a local, comes from money, and owns the bar. My guess is both Nate and Ryan are working for him. It's probably a small drug ring. Someone in the organization is looking for the drugs."

"You are on medical leave. You need to get your ass to the hospital. It could be PTSD, or it could be something else."

"I will, sir."

"Anything else I should know?"

"I'd like permission to investigate. James has to get the drugs from somewhere, and we've known the Gulf Cartel has pipelines into the Tampa area for a while, but Intel hasn't found the connection. I'm here. I can get in and get out. I grew up with these men. I have an advantage." The tightness in her chest eased, allowing her to catch her breath.

"I'll see what I can do. In the meantime, lay low for Christ's sake."

"Any word from Rodriguez?"

"Landed and ready to rock and roll. Stop worrying. They know what they're doing. Your team can do one mission without your smiling face. Hang up, call the police, and follow up with a doctor."

"Roger." She disconnected.

Lieutenant Colonel McGuire had two years before retirement. Older and wiser than the rest of the team, he'd served as her surrogate father since she was fresh out of boot camp. He'd handpicked her and a handful of other Marines to serve in a Special Ops Homeland unit or SOH. In the years since 9/11, the focus of these highly-trained units had shifted from potential terrorist threats on American soil to include eliminating domestic organized crime, like drug trafficking. The government kept the existence of such units classified.

The guy in the hall moved his legs. She pulled the gun from her waistband and moved forward. Trip had no way of knowing when he'd come to, or what, if anything, he'd heard of her conversation. Regardless of her official status on the case, she couldn't risk him telling his employer what he'd heard. He could blow her cover before she got started, or worse, he could run his mouth and endanger her family.

"Get up." She kicked his leg.

"Fuck you. What are you? DEA?" Holding his midsection, he propped himself against the wall.

"I said, get up." Trip aimed the gun between his eyes, needing him standing so forensics would buy that she'd killed him in self-defense.

He pushed to his feet and took one step toward her before she shot him in the head. His body slumped to the floor. It occurred to her she could execute a man without blinking but had a panic attack when surprised. *It's all about control, Marine. Keep control, keep your life.*

Before calling 9-1-1, Trip pulled the disposable cell from her pocket and dialed Nate. "Head's up. Someone broke into the house looking for Ryan's bag."

"Are you okay?"

She walked into the living room. "I'm peachy, but the guy's dead. I thought I should let you know before I call the police."

"I'm on my way. Can you give me a five-minute lead before you make the call?"

"You got three." Trip disconnected and went to the guest room to retrieve her bags. Once the cops arrived, she'd be shit-out-of-luck for clothes. They'd secure the scene, and not allow civilians inside for days.

Trip dropped her bag by the front door and called the police as Nate pulled into the driveway. She put her finger to her lips and motioned to the hall as the emergency operator gave instructions.

"Thank you. No, I don't want to stay on the line. I'm fine." Trip tucked the phone into her pocket and set her gun on the coffee table.

Nate returned to the front room, eyeing the weapon. "Don't recognize him."

Trip couldn't put her finger on his tell but knew he's lied about knowing the perp in the hall. Nate chewed his thumb when worried. Perhaps he'd lost an employee. "I think he might have been at the bar. He looks familiar."

He ran his hands over her arms. "You seem pretty together for someone who just killed a man."

Trip hung her head and closed her eyes, conjuring up the image of Ryan on the gurney in the emergency room. Next, she focused on the memory of her fifth birthday, when Ryan had taken a beating for her after she'd spilled punch on the carpet. Memories of them as kids flooded her mind and tears began to fall.

"Shit. I think I liked it better when you weren't crying." He wrapped his arm around her shoulder and guided her to the couch.

"I'm sorry." Trip rested her head on his chest, sobbing. Not because of the guy in the hall, but because she needed to put on a show for the police and Nate. He'd lied moments before. She couldn't trust him but needed to get close enough to find out why her brother was fighting for his life in the ICU.

Six

NATE HAD NEVER MET A WOMAN LIKE TRIP PEYTON. She'd come a long way from the knock-kneed little girl he had known growing up. The cops had questioned her for over an hour, and she hadn't cracked or changed her story. Trip cried when she spoke of the actual killing, but he knew better. Academy Award winning actresses had nothing on her.

"Gunnery Sergeant Peyton, do you have somewhere to stay for a day or two? We need to process the scene," the detective asked.

"I don't know. I guess I'll book a room." Trip hung her head.

"She's staying with me." Nate put his arm around her.

"What? No, I can't. We hardly know each other."

"You can stay in my apartment. I'll sleep in the main house."

"I need your address, Mr. Benz." The detective held a pen, waiting.

"You have her number. You don't need my address." Nate stood. "Are you finished with her?"

"For now." He narrowed his eyes.

"Trip, grab a bag." Nate maintained eye contact with the detective.

"I can't let you go into the hall."

"I have a bag packed." She stood and moved to the front door.

"Did you pack a bag after you called 9-1-1?" The detective eyed her.

"No. As I told you, I just got into town last night. I haven't had a chance to unpack."

"I hope it's nothing serious." He put his notebook away.

"Me too." She turned to Nate. "Are you ready?"

"Yes." He stood and followed her out. "Ride with me. I'll have someone pick up your car."

"I'm not getting stranded at your place again. Besides, I need to go to the hospital to check on Ryan."

"It'll look better if I drive you."

She stared at him, then slid into the driver's seat. "I'll follow you."

He chuckled and went to his car. This chick might be the death of him if he didn't get a handle on his emotions. Not only had she returned the drugs, but she'd also called him about the break in. Trip surprised him at every turn.

Why had he lied to his boss to protect Trip? Sure, he wanted her, but enough to die over? Nate ran his hands over his face, then slapped his cheeks. "Get your shit together."

He waited for her to catch up before he turned onto Carson's property. Trip chewed on her lip as she followed him down the drive. Watching her in the rearview, Nate overshot the driveway. The car came to a stop with its front bumper resting against an oak tree. "Son of a bitch."

Nate threw the car in reverse, nearly crashing into Trip's rental in the process.

"Whoa there, cowboy." She hopped out of her car and slammed the door. "What the hell, Nate?"

"Sorry about that." He put the car in park and inspected the bumper. A faint scratch marred the shiny black bumper. Carson would pitch a fit when he saw it.

"I'm fine, but I think you owe the tree an apology."

"Yeah, yeah." He grabbed her bag out of the backseat. "How're you holding up?"

"I need to clean up and go to the hospital. I called on the way over. Ryan's in surgery."

"That's good news. Last I heard, he wasn't stable enough for surgery." Nate held the door open.

"Why am I here?" She faced him.

"Because you need a place to stay. I'll sleep in Carson's guest room if you want privacy."

"That's stupid. I don't want to put you out."

He set his hands on her shoulders. "Babe, it's no big deal. I sleep in the main house all the time."

"Right, but generally speaking an almost one-night stand doesn't move in."

He chuckled. "Agreed, but you've got enough on your plate right now. Ryan's my boy, the least I can do is give his baby sister a place to stay."

"Thanks." Her eyes brimmed with tears.

"Those look real." Nate wiped her cheeks.

"Screw you." Trip squared her shoulders, spoiling for a fight.

Nate's chest tightened as the scent of vanilla and spice reminded him of their kiss. His mouth hovered precariously close to her ear. "I didn't mean to insult you."

Trip wrestled her bag from his shoulder. "Mind if I get a shower?"

"It's your place now. Make yourself at home."

She started to say something but turned and walked upstairs.

Nate checked the fridge to make sure she had the basics, then went upstairs to grab some clothes. He didn't plan for her to sleep alone for long but would give her some space for now.

"Hello?" Carson came through the front door without knocking.

Nate met him at the bedroom door.

"What the fuck, man, someone plugged one of the Trevinos at Ryan's?"

"Juan Jr."

Carson grinned wide-eyed. "No shit? You're just telling me this now?"

"I didn't think it wise for you to be involved." He motioned to the bathroom and the sound of running water. "Ryan's sister. She came home and found the guy turning the place over. He attacked her, and she killed him."

"She's here. I'm involved." Carson ran his hand over his head. "We're talking about the chick from the bar, right?"

Nate nodded. "She's going to stay here until the cops finish at Ryan's."

Carson shook his head. "Not a good idea."

Nate lowered his voice, "She's cool. Hell, she called and gave me a head's up about the break in before she called the cops."

"No shit? Huh. Keep her on a leash. I don't need more trouble from a Peyton."

"I doubt she'll be trouble. She's a Marine. The girl worked the cops like a pro. She's like one of the guys. Better than most of them."

Carson smirked. "All women are trouble. Was Daugherty there?"

"No, must have been his night off." Unless he remembered wrong, Trip knew Detective Daugherty quite well back in the day.

"That wouldn't stop that S.O.B. from showing up. I'm telling you, the detective is on the Trevino payroll."

"Nate, where do you keep your extra towels?" Trip walked into the room wearing his robe, her hair dripping down her back.

Carson looked her over slowly and held out his hand. "I don't think we've been introduced. I'm Carson James."

She shook his hand. "Trip Peyton. We went to school together."

"Yeah? You sure? I think I'd remember you."

Nate grabbed Trip's arm and pulled her back toward the bathroom. She might as well have walked out naked, the way the thin robe clung to her damp skin. "In here."

She pulled away. "Sorry, I didn't know you had company."

"Steer clear of Carson," he whispered.

"Gotcha." Trip frowned as he pushed her into the bathroom and closed the door.

Nate shoved some clothes into a bag. The sooner he removed his boss from the apartment, and Trip, the better.

"You were saying something about her not being trouble?" Carson laughed. "Have her come to the house for dinner. She's a lot prettier to look at than you are."

"I'll ask her, but she's going to the hospital to see Ryan."

"Tomorrow then."

"She has some doctor appointment in Tampa. She's here on medical leave."

"If I didn't know better, I'd think you were trying to keep her away from me."

"She's smart. We don't need her up at the main house asking questions." Nate walked downstairs, hoping Carson would follow.

"And you don't think she's gonna ask questions staying out here?" He slapped Nate on the back. "You like this one?"

"I knew her when she was a kid."

"She's all grown up now."

Nate guided Carson toward the door. "That she is."

Growing up, he'd considered her a little sister or a gnat tagging along with him and Ryan. Her constant presence mitigated the amount of hell the boys raised. Looking back now, Trip probably saved him a couple of stints in juvie.

"Any idea why the Trevino boys were at Ryan's?" Carson walked outside.

Nate snapped back to the moment. He didn't need Carson thinking he'd taken a stroll down memory lane. "Someone tipped them off that Ryan was carrying. Marcy said Ryan and Domino met someone at JJ's. I'm not convinced he pulled the trigger."

"Any idea who did?"

"No, but I intend to find out."

SEVEN

TRIP WANDERED THROUGH THE APARTMENT, thankful Nate and Carson had cleared out. Both men aggravated her, for entirely different reasons. She knew Carson's type and avoided it. Nate, Nate was trouble wrapped up in a sexy package.

She pulled the disposable cell from her bag and called her commander through the secure line.

"McGuire."

"Calling to give an update."

"Proceed."

"I killed the intruder in self-defense after my last report."

"Did you get an ID?"

"Juan Trevino, Jr. I don't have the police report."

"I can get it."

The line went quiet. "Sir?"

"Peyton. How confident are you that you can infiltrate Carson James' organization?"

"I'm already in."

"You're a go on this end, but you need to understand you're going it alone. We suspect local law enforcement is compromised. If something happens, get out immediately."

"I understand."

"Keep your damned doctor appointments. If you have another episode, I need to hear about it ASAP."

"Will do." She grinned into the phone.

"Peyton, be careful."

"Aren't I always?"

He laughed. "I'm out."

Trip dropped into a chair and pulled on her boots, making a mental inventory of her gear. She'd need another weapon since the police had confiscated her personal sidearm. Typically, this type of situation called for surveillance equipment, a secure phone, and a team to back her up. Whatever case she built here would have holes with only herself as a witness. Trip had to know why Ryan had the drugs on him. If nothing else, she would save her brother's name.

Trip walked outside and into the blinding Florida sunshine. The richness of the landscape on Carson's compound surprised her. He'd created an oasis for himself. The main house sat a couple of hundred yards from the garage. It reminded her of a hunting lodge, with its thick wooden beams and craftsman details. Yet, it blended with the live oaks, palms, and hibiscus.

Nate and Carson stood beside Nate's car with their heads together. She had no doubt about Nate's role in the organization but didn't know if anyone ranked above Carson or the extent of the syndicate. Discovering the source of the drugs would go a long way in shutting it, and Carson James, down.

"Ready to go?" Nate walked toward her.

"As ready as I can be."

"Nice meeting you, Trip. My prayers are with Ryan." Carson headed toward his house.

Missions, she could handle. Hospitals full of her family, she could not. As much as she hated the thought of asking Nate for help, she had no choice. Leaning on him in her time of need could make him see her as vulnerable. If she played her cards right, she'd have him eating out of the palm of her hand. He'd always suffered from white-knight syndrome.

She waited until Nate turned onto the main road before she spoke. "Would you think me a wuss if I asked you to stay with me at the hospital?"

"No, but I'd be surprised."

"Why?"

"You seem like you can handle anything."

"Anything except my family." A twinge of guilt shot through her for using him as a human shield against her mother. Dammit, she didn't want to care about this guy. The moment she called McGuire, Nate became the enemy or at least a suspect. Trip hated that she had a hard time separating the adult Nate from her brother's childhood best friend.

He patted her thigh. "I won't leave your side."

"Thanks."

"Your mom's not that bad anymore. She's mellowed with age."

"You can say that because you're not her daughter. The woman is pure evil. We already had it out in the emergency room parking lot. I'm not looking forward to round two."

"I got your back."

The two fell silent during the drive to the hospital. Trip tried to distract herself by planning ways to get closer to Carson. Living on his property helped. Cozying up to Nate would seal the deal. She studied his profile as he drove. He'd be quite a catch if it weren't for his chosen profession.

Nate took her hand as they exited the hospital elevator. Any other time Trip might have protested, but given the circumstances, she didn't complain. They followed the signs to the ICU waiting room. Inside sat fourteen of her kin, most of whom she hadn't seen since she left for boot camp. Several people stood to greet Nate, but only her grandmother approached Trip.

She leaned down to hug the frail-looking woman. "Hi, Gramma Ellis."

"My God, your mother said you were in town, but I didn't believe it. I got your letter last week. Why didn't you tell me you were coming home?"

Trip kissed her cheek. "I didn't know I was coming when I wrote the letter. How are you holding up?"

Her grandmother whispered, "I love your brother, but I can only handle the family drama a bit at a time. I'm about done for today."

"Do you have a ride home?"

"One of them will drive me. Where are you staying? Out at the Peyton house?"

Trip nodded, not about to get into her current living arrangement or the reasons for it. "Nate can drive you home when you're ready."

"I'll drive *my* mother home. Some daughters take care of their mommas," Dixie yelled as she crossed the room.

Trip turned in time to catch the glare in her mother's eye. She'd seen that look many times in her lifetime. Dixie, not the brightest bulb on the tree, preferred to assess her victims. She'd study them, looking for any outward sign of weakness, the chink in the armor. Her attacks were tactical with the precision of a laser.

"Some people don't leave their families in times of crisis." Dixie set her hands on her hips.

Trip stiffened and grabbed Nate's hand to keep from decking her mother. She couldn't understand why the woman insisted on harassing her at every turn. What had she done to deserve such hatred, besides being born? "Mom."

Grandma Ellis said, "Give it a rest, Dixie. You haven't left the hospital since he got here, and you ain't about to now."

Nate cleared his throat. "How's Ryan doing?"

Dixie flashed Nate a smile. "He's out of surgery. They screwed his pelvis back together, repaired his intestines best they could. They say he tore his leg off, but for a piece of muscle. Messed him up bad."

"He's tough. He'll get through it." Nate squeezed Trip's hand.

"They say if he makes it he won't walk again." Dixie blew her nose into a worn tissue.

"They don't know how stubborn he is." Nate shook his head. "Can we see him?"

"Only family, but you're more of a brother to him than she's ever been a sister." Dixie pointed.

Trip hung her head. Out of respect for her grandmother, she'd take her mother's insults without throwing anything back. As long as Dixie kept her hands to herself, Trip would play contrite.

Her mother raised her chin in triumph. "Two at a time can go back. I'll tell the nurses you're his brother and sister."

"Thanks, Dixie." Nate ran his thumb over the back of Trip's hand.

A nurse escorted Nate and Trip into the Intensive Care Unit. Trip caught every third word as the nurse explained Ryan's condition: fractured spine, open-book pelvic fracture, shattered heel.

Trip stood beside Ryan's bed, her eyes following the wires and tubes from his body to machines. They had taped his eyes shut, and strapped his arms down. The sucking and whooshing of the ventilator reminded her of standing beside a much smaller patient many years ago.

Images of her tiny daughter flashed unwelcome through her head. At less than five pounds, Sarah went from the womb to an incubator. Her little lungs hadn't had time to develop before she came into the world. In her brief life, Sarah had fought hard to survive, but in the end, she was too small. All these years later, the week she spent as a mother haunted Trip's dreams.

This can't be happening. Not Ryan, not like this. Her knees went out from under her.

Nate wrapped his arm around her shoulders. "Whoa, hon."

Trip whispered, "I'm all right."

Nate tightened his grip. "You don't have to be strong for me."

She set her hand on Ryan's. "Hey, big brother. I need you to wake up soon. I don't know how much longer the family can be in the same room before someone goes to jail."

Nate brushed tears from his eyes. "Hey, man. You got to be tough if you're going to be stupid."

Trip turned to Nate, unsure of what to make of his words. While they had a certain poetic ring to them, she didn't care for him calling her brother stupid. The expression on Nate's face stole her breath. Maybe her mother spoke the truth. He was more of a sibling to Ryan than she had been.

"I love you, man. You get better so we can make Mardi Gras again this year." Nate patted Ryan's shoulder and turned away.

Trip kissed Ryan's cheek. "I love you, Ry."

As Nate led her from the room, she glanced over her shoulder, wondering if it would be the last time she saw her brother alive.

"He'll make it." Nate held the door open.

"I hope so." Trip collapsed into a chair in the hall, not ready to face her family again. Had she not been sent home, she'd be somewhere in Mexico now. Would weeks or months have passed before she learned what had happened to Ryan? She loved her job, but what about her grandmother? The woman had grown old. How much time did she have left? *Where will I be when she dies?*

Nate knelt. "Are you okay? You look pale."

Her chest constricted and her lungs burned as she tried to draw a breath. Trip pressed her hand to her sternum and leaned forward. Fireflies danced in the corners of her eyes and her heart pounded in her ears.

"Trip?" Nate grabbed her face and forced her to look at him. "Trip? Can you hear me? Nurse! Someone help."

"The Marine can't handle seeing someone in ICU?" Dixie laughed behind them. "Don't worry about her. She does this shit for attention."

"That's enough, Dixie." Nate frowned over his shoulder.

Great. Nate stood up for her just like old times. Why couldn't her mother go away, give her five minutes to get her shit together before having to defend herself?

If the situation reversed, and Trip was fighting for her life, Dixie would console Ryan. Her mother had the capacity to love. Trip had learned at an early age she could starve for lack of love as easily as for the lack of food, so she found sustenance on her own.

Two nurses came from behind the counter to assist, but Trip waved them away. "I'm fine. Just lightheaded."

"You sure?" Nate didn't look convinced.

Dixie threw her hands up and walked back into the family waiting room, cursing loud enough to be heard three floors down.

Trip whispered, unsure if she wanted the answer. "Is she clean?"

"Yeah, as far as I know." The space between Nates brows creased. "What's the story between you two?"

"I wasn't like her." Four simple words summed up layer upon layer of animosity between mother and daughter. Trip knew it deep in her soul. Dixie punished her for being different, but more than that, she punished her for leaving.

EIGHT

NATE'S ARM ACHED FROM LACK OF USE, but he didn't want to move and wake her. Trip had given him a hell of a scare but refused to see a doctor. In fact, she refused to talk about what had happened.

She looked younger when she slept, the hard exterior melted away to reveal the real woman. The way her hair splayed out on his shoulder made his palms itch to run his fingers through it.

Trip opened her eyes, and the peace left her face. She blinked a couple of times and pulled away as if confused as to why he sat so close. It unnerved him how quickly she could lock her emotions somewhere down deep where he couldn't touch them. *Or touch her.*

She stretched her arms over her head and yawned. "Any news?"

"No." Nate leaned forward and set his elbows on his knees.

Trip grinned. "Were you watching me sleep?"

He hated her fake grin and the teasing tone of her voice. "Is it PTSD?"

"It's lack of sleep, worrying about Ryan, too much caffeine, not enough food, my mother…Shall I go on?"

Nate shook his head. "I get it."

"I should go to the waiting room in case the doctors come to speak to the family." Trip stood and stretched.

"You sure you want to go back in there?"

"No" She plopped down beside him. "Thanks for staying with me. I'm sure you have other things to do. I'm okay."

Nate checked the time. "It's late. Why don't I stay a while longer, then take you home to get some sleep? We can come back in the morning."

"I can stay, you go home and sleep. Anything can happen, and I don't want to leave." She met his eyes with a cold expression. "This isn't a *we* thing. Ryan's *my* brother."

Nate shoved his hands in his pockets. "I'll give you some space."

Trip grabbed his arm when he went for the door. "Wait. I'm sorry. You don't need to go. I don't need space."

Her change in tone stopped him. Try as he might, he couldn't figure her out. One minute she acted as if she hated him, the next she said the right thing to keep him by her side. "Okay?"

She leaned forward with her head in her hands. "I'm sorry. I hate relying on you. I mean, I hardly know you anymore. Why are you being so nice?"

"I happen to care about your brother. I like to think he would look after my sister if I couldn't."

"So, this is about doing right by Ryan?" Her brows rose.

"You're a huge pain in the ass, but you're growing on me." Nate pulled her close.

Trip slid her arms around his waist. "Thanks, I guess."

Nate walked hand in hand with her into the family waiting room. Trip had to feel like an ant frying under a magnifying glass then they turned to her. "Any word yet?"

"No change." Dixie eyed her daughter.

Trip glanced between two empty chairs beside her mother and one empty chair on the other side of the room. She squeezed Nate's hand, then released it and sat beside Dixie. "Do you need anything, Momma?"

"No." Dixie moved to the far side of her chair. "When did you get into town?"

"Yesterday."

Nate seated himself beside Trip.

She reached for his hand as she glanced at her curious relatives, then turned back to her mother. "How have you been?"

"I retired last year. Eugene and I are engaged. He treats me real well."

"That's great. Is he the guy who was at the hospital last night?"

"No, Eugene's a truck driver. He's in Wisconsin on a run, should be home in a few days. He's real broken up about Ryan." Dixie blew her nose and stuffed the tissue into her purse. "Are you staying at Ryan's?"

Trip hesitated and lowered her head.

Nate said, "Dixie, someone broke into Ryan's place, tore through it. Trip walked in on them."

Dixie's eyes went wide, and she covered her gaping mouth.

"He attacked me and I shot him," Trip whispered.

"You killed someone in Ryan's house?" She leaped to her feet. "Did you call the police?"

"Of course, I called the police." Trip sighed.

"You didn't let them search the place, did you?"

"Let them?" Trip shook her head. "Are you for real? It's a homicide investigation, how am I supposed to keep the police from searching the house?"

"You stupid little bitch," Dixie's voice rose.

"Relax, Momma. The dead guy tore the house apart. If he didn't find what he was looking for, I doubt the cops did."

Nate motioned for Dixie to sit. She needed to calm down before she drew the wrong kind of attention. "Trip called me first, I was there when the police arrived. There was nothing in the house."

"Trip? Who the hell is Trip?" She glared at her daughter. "Is that what you're calling yourself now?"

"It's a military thing, my initials—"

"It's stupid. What kind of name is that?" Dixie plopped back down. "It's a good thing you called Nate. You don't have a lick of sense. Ryan don't need possession charges when he gets out of here. Did you think about that before you killed someone in his house?"

Trip sighed. "It's half my house, too."

"You gave up rights to anything in this family when you left." Dixie leaned closer to Trip. "What were you thinking bringing this kind of thing down on Ryan?"

"I was thinking the guy had a gun and tried to kill me."

"Oh, he had a gun, and somehow you managed to shoot him first?" Dixie's eyes narrowed. "I bet this is nothing new to you. I bet you've killed loads of people, haven't you, little girl? I bet you get off on it, like some psycho."

Trip clenched her jaw and turned her head.

Nate lowered his voice to a whisper. "We don't need to discuss this here."

Dixie frowned. "Who was it? Anyone I know?"

Nate sighed and ran his hand over the back of his neck. "A Trevino."

Dixie gasped her hand on her chest. "Oh, baby girl. Do you know what you did?"

"Not at the time, but I do now. I'm staying at Nate's until it's safe."

"It'll never be safe, not for you, or me, or any of us." She motioned to the room full of eavesdropping people.

Before Nate could speak, a doctor came into the waiting room. "Family of Ryan Peyton?"

"Right here." Dixie stood and swooned as if she'd faint.

Trip caught her mother before she could fall.

Nate shook the doctor's hand. "Nathanial Benz. How is he doing?"

"We are keeping him in an induced coma for the time being. With his spinal injuries, we don't want him moving. To be frank, he's doing better than we expected. If his vitals remain stable, we will operate on his spine tomorrow or the day after."

Dixie buried her face into Nate's shoulder.

Since no one else had questions, Nate continued, "When will you wake him?"

"One thing at a time. We can try after the surgery, but I wouldn't expect much communication. He'll know you are here, but he'll still have a breathing tube and not be able to speak."

Nate feared the answer but had to know. "Is he... Did he have any head injuries?"

"Surprisingly, no. I understand he wasn't wearing a helmet. Other than some bruising around his neck, he didn't suffer any head trauma. We're concerned about infection and surgical complications, but he is holding his own."

"He's gonna make it?" Dixie's expression brightened.

"I can't answer that, but I am more optimistic than I was yesterday. Your son is a fighter."

She broke down in tears clinging to her daughter. Trip held her as if she didn't know where to touch her.

"Thanks, doc." Nate shook his hand again.

"Is it safe to go home and get a change of clothes?" Trip asked.

"Again, I can't make promises, but he should be all right tonight. Take care of yourselves. You're no good to him if you're exhausted. He'll need you for the long haul." The doctor patted her shoulder and left the room.

"Momma, why don't you let Nate and I take you home for a quick shower? You'll feel so much better."

"It's too far, almost an hour each way. I'd never forgive myself if something happened." Dixie wiped her eyes.

Trip nodded. "There's a hotel across the street. I could get you a room."

"I suppose that would be all right. Nate, will you stay here and call me if anything changes?"

"Yes, ma'am."

Dixie hugged him, then mother and daughter left the ICU waiting room like the walking wounded. Nate didn't pretend to understand their relationship. He couldn't wrap his head around having an addict for a mother. His mom walked on water to get to church every Sunday. He'd grown up in and out of the Peyton house, but Ryan never wanted to discuss it. They had a sort of unspoken code—when things were bad Ryan stayed at his place. Nate had worried about Trip but had never intervened. He couldn't help but wonder how different their lives would have turned out if someone, anyone, had stepped in.

NINE

TRIP SAT ON THE BED WHILE HER MOTHER took a shower. She wished she'd thought to bring a change of clothes for Dixie, or thought of anything other than how to avoid her. Thankfully, the hotel's front desk had extra toothbrushes and deodorant. The majority of their business came from the families of patients. The thought left her gasping for air. She didn't like hotels but prayed they would need the room for a long while. *Ryan's going to pull through this. He has to. He's the glue that holds us together.*

Dixie came out of the bathroom wearing one towel around her chest and another on her head. Long ago, before drugs ruined her skin, she was a beauty. Her graying blonde hair still hung to the center of her back. Her blue eyes had clouded and hidden beneath sagging skin. Time had not been kind to Dixie.

"I always loved your hair." Trip smiled.

"I'm surprised yours is long, I thought they made women cut their hair in the Marines?"

"I have to wear it in a bun when I'm in uniform."

Dixie rolled her eyes. "I always wanted a blonde-haired baby girl. Izzy's hair is light like yours was when you were little. Maybe *hers* will stay that way."

"Tell me about Izzy. Nate mentioned her."

"She's two months old and a pretty little thing. Big blue eyes, like her daddy. Not gray, like yours. She's a good baby, too. Hardly ever cries."

The pride in her mother's eyes stung. Trip couldn't help but wonder what her daughter would have looked like had she survived. "I can't wait to meet her."

"Marcy, her mother, loves Ryan. They make a good couple, but you know your brother. He's as stubborn as a hound dog on a scent. Says he won't ever get married."

Trip grinned, remembering her last conversation with Ryan. He definitely didn't seem ready to settle down. "Where's Marcy? I haven't seen her since the accident."

"I don't know. Her sister called and asked if I could take Izzy for a couple of days. She said Nate dropped the baby off the night of the accident. She hasn't seen or heard from Marcy since."

"That's odd." Trip didn't think it strange at all. Anyone with eyes could see that Marcy had a problem. She probably went on a bender after the accident. Seeing someone you love that severely injured on the side of the road would rattle anyone, but it could push an addict over the edge.

"She'll turn up. She always does. Maybe this will be a wake-up call for Ryan. Nearly dying has a way of making you take stock of your priorities." Dixie hung her head. "He has to make it through this."

"He will, momma. Like Nate said. He's stubborn."

"What about you? Are you seeing anyone?" Dixie dried her hair, then dropped the towel on the floor.

Trip hesitated. She could talk about Ryan but didn't want to share personal information with a woman who had done nothing but pick fights. "You're pretty chatty. I thought you hated me?"

"Hate? You're my daughter. I don't hate you. I might not like you all the time, but I don't hate you." Dixie smiled saccharin sweet. "Can't we try to talk like we used to when we were little?"

Trip cringed inside remembering the times when Dixie would give her a blow by blow of her personal life. She'd known secrets about every man her mother had ever dated, up to and including the size of their dicks. "I guess."

"So, tell me about your life. What's his name? The man you don't want to tell me about."

She wanted to believe that things could change, that she could have some semblance of a relationship with her mother. She'd set boundaries, of course. Some things would remain off limits. "There's no man. Dating in the Corps is hard. I'm always working, and we aren't allowed to go out with other Marines unless we're the same rank."

"That's just ridiculous." She dressed in her dirty clothes. "How do they expect you to meet a man?"

Trip decided on her first boundary—any discussion regarding men. "I'll bring you some things from home if you tell me what you need."

"Oh, thanks, but no. My house is a mess. I'll make do."

Trip's heart sank. Some things didn't change. Dixie's place may be a mess, but Trip would bet her right hand her mother had something in the house she didn't want her to see. Ryan had assured her Dixie had cleaned up years before. If she didn't have drugs, what could it be? Her hopes of making amends with her mother began to seep away.

She rummaged through her bag and pulled out a brush. "Here, Momma."

"Thanks. How long are you staying?" Dixie sat at the desk and pulled the brush through her hair.

"A month or so. I have some appointments in Tampa." Trip flipped through the hotel info book. "Hungry? We could order pizza. It has to be better than hospital food."

"What kind of appointments?"

"Nothing serious. Checkups."

"You still can't lie for shit. Tell me what's going on?" She tossed the brush at Trip.

"I had a situation where four of my team members were killed. My commander wants me to take some time off to make sure I don't have post-traumatic stress." She'd not spoken of the losses since she gave her report. The sudden urge to tell someone what happened surprised her. Maybe getting it out would help. Maybe her mother would offer some jewel of wisdom.

"That PTSD stuff is bullshit. I've been through hell and back, and I don't have nightmares about it." Dixie pursed her lips. "You don't have PTSD."

Trip had visited Hell too many times to count and, yes, she had nightmares. Some things that happened to you never went away. Some wounds cut too deep to heal no matter how deep you buried them, but she didn't have the strength to argue. *I'm an idiot. Why did I think she would understand?*

"You're in a dangerous job. People die. I see the boys coming home in coffins on the news all the time and wonder when they are going to call and tell me you…" Dixie bowed her head. "We should go back and check on Ryan."

"I missed you, Momma."

Dixie's brows rose. "Could have fooled me, little girl. But what's done is done."

Trip sighed. Whatever moment the two had shared left as unexpectedly as it had come. "Tell me about Juan Jr."

"Juan Jr.? What about him?"

"That's the man I shot."

Dixie took a step back. She shook her head and pointed at Trip. "You didn't kill *a* Trevino. You killed *the* Trevino. Now that…that will cause some PTSD. They are mean sons of bitches. Juan's the leader's son. His *favorite* son. His brothers are crazy Mexicans. I hear they run drugs up and down the East Coast. Rumor has it they are cousins of El Guapo, or whatever his name is. You know, that cartel lord? You stay close to Nate and get your ass out of town as soon as you can."

"El Chapo?"

"That's him, the one who chopped people up for fun." She made the sign of the cross.

Trip ran her hands over her face. She doubted the guy she killed had ties to El Chapo. The guy went down like a sack of flour. Though, Dixie Dixie's reaction concerned her. Plus, Nate had lied when he said he didn't know him.

"We should get back to the hospital." Anxiety came off her mother in waves.

"You should take a nap. You heard the doctor, you have to take care of yourself."

Dixie slid her feet into her flip-flops. "Uncle Donnie is coming down from Orlando. I want to be there when he gets here."

Trip couldn't help but stare at her mother. "Why in God's name is *he* coming?"

"He's a paramedic. He can talk to the doctors, keep an eye on things."

"Mom, no, please." Trip's mind reeled at the thought of being in the same room with him. After all this time, after facing everything she'd faced, Uncle Donnie made her skin crawl.

Dixie set her hands on her hips. "Do *not* start that business again now. It was twenty years ago."

"I can't deal with him and Ryan at the same time." Trip hugged herself. Her stomach clenched and threatened to spill its contents.

"This isn't about *you*. This is about me needing family here."

Trip whispered, "Family? He's a child molester."

Dixie rounded on her. "I will not have you causing a scene. If you can't deal with it, then leave. He said he didn't mean it, and that's it."

"He didn't mean to put his hands on me when I was four years old, or when I was six? Oh, I know, he didn't mean it when he raped me at thirteen. Are you fucking kidding me?"

The slap came out of nowhere, whipping Trip's head to the side.

Dixie screamed, "Shut up."

Trip brought her hand to her cheek to ease the sting, but nothing could ease the sting in her heart. "I should have known better than to try to reconnect with you, you selfish bitch."

Dixie looked her over from head to foot, then up again. "You know what your problem is? You can't ever let anything go. Poor little Trixie, always the victim. Life's not fair, people make mistakes, suck it up and deal with it, or run away like you always do."

It took every ounce of Trip's training to swallow her mother's words. She made sure Dixie hadn't left anything in the bathroom, stuffed the key card into her pocket, and walked out of the room with her shoulders squared and chin high. She'd be damned if she let that woman see the pain she'd caused.

Trip silently berated herself for hoping that she could talk to her mother about her life. Unless the topic of conversation centered on Dixie or Ryan, the woman didn't care. She never had and she never would. Trip had no one to blame but herself. She knew better than to open up to her mother. Now that she had, it was only a matter of time before her words came back to haunt her. She'd shown the chink in her armor and Dixie would never let her forget it.

Dixie followed her to the lobby and scoffed as Trip checked out. No way in hell would she leave the room in her name unattended. She suffered a stab of guilt when her mother sniffled behind her, but Trip couldn't do this. Trip couldn't allow her mother to force her to sit in the same room as that monster, to pretend nothing ever happened, and to smile when he used a hug as an excuse to feel her up.

"Someone else could have used the room," Dixie said as they walked back to the hospital.

"I'm going to look in on Ryan one more time tonight, then I'm calling Nate to pick me up."

"What-the-fuck-ever." Dixie hit the button for the fifth floor. "I'm sorry I'm not perfect, but I'm the only mother you got."

"I'm a little old to need a mommy." Trip stepped out of the elevator and into the man who had haunted her nightmares since childhood. His long hair had turned from brown to gray, but she remembered how it smelled, like cigarettes and beer sweat. He'd grown soft around the middle, but still wore his jeans slung low on his hips. His walk had the same swagger, and his grin still lifted on the right side of his mouth. Everything about him told her that he still thought himself God's gift to women—and prepubescent girls.

"Trixie Rae, come on over here and give Uncle Donnie a hug." He held his arms out wide.

The hungry look in his eyes sent a shiver down her spine. Standing near him stripped away the years and her confidence and left the little girl he'd molested behind. He'd taken his time grooming her. The touching started innocent enough, but over the years it morphed into something dark and shameful. Trip sidestepped him, keeping her eyes on the double doors that lead to the Intensive Care Unit. "What's the matter, baby girl? That's no way to treat me after all these years." He grabbed her arm.

She turned on her heel, throwing the momentum into her swing. Her fist landed in the center of his face causing him to fall on his ass and his nose to erupt in blood. "Don't ever touch me again, you sick fuck."

"Security. Security." Dixie rushed to his side.

Several of the extended family filled the hall, looking from her to Donnie with shocked expressions. One of her larger cousins came at her swinging, but another grabbed him from behind before he could land a punch. "Whore." "Trash." "Crazy bitch." Everyone spoke at once.

Trip turned for the doors, but before she could reach them, two security guards arrived. Cousins, aunts and actual uncles shouted she'd assaulted an innocent man. One of the guards loomed over her, and she nodded.

"I hit him."

"Come with us." He took her arm and led her away.

She didn't bother to struggle. It would only make things worse.

They ushered her into a small room and closed the door. A moment later Donnie and her mother came in. For once, her mother had nothing to say. Instead, she clung to him, fussing over his crooked nose.

The heavier security guard turned his attention to Donnie. "Do you want to press charges?"

"Yes," Dixie said.

"No. It's all good. I wouldn't want it getting out that I got clocked by a woman." Donnie chuckled in his good-old-boy way.

"Go to the ER and get that nose looked at." The guard sighed when they left the room. "Care to tell me what happened?"

Trip shrugged. "Short version is, I haven't seen him since I was a kid and he put his dick in my mouth. My brother's in ICU, and I'm a little stressed. He put his hand on my arm, and I snapped."

The guard cleared his throat and pulled out a notepad. "What's your name?"

"Gunnery Sergeant Trip Peyton."

He sdid a double take. "Active duty?"

"Yes."

"I did three tours in Iraq."

"I spent a couple years in the sandbox, myself. My unit lost some good people."

He nodded. "Are you home because of your brother's accident?"

She shook her head. "I was here when it happened. I'm on medical leave. Seems some of the stuff followed me home. I'm seeing a shrink in Tampa. This, tonight, had nothing to do with PTSD."

The guy pressed his lips into a thin line and nodded. "I hear what you're saying. They discharged me when I started having nightmares after my Humvee ran over an IED. I was pissed at first, but I've learned that nightmares are part of it, just like having a short fuse."

Trip hung her head. "You're right. I've been edgy ever since I got back to the states."

He wrote something on the pad. "I'm supposed to call the police and trespass you from the facility."

Trip knew coming home would hurt, but she never imagined it would ruin her career. Something like this could jeopardize her security clearance. "I understand."

"However, given the circumstances, I'll leave you with a warning, but you need to go home tonight. Keep future visits short, and no more assaults."

"Thank you." She stood and offered her hand. "I really appreciate it."

His firm handshake and rigid posture reminded her of her real home. She needed to get back to sanity, back to the Marines.

Ten

NATE PULLED INTO CARSON'S DRIVEWAY and cut the engine in front of the garage. Trip hadn't said a word since she emerged from the room with the security guards. He'd seen her deck Donnie but had no idea why. Not that he cared, the guy was a class-A douche bag, but it struck him as odd that she'd snapped. PTSD or not, she could handle herself in tough situations, at least until tonight.

"Ready to talk?" The look in her eyes gave him pause. He should back off and let her come to him, but something else had happened to cause her reaction.

"I'm a damned idiot. How's that?" She stepped out of the car.

Nate met her by the front door and entered the alarm code. "What started it? Did you and Dixie get into it at the hotel?"

"Yeah, you could say that, but that's not why I hit him."

"What happened?" He followed her inside.

"I managed to get myself out of criminal charges, but I'm not exactly welcome at the hospital for a while." She sat and removed her boots.

Once again, she avoided his question. The walls slid into place around her, locking him out. Everything about her had changed in her time at the hotel. She struggled to hold back tears. Her posture screamed of exhaustion and frustration. Trip cursed and yanked at her boot laces. Nate recognized a woman on the verge of a breakdown. "What do you need?"

She stopped moving and looked at him as if he'd told her he'd just seen a leprechaun.

He sighed and drew her into an embrace. "Hasn't anyone ever asked you that?"

"No. I don't think they have. Some alone time, if you don't mind."

"Why don't you relax? Get a shower or sleep. I need to check in on Carson." Nate eased back to go.

"I think I'll crash." Her hands slid up his back, and she turned her face toward his. "Carson's a big boy. Join me?"

She'd done it again, changed her mind on the head of a pin and left him with whiplash. "In bed?" As soon as the words fell out of his mouth, he cringed. *Smooth, Nate, real smooth.*

"Yes, in bed. I'm too keyed up to sleep, and I don't want to be alone." She slipped her fingers beneath the waistband of his jeans.

"You just said you needed alone time."

She shrugged. "I don't want to think right now. If I'm alone, there's nothing to stop my brain from overloading."

"Come with me." He took her hand, leading her to the door.

"I'm barefoot, where are we going?"

"You don't need shoes." He tugged her hand when she hesitated. This woman needed someone to take care of her, and he happened to be in a caring sort of mood.

She followed him out of the apartment and down the sidewalk, to the back of the main house. As they rounded the corner, flood lights came on illuminating the pool.

"I don't have a bathing suit."

"You don't need one." He climbed the steps to a cedar deck surrounded by tropical plants in enormous ceramic planters. Nate opened the control panel and pushed buttons until the flood lights winked out and softer spots lit the edges of the deck. A hot tub sputtered to life behind him.

Trip folded her arms across her chest and shook her head. "I'm not going in Carson James' hot tub naked."

"Never figured you for a chicken." Nate pulled his T-shirt over his head. He had no doubt she'd join him, given the right incentive.

Trip watched him, then glanced at the darkened windows, and back to him. "You're serious?"

Nate dropped his jeans and boxers at the same time. "As a preacher on Sunday."

"Really? You're going to talk about preachers when you're standing there naked?" She glanced at the second story windows again.

Nate stepped into the steaming water but didn't take his eyes off her. "If you're shy, leave your bra and panties on. They cover as much as a bikini."

Trip put her hands on her hips. "I'm not shy."

God, she's even more beautiful when she's irritated. Even in the dim light, he made out the crease between her brows and her petulant frown. "Looks that way to me."

She grumbled as she shimmied out of her jeans and panties at the same time. The T-shirt came next and bra. True to her word, she didn't cover her chest as she walked forward. "Is this thing clean?"

Nate admired her lean form. Exhausted and disheveled, she still managed to steal his breath. Her eyes reminded him of a storm in the distance. The way she curled her lip made his lower abdomen tense. "Yes, babe, it's clean."

She sank into the opposite side of the hot tub, though he didn't expect anything else. Whatever the cause, her argument with Donnie and her mother had hurt her. As much as she tried to play it off, her eyes told a different story. She had the same haunted look she'd had as a little girl.

Trip blew out a breath and smiled. Her wet hair clung to her shoulders and chest.

He couldn't take his eyes off her. "Feels good, doesn't it?"

She rested her head against the edge and closed her eyes. "Uh huh."

The bubbling water splashed her chest just above her breasts. His dirty mind didn't give a damn about her current mood, but he cared more than he should.

Nate wanted to go to her, to touch her, but he bided his time. If only he could break through her defenses and get to know the woman that hid under layers and layers of defense mechanisms and pain. She'd run if he pushed for more than physical intimacy. *She'll run, and I'll follow like a damned lost puppy.*

He mimicked her, resting his head and closing his eyes. A long, silent moment passed between them. He could imagine many such moments in the future if she'd let him in.

The stars shone overhead along with a half-moon, lighting Trip's skin as she moved to him, her hands on either side of his thighs. "You sure no one's watching?"

Nate shrugged. "The house is dark. If Carson is alone, he's sleeping. If he's not alone, he's too busy to pay attention to us."

She climbed into his lap and ran her hand through his damp hair. This girl could do so much better than him. She played in the majors, while he still knocked balls off tees.

Nate mused at how his hands trembled tonight like they had the first time they kissed. He wrapped his arms around her waist, waiting for her to make the next move.

Trip pressed her lips to his. Like the woman herself, the kiss was rough and demanding, with a sweetness underneath that undid him. He ran his hands down her back and cupped her firm ass, pushing her forward against him. She drew his lower lip between her teeth and bit down until he moaned. She curled her fingers around his length, stroking him until he broke the kiss.

Trip whispered, "Condom?"

"In my wallet, but I don't trust them in here."

"Don't be ridiculous, they work in water." Trip came to her knees and reached behind him for his jeans.

"Babe, slow down." He pulled her back into his lap. Screwing a stranger was one thing, but he desired something more than sex with Trip.

"Why?" She wiggled, sending a bolt of electricity through him.

"There's no rush." He wanted to take his time and get to know her body. More so, he wanted to chip away at her defenses until her walls crumbled. He ran his hand up her thigh. "Just let me touch you."

"You didn't bring me here for sex?" She bit her lip as if holding back laughter.

"There's more to sex than inserting tab A into slot B." He ran his finger over her folds and circled her sweet spot. "Let me take care of you."

She reached for his erection, but he grabbed her wrist and put her hand on his shoulder. "Not in the hot tub, house rules." He pushed his finger inside her, then back to her nub.

Trip kissed him again, moving her entire body against his. He closed his eyes and returned what she gave. She held the back of his head, tugging his hair until he moved his head where she wanted it. All the while, he worked her beneath the water. Her thighs tensed, and she dropped her face to his shoulder, biting him gently.

The way she moved drove him crazy, hips rocking back and forth, her breasts pressed against his chest. It took every ounce of self-control not to set her on the deck and dive between her thighs. He couldn't take advantage of her in her current emotional state, even with her asking for it. She deserved more, and he wanted to give it to her.

Her back bowed, and she held her breath. Color stained her cheeks and chest. She gasped and cried out, coming apart in his hand.

Trip pulled back, but he persisted until she jerked her hips to the side. "Stop, please, stop."

Nate wrapped his arm around her and eased her against his chest. "You're so beautiful."

She nuzzled her face into his neck. "Give me a minute, and I'll return the favor."

"I'm good, babe." Nate caressed her back until she stilled in his arms. He wondered what she was thinking but didn't dare ask.

Eleven

TRIP RESTED HER HEAD AGAINST NATE'S SHOULDER, her mind racing. *What does he want from me? Why did he refuse to have sex? He wants me. The proof is stabbing my side. Why did he hold back? What sort of man is content getting a woman off with nothing in return?*

Trip needed to complete the mission and get back home, back to where things made sense. *Can I get close to Carson while getting naked with Nate?* The more thoughts that tumbled through her mind, the more she convinced herself any emotional attachment to Nate would compromise her mission, but he provided her with an *in*. She could do this, do Nate, without developing feelings. *What choice do I have?*

"I don't think my legs will work well enough to walk back to the apartment."

Nate kissed the top of her head. "You can stay with me here."

"Sounds good." Trip eased back and waited while he climbed out of the hot tub and hustled inside what she assumed was a bathroom.

He returned with a towel around his waist and another in his hand. Trip stepped out of the water and dried herself before wrapping the towel around her body.

Nate pressed his hand to the small of her back and led her through the bathroom and down a hall. The bedroom took her breath away. An enormous four-poster bed sat in the center of the room, a small seating area off to one side. The rich fabrics had a masculine feel despite the deep red color.

"Wow." Trip ran her hand over the carved post.

"Carson has good taste." Nate tossed several throw pillows on the floor.

"He decorated this room?" The idea of Carson James poring over fabric samples and paint chips made her grin.

"He has good taste in interior decorators." Nate moved to a chest of drawers and pulled out a T-shirt. "You can sleep in this."

"Thanks." Trip slid the shirt over her head and turned as he stepped into a pair of silk boxers. "Do you have an extra pair of those? I don't want to wander the house with my business uncovered."

He handed her a pair. "I'll get your clothes if it will make you more comfortable."

"Thanks, but these will work." She slid the boxers on and crawled into bed. Her body felt heavy and boneless. Hot tubs and orgasms had a way of doing that to a girl. She sighed into the soft sheets. "I'm exhausted."

"Me, too." Nate stretched out beside her. "Come here."

Trip scooted closer, and Nate wrapped himself around her body. His warmth provided comfort, but the closeness threatened to suffocate her.

She wiggled to put some space between them. "I can't sleep like this."

"Like what?" A smile played across his lips as he pulled her even closer.

"I hate it when people breathe on me." Trip struggled to break free, but he held her in place.

"Go to sleep, Trip."

"So, help me, if you snore…"

"Go to sleep, Trip." His voice turned husky, freaking sexy.

Sleep evaded her. She couldn't relax while held hostage in Nate's arms and legs, it made her antsy like she'd come out of her skin. Trip brought his hand to her mouth, kissed it, and sighed.

"You okay?"

She turned to face him. "I don't know."

"Want to talk about it?" He smoothed her hair back from her brow.

"Not really." She brushed her lips across the dimple in his stubbly chin, then dipped her head to his neck and sucked the skin between her teeth.

Nate made a growling sound in the back of his throat. "Thought you were exhausted?"

"What can I say? You turn me on." She slid her hand down his chest. "Fuck me, Nate."

He sighed and wrapped his fingers around her wrist. "Anyone ever tell you that you have a potty mouth?"

"Once or twice." She ran her foot up and down his calf. "Are we going to have sex or what?"

He brought her hand to his mouth and kissed the back of her hand. "Turn around."

"I can do that." She turned in his arms, her back to his front. "Do you have a condom?"

Nate reached behind him for his jeans and pulled a foil packet from his wallet.

"Thanks, better safe than sorry."

"Mmm hmmm." Nate slid his hand up her shirt and cupped her breast. Behind her, he fumbled with his boxers. "Get naked."

She managed to pull the waistband to her thighs before he pinched her nipple hard enough to elicit a moan. He tugged them down her legs as far as he could reach, and she kicked them off somewhere beneath the covers at the bottom of the bed.

Nate clamped a hand on her hip and pushed her forward. His lips on her ear, he whispered. "Reach down between your legs and play with yourself."

Her heart skipped a beat. If she could have an orgasm from words, the tone of his voice would have done it. She ran her fingers over her sex as he suited up and guided his erection between her cheeks.

"You're so wet." He nudged her entrance. "Is this what you want?"

"Yes." She pushed against him, but he pulled back and pinched her nipple again.

"Uh, uh, uh…"

She whimpered, still working her fingers over her sex.

Nate moved forward, sinking inside her enough to tease. His hand closed over hers, pressing her middle finger against her nub. He captured her earlobe in his teeth as he rolled her sore nipple between his fingers.

The combination of sensations threatened to send her into overload. Nate's tight grip restricted her movements. She arched her back and writhed between their fingers and his hips, forcing him deeper but not deep enough. "Please, Nate."

"What's the matter, baby?" He bit her neck hard enough to leave a mark.

"Give it to me." She hated the whine in her voice.

He thrust deep a few strokes, then resume the slow, shallow pace.

The pressure built in her core. "No, please, don't stop."

Nate shifted his weight and pushed her to her stomach. He came to his knees behind her and grabbed her hips, yanking them from the bed. His fingers dug into her flesh as he drove inside her in one hard thrust. The combination of pleasure and pain tore a moan from her before she could stop it. He set a quick pace, grunting each stroke as if to punctuate his dominance.

Her body tensed. "So close, don't stop."

Nate gave her no warning before his hand came down on her ass. The sound reverberated through the room and her body. She cried out, though she didn't know if pleasure or pain made tears spring to her eyes. The second slap didn't shock her, but it stung the already tender flesh. The third rocketed through her at the same time the orgasm exploded through her core. She gripped the sheets and buried her face in the pillow. Before the orgasm subsided, Nate wrapped her hair around his hand and yanked her upper body from the bed, holding her to his chest.

With one hand on her neck, the other between her legs, Nate shook as he went over the edge. When his body stilled, he pressed his lips to her ear. "You're so beautiful, so fucking beautiful."

Trip sagged in his arms. Her head rested against his shoulder as tears streamed down her face. She'd never experienced anything quite like what had happened. Nate had destroyed a carefully constructed barrier, the part of herself that allowed her to maintain control of her body. He'd started in the hot tub and didn't stop until he'd turned her into a mass of rubbery muscles and tears.

"Babe, did I hurt you?" He eased Trip to the bed and held her to his chest as she wept.

She shook her head. "No. That was…"

"Incredible." Nate kissed the top of her head. "I got you, cry it out. I'm not going anywhere."

Trip fought to remain awake until Nate loosened his grip, sound asleep. She'd lost herself in sex, but it couldn't happen again, nor would she allow it to compromise her mission. This was the perfect opportunity to explore the house. She moved an inch at a time until she managed to disentangle herself from him. He rolled onto his back but didn't wake. Morning sun filtered through the blinds, giving her enough light to find her clothes and the door.

She tiptoed down the hall, peeking into each room along the way. Trip had no idea what she hoped to find but damned sure didn't expect to find Carson James in the kitchen. He stood with his back to her and his head in the refrigerator.

Trip took a step back, planning to return to Nate's room.

Carson turned and grinned. "Good morning, sunshine."

"Good morning." Trip folded her arms across her breasts. While she seldom wore a bra, the way he eyed her made her uneasy. "You're up early."

"Hard to sleep with all the screaming going on."

She dipped her chin. "Yeah, sorry about that."

"Don't worry about it. I don't need much sleep." He set a carton of eggs on the counter. "Hungry?"

"Starved."

He motioned to a barstool. "Have a seat. Nate will sleep until noon unless you wake him."

"I hope you don't mind me staying out in the garage apartment for a few days." She seated herself on the stool and ran her hand over the smooth marble bar. The kitchen belonged in a magazine with its stainless-steel appliances and high-end finishes.

Carson poured two cups of coffee and placed one in front of her. "You're welcome to stay here. Nate's apartment smells like exhaust fumes and sweat socks."

"I'm used to it. The barracks smell the same, along with a cloud of bleach." She cradled the warm mug.

"Marine, right?" He sized her up.

"Yes, for the last fourteen years."

"How long are you on leave?" He pulled a frying pan from the rack and set it on the stove. She couldn't help but notice the way his muscles rippled when he stretched.

"A month or two." Trip sipped her coffee. The blend had a full flavor that spoke of quality, nothing like the swill in the galley.

"Long time. Medical leave?" He layered bacon into the pan.

"Something like that."

"How do you like your eggs?" Carson glanced over his shoulder. His bright blue eyes reminded her of a little boy with a secret. *This guy's trouble.*

"Fried is fine, but break the yolks. Can I do anything to help?"

"Keeping me company is enough." He pulled a second pan down. "I'm sorry about your brother. He's a moron about half the time, but he's a good guy."

"Thanks." Trip turned and surveyed the room. This part of the house had the same masculine quality as the bedroom. Saddle colored leather furniture and a massive stone fireplace took up the majority of the space. She could do without the hunting trophies on the walls, but they suited the décor.

"Souvenirs from trips to Africa with my father." Carson pointed to a warthog mounted to the wall. "That one almost took me out."

"Ugly sucker." Trip smiled and took another sip of coffee. "Do you go often?"

"Not since my dad died three years ago." He turned to the stove.

"Sorry for your loss."

"Don't be, he was a mean son of a bitch." Carson cracked several eggs into the pan. "Be gentle with Nate. He's not as tough as he looks, not when it comes to women."

"Nate knows I'm only home for a visit." She puzzled over his words. Carson James worried she would break Nate's heart?

"He doesn't do casual well." Caron turned and must have caught the worried look on her face. "I mean one-night-pussy is one thing. He doesn't fall easy, but when he does…he does."

"I won't make him any promises I can't keep."

"Fair enough." He put bread into the toaster. "Me, I only do casual. After hearing you last night, I'd love to take you for a test drive."

Trip choked on her coffee. "I'm not a test drive sort of girl."

"No, I didn't think you were." He put the bacon on a plate and added two hard fried eggs. "How long have you had PTSD?"

Trip sat back and sighed. Carson James was smarter than she'd given him credit for. "I honestly don't know when it started."

"I know when mine started, only they didn't call it that back then. I was eight and saw my mother die in a car accident." He added toast to the plate and slid it to her as if they discussed the weather. "I manage pretty well, but some days are harder than others. There's medication that helps."

"Thanks." The food looked great, but her appetite had waned. "They have me on something now, but I'm not a fan of taking meds."

Carson opened a cabinet and retrieved several bottles of prescription medication. "I'm used to it."

Trip took a large bite of eggs, trying to hide her curiosity. People in their thirties didn't take that much medication unless they had an illness.

"The best-kept secret in Crystal Beach." He chuckled and took a handful of pills. "I have leukemia. The docs told my folks I wouldn't live to twenty. They were wrong. I've outlived them all."

TWELVE

Nate reached for Trip in his sleep only to find an empty bed. Her scent lingered on the pillow, making him miss her that much more. He couldn't remember the last time he had slept beside a woman. Waking alone left him disappointed.

His cell phone rang, and he glanced at the clock. He'd forgotten it was Saturday, time for his weekly call. "Hey, Sweetheart."

"Hi Daddy, guess what?"

Sophia's voice brought a smile to his face. "What?"

"Papa said I can have a horse of my own."

Nate sat upright and rubbed the sleep from his eyes. "He did, huh? I think you're a little short for a horse."

"I've grown three inches since you were here. Gramma marks it on the wall. I can prove it. I'll send you a picture so you can see."

She'd grown three inches in his absence. Three more inches he'd missed. "I believe you, Sophie. Promise me you will be careful riding."

"I will, Daddy. When are you coming to visit?"

"Soon, I promise. Have you been behaving yourself?"

"Yes, Daddy."

"Going to Sunday school?"

"Uh-huh."

"I love you, baby." He turned when the door opened, and Trip walked in.

"I love you more." Sophia giggled.

"Not possible."

Trip pressed her lips into a firm line and turned for the door. Had she heard his end of the conversation?

Sophia groaned. "That's not how you answer. You're supposed to say, 'I love you more.'"

"Is it? I must have forgotten. I need to go. Can I call you later?"

Trip walked out of the room. She'd heard enough to jump to the wrong conclusion.

"Sure, Daddy." Sophia disconnected the call.

The disappointed tone in his daughter's voice tore through him like a bullet straight to his heart. Nate hopped out of bed and followed Trip. He found her in the kitchen with Carson, washing dishes.

"Trip, can I talk to you?" Nate frowned at the two plates and two glasses. *How cozy.*

She glanced over her shoulder. "Sure, what's up?"

"Alone?"

She took a soapy pan from Carson and rinsed it. "I'm earning my keep. Talk here."

"I think you got the wrong idea." Nate moved behind her and set his hand on her shoulder.

She shrugged it off. "I don't care who you talk to. It's none of my business."

Carson glanced at them and grinned. "Sounds like she got the right idea. You should know to turn your phone off if you're not sleeping alone. Kills the mood when another woman calls."

"I was talking to my niece."

Carson's grin widened. "Which niece? Tabitha? Candy? Or the redhead?"

Leave it to Carson to throw a rattlesnake into a foxhole. Before Nate could reply, Trip shot him a dirty look and dried her hands. *What a fucking mess.* He remembered why it had been so long since he'd had a woman sleep over.

"I need to get back to the hospital."

"I heard you were banned from the hospital. Hell, I heard you were arrested." Carson chuckled.

"All lies." She leaned in and kissed Carson on the cheek. "I might just take you up on your offer."

He slid his hand to her hip. "Which one?"

Trip cocked her head to the side and pursed her lips. "I haven't decided, maybe both?"

Nate poured himself a cup of coffee, pretending to ignore the two of them. Carson did his best to piss him off, and Trip took the award for pain in the ass. Nate cleared his throat. "I'll drive you, make sure you don't deck anyone today."

"You can borrow one of my cars. I've seen that rental piece of shit you're driving. I wouldn't trust it to get you to Tampa." Carson opened a drawer and pulled out a key ring. "Black BMW parked out front."

Trip caught the keys. "Thanks."

Nate focused his attention on his coffee as she turned and walked out the door wearing his T-shirt and boxers. He counted to twenty before he opened his mouth. "Thanks, Carson."

"What'd I do?"

"Leave that one alone. She's going through a lot of shit right now."

"We all are. So?"

"I like her."

"I know you do, why else would she be sleeping in my house? Don't get attached."

"What did you offer her?" Nate refilled his mug, pretending the situation didn't piss him off. On some level, he wanted to believe that Carson wouldn't do anything to hurt him, but the man made a hobby out of irritating the people closest to him.

"My cock and a room here."

Nate stared in disbelief. "Look. She's not some bar whore. She's smart. Too smart to be sleeping in the same place business activities occur."

"The house is clean."

"Stay out of her pants."

Carson chuckled. "Relax, man. She's not my type. I like 'em with more boobs than brains."

"What's going on, Carson? You warned me to keep her out, now you want her here?"

"I don't know. There's something about her." Carson folded his arms across his chest. "I trust her."

"You don't trust anyone. What gives?"

"Maybe I'm tired of your ugly face, and I want a woman around to talk to."

Nate didn't like Carson's interest in Trip. Be it jealousy or concern, the idea of her and Carson laughing over breakfast set him on edge. "You have plenty of women to talk to."

"Bar whores are not for talking, Nate."

"I'll bring her stuff here after she leaves for the hospital." Nate poked around in the fridge.

"Any word on the Trevinos?"

Nate grabbed the Cocoa Puffs and a bowl from the cabinet and sat at the bar. "There's talk of retribution for Little Juan."

"Damn. Since when do they retaliate against innocent women?"

Nate sighed. "Since the person who pulled the trigger is related to one of your known associates. The cops ruled it self-defense, but the Mexicans don't believe it."

"I asked for a sit-down with Juan Sr. but haven't heard back. Seems Padre is locked away, mourning Junior."

Nate shoveled a spoonful of cereal in his mouth. "He had to have come at her for her to shoot him, but I swear I never saw anything like it. She was stone solid when I got there."

Carson furrowed his brow. "Military bearing."

"It definitely wasn't her first kill."

"Did you know she has PTSD? That's why she's home on leave."

Nate choked on his cereal, coughing until he caught his breath. "She hasn't said, but I figured. How'd you find out?"

"I asked her."

"And she told you?" Nate's heart thudded into his lap. How could she tell Carson something so personal? Getting anything out of her had been like cracking a safe.

"Like I said, don't get attached. She's passing through."

"I know."

"You know you can fuck her and not fall in love, right?" Carson slapped his shoulder.

"Yes, I know." Nate focused on his breakfast.

"How can you eat that shit? Nothing but chemicals and sugar." Carson headed for the stairs. "I'm gonna go work off some of this energy. After listening to Trip moan half the night, I'm keyed up."

"Not funny, man. Not funny."

Carson chuckled as he walked upstairs.

Nate's cell rang, and the screen showed an unknown number. "Yeah?"

A female voice filled his ear, a hysterical female voice. "Nate, it's Dixie. Ryan. He's gone."

"What?" Nate stuttered. Last he'd heard, Ryan's condition had improved. The docs had taken him in for surgery. "What did you say?"

"Ryan's dead."

The words slammed into him. He'd lost his best friend.

"Nate?"

"I'm sorry. What do you need?" Nate stood and ran to the door. He had to catch Trip before she left for the hospital. She didn't need to walk into a room full of grieving family unprepared.

"I need my son back, what do you think I need? I need help. I don't know what to—" A male voice interrupted her tirade. "Hang on, Nate."

He ran out of the house, rounded the corner and skidded to a stop in the BMW's empty parking spot. "Dixie. I'm on my way."

"Don't bother. Ryan's friend Carlos is here, said he can help. He just went through this with his brother."

Nate cursed under his breath. "Listen to me. He's not a friend of Ryan's. Keep him away from Trip. She's on her way."

"I don't have no daughter. Are you sucking her? Is that why you're so concerned all the sudden? Don't get involved with her, Nate. She doesn't deserve to be a part of my family."

You got that right. Nate disconnected the call and ran to his bike. Carlos Trevino had no business anywhere near the Peytons, no business other than to hurt Trip for killing his brother.

THIRTEEN

TRIP STEPPED OUT OF THE HOSPITAL ELEVATOR and into the seventh circle of Hell. The tearstained faces of her family told her all she needed to know. Her grandmother caught her eye and stood, shaking her head. A million questions filled her mind. *How? What? Why?* None of that mattered. What mattered was her brother, and he was dead.

Trip took a step toward her distraught grandmother, but Dixie blocked her path. The pain in the woman's eyes stole her breath. The hurt turned to fire and her mouth twisted into an ugly snarl. Trip had faced down much worse than her mother, but she took a step back.

Dixie poked her finger into Trip's chest with each word. "You don't belong here. I want you to leave."

"Momma, I'm sorry." Trip's throat grew tight, choking her words. More than anything she wanted to hold her mother, to grieve, to be a part of the family for once.

"Sorry? You're sorry? Save it," Dixie screeched.

A man Trip didn't recognize stepped in front of her mother. "You must be Trixie. I'll walk you out."

"No, Carlos, don't waste your time on her, she's trash."

Trip turned to leave. Her chest hurt but not from a panic attack. She remembered this feeling, the sense of the world ending and being unable to hold onto someone she loved. The finality that only death could bring. She'd never see Ryan's eyes twinkle as he told a joke, or hear his laughter.

"It's no bother." The stranger stole her back from her grief. He pressed his hand to her shoulder and guided her to the elevator.

The small gesture of kindness undid her, and her knees threatened to buckle. "Thanks."

"I'll see you to your car." He pushed the button, and the doors closed in front of them. He studied at her with a concerned expression, but his eyes remained cold. The line of his jaw sparked a memory.

Trip hung her head and wiped her eyes with the back of her hand as she assessed the situation. Carlos stood a foot taller and outweighed her by at least seventy-five pounds. Unlike Juan Jr., he didn't have an ounce of fat on him. This guy could easily overpower her. He flexed his fingers at his side but kept his eyes on the door. A slight bulge in his jeans above his boot told her he carried a weapon. His leather coat obscured his lower back and sides, but Trip would have bet her grandmother's pearls he had a second gun.

The doors opened, and Trip stepped out into the lobby. "I need to use the ladies' room."

The muscle in his jaw tensed as he followed her to the restroom.

"You don't have to wait for me." Trip pushed the door open, determined to get away from him.

Carlos folded his arms. "We need to talk."

"Oh, you want to talk about Ryan?" She smiled, playing dumb. "I'll be right out."

Inside the restroom, Trip pushed her emotions to the back of her mind and focused on escape. She surveyed the bathroom. No windows, one way in and out. She could wait him out, pull the medical emergency cord, call the police...and say what? "Hi, this guy has a gun and insists on walking me to my car." She dialed Nate on the burner phone. No answer.

Trip stepped into the handicap stall and locked the door. The red emergency cord hung within easy reach. If he burst in, she could pull it, but help wouldn't come before he shot her. She scrolled through the call log, noting the most frequently dialed number, assuming it was Carson.

"Carson James."

Trip whispered. "Carson, this is Trip. Did Ryan have a friend named Carlos? Big guy, Latino?"

"Why?"

She didn't like the alarm in his voice. "I'm in the bathroom. He's insisting on walking me to my car."

"Don't go with him. Call Nate. He's on the way to there."

"I did, no answer. I take it he's not a friendly."

"Stay put." Carson disconnected.

A cell phone rang from the hall. She strained to listen to the conversation but couldn't make out the words. Trip took a chance and dialed Nate again.

"Yeah?" He sounded irritated.

"Nate, where are you?"

"In the hospital, where are you?"

She rested her head against the wall, imagining her blood and brains splattered on the cold white tile. "Locked in the bathroom with an armed guy named Carlos waiting to walk me to my car."

"Which bathroom?"

"Lobby, to the right of the info desk."

"Are you armed?"

Trip's pulse rang in her ears. Each second brought her one step closer to the end. "No."

"Damn it. Stay put."

The bathroom door swung open and heavy footfalls echoed in the space. Trip pulled the cord and climbed onto the toilet. She held her breath and waited as the footsteps came closer. The door opened again. *Please, be Nate.*

She peeked over the stalls but couldn't catch sight of the newcomer.

"This is the ladies' room, sir." A male voice bellowed. "Did you pull the emergency alarm?"

The door opened again, and several additional people filled the restroom, but Trip stayed put.

Carlos said, "No, sorry. My girlfriend came in here, and I came to check…"

"Where is she now?"

Trip forced tears to her eyes and called from the stall. "I'm here."

"Do you need assistance?" The male nurse tried to push the stall door open. "Can you unlock the door?"

Trip slid the lock open and pressed herself against the back wall. If bullets started to fly, the position would buy her an extra couple of seconds.

The nurse opened the door halfway and peeked inside. "Do you need assistance?"

She nodded her head, forcing her eyes to go wide when she nodded toward Carlos's position. She lowered her voice to a squeak. "I need a female nurse."

A woman pushed forward and joined her in the stall. "Are you ill?"

Trip shook her head and collapsed onto the floor, sobbing.

"Everyone out," the nurse shouted. She knelt in the small space. "What happened?"

Trip waited until the door closed behind Carlos and the emergency response team, leaving her alone with the nurse. "That guy…he's armed. He tried to…to…hurt me. My real boyfriend is on his way. I was so scared, I pulled the cord. I didn't know what else to do."

The nurse retrieved a phone from her pocket and called security. While she relayed the information, Trip's phone rang.

"I'm outside, but they say you were having some sort of emergency?" Nate said.

Trip stood and went to the door. "He's with me, can he come in please?"

The medical personnel and security in the hall looked at each other, then the apparent leader nodded, and motioned for Nate to enter.

"I'm okay, sorry for the trouble," Trip said.

Nate pushed her into the bathroom and ran his hands over her arms. "What happened?"

She hugged him, whispering, "Later."

Armed security and two actual police officers came into the bathroom. Thankfully, the hospital security guards weren't the same as she had met the night before. Nate held her hand while she relayed the fictional version of the story to the officers. It struck her that Nate sat by while she lied to the police for the second time.

"The suspect evaded us. Are you willing to come to the station to file a formal report?"

Trip slumped. "Tomorrow. My brother just died. I need to be with my family."

"Miss, I am sorry for your loss, but—"

"She said tomorrow." Nate slid his arm around her shoulder. "She's had enough trauma for one day."

The policeman opened his mouth to argue but met Nate's gaze and frowned. He pulled a business card from his shirt pocket. "Have her call this number."

Nate took the card.

She frowned and buried her head in Nate's shoulder. "I really need out of this bathroom."

"Of course, again, I'm sorry for your loss, Ms. Peyton."

She walked pressed against Nate until they reached the parking garage. Once out of the relative safety of the hospital, she pulled away and surveyed her surroundings. No sign of Carlos, or whatever his name was, she turned to Nate. "Where are you parked?"

"Third floor. Why don't you tell me what happened?"

"Later, when I am sufficiently armed and less in the open."

Nate sighed and reached for her. When she ignored his hand, he sighed and stuffed it in his pocket. "We'll take Carson's car."

"I'd rather you follow me." She had no idea why she argued, other than to push him away.

Nate pushed a button on his key ring, and a car in her row beeped. He strode past her toward the flashing lights. Trip followed, cursing Carson for having the second set of keys. She plopped into the passenger's seat and locked the door.

Nate put the car in reverse and backed out of the space, then hit the gas and sped through the garage. Once on the street, he glanced at her. "Talk."

"I need to call Carson."

"The hell with Carson, talk to me." Nate slammed the car into fifth gear.

"Ryan is dead." She turned her head toward the window.

"I heard. I'm sorry. I don't mean to disrespect Ryan, he's my best friend, but right now I need you to tell me about Carlos."

"He was with Dixie. He offered to walk me to my car after she threw me out. I noticed he was armed and…" She turned in her seat. "I went to the bathroom to buy time and called you, then Carson."

"Good instincts." Nate merged into traffic on the interstate and the tension in his shouldered eased.

"He was going to kill me?" She knew the answer before she asked the question, but asked anyway. Confirmation of her fears would make them real, not something produced from grief and anxiety.

Nate pressed his lips together as if trying to find the words.

"I take that as a yes." She turned back to the window. "The cops have my personal weapon. I need a gun, maybe two. Something small enough to carry."

"I'll get you something cute but deadly." He ran his hand over her shoulder.

She closed her eyes and recalled her would-be murderer's features. He seemed so familiar, but how? Then it hit her. "Is Carlos related to the guy in Ryan's house? Juan?"

Nate nodded. "Brothers."

The second blow to the gut came out of nowhere. Not that Nate had lied, she knew he had, but that it disappointed her. *He's up to his ass in dirty business. Lying is the least of his crimes.* "You said you didn't know the guy in Ryan's house."

"And you said you fired in self-defense." Nate shot her a look.

She shrank back in her seat, unable to hold onto her self-righteousness. "Anything else I should know?"

"I could ask you the same question."

Trip shook her head and sank into her thoughts. She'd underestimated Nate more than once. Had she let her guard down because of everything else going on? Did it have something to do with coming home? No, this had to do with Nathaniel Benz. The man, not the place, brought her a sense of home. She'd grown up tagging along with Ryan and Nate, watching them run the streets and laughing with them when they didn't get caught. She'd trusted him since she was a child.

"You okay over there?" His eyes softened.

"I didn't have a panic attack." The realization startled her.

"I didn't think you did."

She sat back and smiled. "No. I mean, I got through that without having a panic attack. I was worried I'd flip out anytime I was in danger, but I didn't. Maybe the anxiety isn't as bad as they think."

Nate gave her a weary look. "PTSD can be tricky. When's your doctor appointment?"

"I moved it to Thursday morning." Her smile faded. "Carson told you?"

"I suspected it, but he told me." Judging by his grim expression, her supposed illness worried him. He took her hand. "Until we sort this out, you'll stay at Carson's. If you have to go somewhere, I'll go with you."

She wanted to pull her hand away, but the physical contact eased her battered heart. "I don't need a bodyguard."

"And I don't need to bury another friend."

The way he said *friend* made her cringe. She eased her hand away. Better to hurt and heal than to risk more pain. "Friend? I thought we were just screwing each other?"

"That too. Listen, the call earlier…"

"You don't need to explain. I'm okay with fuck-buddies."

"It was Sophia. She's not my niece, she's my daughter."

Trip studied his profile. The tension had returned to his shoulders and jaw. He'd tipped his hand and showed his cards. She braced for more, expecting him to say something to make her feel even more like an ass.

"No one knows she's my kid, not even Carson. Her mother died in childbirth."

Trip's heart missed a beat. *Yep, I'm a complete ass.* "You keep her hidden to protect her."

Nate kept his eyes on the road, but they glistened with unshed tears. "I'm banking everything I make. I'm close to having enough to get out."

Trip sat, unable to form a word. She'd never seen him slip. He couldn't have risen so high in Carson's organization by being sloppy. He'd told her two dangerous secrets. Those secrets weighed on her shoulders. He trusted her, but why? How would that play out while she built a case against him and Carson?

Fourteen

WHAT IS IT ABOUT THIS WOMAN that compels me to do and say stupid shit? Nate kicked himself from the moment the words fell out of his mouth. Leaving his daughter with his parents and keeping her a secret for the last five years had happened out of necessity, but he hated himself for abandoning his child.

Sharing his secrets meant something to him. He wanted her to know the truth, but her silence unnerved him. His thoughts drifted back to Trip and Carson in the kitchen. *How cozy. Have I completely misjudged her?*

He parked the car. "We should get your things and move you into the main house."

"I won't say anything."

He paused, unsure if she referred to his planning to run, Sophia, or both.

"You did the right thing, keeping her safe."

"Thanks." Her words soothed his fear, but only time would tell if he'd made a mistake. Nate helped her from the car, surprised when she didn't poke fun at his attempt at chivalry.

"Can we stay here for a little while? I need some time."

"Of course." He led her into the garage apartment. *What an idiot. I should have said something about her loss. My loss.* The reality that his best friend had died hadn't sunk in. How could it have? He'd been too busy getting her out of harm's way and spilling his guts. Things were happening too fast. Sooner or later he would find a quiet moment to grieve.

Trip wandered into the bedroom and collapsed on the bed, hugging the pillow to her middle.

"I'll give you some privacy." Nate turned to go.

"No, stay, please." She curled around the pillow. The lost look in her eyes softened her features, reminding him of the way she looked while asleep, so innocent and young.

"Sure." He stretched out beside her, careful to keep a safe distance. "Do you know what happened to Ryan?"

"I didn't get the chance to ask." She reached behind her for his hand and pulled his arm around her.

Nate pulled her back against his chest and held her, burying his face in her hair. "We'll get through this. I won't let them hurt you."

She sighed into the pillow. "Don't get attached to me, Nate. I'm going back to Lejeune as soon as I'm cleared for duty."

"Ma'am, yes, ma'am." He believed her. Whatever was or wasn't between them could only last a short time. She'd leave, and he'd get on with his life. Yet, when she turned to him for comfort and relaxed in his arms, he wanted to hope.

She rolled over and met his eyes. The little girl he once knew peeked from behind the woman she'd become. He searched her face and saw her vulnerability, her fears, her feelings for him. She had drawn him into her orbit that night at JJ's and hadn't let him go. His eyes drifted closed, and he kissed her.

The kiss started soft, but as with most things involving Trip, turned hard and desperate in the span of a breath. Nate lost himself in a tangle of tongues, limbs, and flying clothes. He had to have her, to bury himself inside her and forget his pain.

He pushed Trip to her back and tucked her beneath him. Nate settled between her thighs and thrust inside her. This is what he needed, what they needed. An affirmation of life, something to remind them they hadn't died with Ryan, that death hadn't stolen everything.

She wrapped her legs around his waist and scored his back with her nails. Nate welcomed the pain, the urgent race to the finish line. He closed his eyes and focused on the feel of her as their bodies slammed together. Her toned, muscular thighs clenched tighter around his waist. Trip tugged his hair and bit his shoulder, clinging to him as if he were a life preserver in a raging sea.

Nate turned his head as tears fell down his face, tears that he had held back since the night of Ryan's accident and Marcy's death. He hadn't cried in front of a woman since his daughter was born. Shame overwhelmed him.

Trip cupped his cheek and turned his face to hers. Nate expected disapproval. Instead, she offered a soft smile and pulled him to her chest. Still joined, he let go of his emotions.

Nate had no idea how long they stayed like that, holding each other, both with tears in their eyes. The release left him exhausted.

He eased to his side. "Sorry."

"For what?"

"I don't usually cry like a bitch in the middle of sex."

"I won't tell anyone if you don't." She snuggled closer.

Nate held her as her breathing evened out and her body gave in to the fatigue of grief. Of course, he'd have to let Trip go when the time came, but he'd be damned if he'd let anything happen to her between now and then.

Nate woke to Trip nuzzling into his chest. He pulled her close, kissing the top of her head. Yes, he'd let her go if he had no choice, but he'd play dirty to keep her as long as he could.

"Hey." She kissed his chin.

"How'd you sleep?" He brushed her hair back from her face.

"Like a rock. What time is it?"

Nate pushed himself up to check the time. "Five-thirty. We should grab some food."

The front door slammed open, and it sounded like a horde of people wrestled their way inside. Nate slid his hand into the nightstand drawer and pulled out a handgun. He handed it to Trip and pulled his double barrel from beneath the bed. Generally, the *click-click* sound of someone cocking a gun was enough of a deterrent for an intruder. However, whoever headed toward them didn't stop.

"Whoa, stand down," Carson called from the hall.

Nate stood and came face to face with his boss and a bloody Carlos Trevino. "What the hell?"

Carson motioned to Trip. "Is this the guy?"

She shrank back and pulled the blankets to her chin. "Yeah?"

Carson released Carlos. The man slumped to the floor. Evidently, his injuries extended well beyond his face.

Trip's terrified expression made Nate want to deck Carson, the selfish son-of-a-bitch. She didn't need this, not on top of losing Ryan. Nate took a step, inserting himself between the men and Trip. "Who did this?"

"I did." Carson pulled a pistol from the back of his jeans, pressed the barrel to Carlos's temple, and fired.

Trip gasped behind him, loud enough to be heard through the ringing in his ears. Nate stood in shocked silence while his brain refused to process what had happened.

Carson grinned and lowered the gun. "Nate, clean up on aisle five. Trip, darlin', come with me."

Nate balled his fists at his side. His pulse pounded in his ears as fire surged through his veins. Had it not been for Trip trembling beside him, he would have put an end to Carson's insanity once and for all. "Are you crazy? Two Trevino brothers dead? This will cause a war."

Carson waved the gun in Nate's direction. "You got a little pussy, and you think you can talk to me like that?"

The alcohol on Carson's breath gave Nate pause. He was a SOB when sober but downright psychotic when drunk.

"Put the gun down." Trip called from behind him.

Carson's eyes went wide for a fraction of a second before he burst out laughing. He tossed the gun onto the bed and raised his hands. "Stand down, soldier. You can't shoot a man after he made you breakfast."

"I'll shoot you where you piss if you call me 'soldier' again." She lowered the gun. "You don't clean up your own mess?"

Carson grinned. "That's why Nate's on the payroll."

Nate hung his head. Times like these he hated Carson and the world he lived in. Nate's face heated, and he couldn't bring himself to look at Trip. He could only imagine the look of disgust in her eyes.

"I'll stay and help." She moved to Nate's side.

"This isn't women's work." Carson's grin faded.

"Please don't add male chauvinist to your growing list of character flaws." Trip wore a shit-eating-grin that softened the blow to Carson's ego.

"Suit yourself, but I expect both of you to join me for dinner. Potatoes are in the oven. I'll put steaks on the grill when you get there." He turned and left.

Trip sank to her knees and covered her face. Her shoulders shook with silent sobs. Nate slid his hands under her arms and helped her stand. She stiffened her spine as if forcing her emotions away, but failed and crumpled against him.

"Babe, go take a shower. I got this."

"I'm okay. I'll help." Trip glanced at the dead man and started to tremble.

He had watched her force tears and feign trauma the day she shot Juan Jr. This…this was different. "I'm not asking. You've been through enough."

"He shoots a guy in your living quarters and expects you to clean up his mess?"

"It's what I do." He turned from her.

She forced him to meet her gaze. "It sucks. I don't care who he is, or that he's sick. He's a bastard."

Nate's mouth went dry. "Sick?"

She lowered her eyes.

"Carson told you he's sick?"

She nodded.

"Besides his medical team, you're one of the three people he's told." Nate didn't know what to make of this news. His boss didn't invite people into his house, and he never shared his secrets. "Be careful with Carson. He can be charming, but he's—"

"Unpredictable?" Trip wiped her eyes. "I think he killed Carlos for me."

"I think you are right."

"Should I be worried?"

He pulled her close. "For some reason, he's brought you into his inner circle. He won't hurt you unless you betray him."

FIFTEEN

HE WON'T HURT ME UNLESS I BETRAY HIM? Trip knew Carson's type. Dangerous men with a sense of entitlement, little boys trapped in grown-ups' bodies who'd traded in their BB guns for the real thing. She'd do what she had to do to complete the mission, but she had to get her shit together first.

Trip stood under the water until her skin turned pink, but she couldn't wash away the memory of the dead man in the other room. Maybe they were right, maybe she'd lost her mind. She'd killed before, more than a few times, but had never reacted like such a girl.

She rinsed the shampoo from her hair and turned off the water. Somewhere in the distance, her cell phone rang. At first, she decided to ignore it but thought of McGuire.

Nate called from the bedroom. "Your phone's ringing. Want me to get it?"

"No, let it ring." Trip grabbed a towel and wrapped it around herself. She didn't need him to answer a call from her commander.

She stopped at the door and listened as Nate talked into her phone. From the tone of the conversation, her mother had called to vent. Trip's frustration with Nate answering her call dissolved into self-doubt. She turned and wiped the fog from the mirror. Trip hardly recognized her own reflection. Her hands trembled as she clutched the sink for support. *How in the hell am I going to make it through dinner with Carson? He won't appreciate the tears.*

Nate knocked and opened the door. "That was Dixie. They're having a family gathering. Do you want to go?"

"She called to invite me?"

"Seems that way."

Trip sighed. "I'd rather not spend hours with my family, but you can go if you want."

"I told you I would stay with you." Nate frowned. "But is dinner with Carson the lesser evil?"

"A seven-day cruise on a ship through Hell with Satan navigating would be a lesser evil."

He laughed and shook his head. "Why don't you get dressed and go to Carson's? I'll be there shortly."

"I'm no expert, but it takes longer than a few minutes to clean up a murder scene and dispose of the body."

Nate folded his arms across his chest. "I may be in charge of cleaning Carson's messes, but I have people to do the heavy lifting."

"I'm sorry, I didn't mean to offend you. I forgot about the cleanup crew."

He stepped closer and set his hands on her shoulders. "Don't apologize. I'm far from offended."

She nodded and bowed her head.

"Are you okay? You seem pretty shaken up."

Trip considered his question, a question she had grown tired of answering. *No, I'm not okay.* "I'll be fine. It's been a long day."

He wrapped his arms around her, pressing her cheek to his chest. "Don't lie to me. I can see you're upset."

"I should get dressed."

Nate released her but stayed close as she threw on a pair of jeans and a T-shirt. Trip thought he might follow her to the door, but he turned when she walked downstairs.

Mabelle the Basset Hound kept her company as she walked down the sidewalk toward the main house. She couldn't help but smile as the dog hustled on her stubby legs. Trip could relate to the worried look on the dog's face. She too felt as if hers was sliding from her skull.

Trip knocked on Carson's front door, rethinking her choice to have dinner instead of going to the wake.

"Come in."

The scent of fresh-baked bread greeted her the moment she stepped inside. *No not bread, something sweet and full of cinnamon.* She wandered into the kitchen and leaned against the wall, watching a barefoot and bare-chested Carson take a cake out of the oven.

He turned and grinned. "Feeling better?"

"Why does everyone keep asking me that?"

"Either you got soap in your eyes, or you had a good cry. My bet is on the latter." He set the cake on a rack and moved back to the stove.

Trip frowned and climbed onto a barstool. "My brother is dead."

"I heard." He turned. "I'm sorry. That sucks, but life goes on."

She nodded. He had a point.

"Drag that pretty little ass of yours over here and stir the sauce while I check on the steaks."

She took the spoon and stirred, slopping some of the sauce onto the stovetop.

Carson hissed behind her and placed his hand over hers, leaning in to whisper into her ear. "Slow, like this."

"I got it, thanks." Trip frowned, unable to move from between him and the hot oven.

He set his other hand on her hip and pressed his chest to her back. "You're tense."

Trip pushed his arm away and turned with the spoon in her hand. "I am, and you're not helping. Can the shit. Okay?"

"Okay. Don't let it burn." He grinned and motioned to the saucepot. "When's your birthday?"

"Why? Do you plan to look up my sign?"

"You can tell a lot about a person by their sign."

"July thirty-first. I'm a Leo."

Carson chuckled. "I could have guessed that. If not Leo, then Scorpio. What year?"

"It's not polite to ask a woman her age." She turned and caught the look in his eye. *Sign my ass, he wants to know my birthdate. But why?* "Eighty-four."

"In case you haven't noticed, I'm not polite."

"I noticed." She motioned to the door. "You better go check the grill. I smell smoke."

He opened his mouth as if to say something, but she turned her back to him.

The sliding glass door opened and closed behind her before she released her breath. "Damn men."

"What did I do now?" Nate walked into the room and put a six-pack in the fridge.

She set the spoon aside. "Nothing, I think it's sticking to the bottom of the pan."

Nate glanced at the sauce. "It's supposed to do that. Keep stirring until it reduces to a few tablespoons."

"What is it?" Trip wrinkled her nose at the concoction.

"Béarnaise." Carson returned to the kitchen and pushed her aside. "At least, that's what it was before you took over."

Trip took the opportunity to return to her stool. She'd never learned to cook and had no intention of doing so now. The men had apparently spent a lot of time in the kitchen together, judging by the way they ducked and wove around each other. "You two do this often?"

Carson glanced over his shoulder. "You mean shoot someone and then make dinner? Not as often as we should."

Nate glared at him.

"What?" Carson grinned. "Too soon?"

Trip took the opportunity to press for answers. "Nate, what did you mean when you said two dead Trevinos would start a war?"

Nate's spine stiffened.

Carson leaned against the counter, looking between them. "Nate worries too much. Want a beer?"

"I think he has to do the worrying for both of you."

Carson grabbed three cold bottles from the fridge, offered one to each. "I suppose that's true. How about you, sweetheart. Are you worried?"

"Yeah, I'm worried. I don't know what I walked into, but people keep dying." Trip took a long pull from the bottle. It hurt to add Ryan to the growing list of casualties. She wanted to ask what happened the night of Ryan's accident, if it was an accident, but didn't dare push too hard too fast.

Nate said, "Babe, I told you. You're going to stay here until we settle this."

Carson nodded. "No one is stupid enough to set foot on my property without permission. You'll be safe here."

"I appreciate that, but I can't sit around here. I have things I need to take care of, doctor appointments…" *And Ryan's funeral.*

"None of that matters if you're dead." Carson poured the contents of the saucepan into the blender. "Go get the meat off the grill. This will be ready in five."

Sixteen

NATE'S APPETITE LEFT THE MOMENT TRIP ASKED about a war with the Trevinos. Unlike some people, who ate their stress away, Nate's hunger had an inverse relationship with his stress level. Since Trip walked into JJ's, the idea of food made him ill.

"Watching your girlish figure?" Carson motioned to Nate's plate.

Trip studied him for a moment, then pushed away from the table. "Where do you keep your plastic containers?"

"You barely touched your food. What is up with the two of you?" Carson frowned as he shoveled another hunk of steak into his mouth, chewed, and continued talking. "I don't use plastic. Hot food in plastic containers causes cancer."

Nate shook his head and stood to join Trip in the kitchen. He pulled several glass bowls from the cabinet. "They say grilling meat over charcoal causes cancer, too."

"That's just plain old bullshit. The cave men grilled and they didn't have cancer. It's a chemical thing." Carson took another bite.

"I'm pretty sure the cavemen didn't have charcoal." Trip grinned.

"This is how it's going to be? The two of you knuckleheads ganging up on me?" Carson pointed his fork at Trip. "You, I'll excuse because you're cute, and I'm pretty sure you could kick my ass."

Nate put the leftovers away. "Carson James afraid of a girl?"

"Fuck, yeah. Have you seen the guns on her?"

Trip put her hands on her hips. "I'm standing right here."

Both men chuckled. Nate set his hands on her shoulders, massaging out the walnut size knots in her muscles. "You need to call your mother. She'll need help with the planning."

Trip took a step away. "I doubt she needs any help from me, other than cash for the funeral. I still can't believe she invited me over tonight."

Carson joined them in the kitchen. "She invited you because I told her to. A condition of my taking care of the funeral. Lurch is setting up the memorial."

"Lurch?" Trip tilted her head. "Who's Lurch?"

"Old man Sievers' son, Daniel. He's a tall, lanky SOB and about as sharp as a marble, but a good guy." Carson set his plate on the counter. "He's going to split the ashes and return some to me and some to Dixie."

Trip leaned against the kitchen island for support. "They're cremating Ryan?"

Nate took her hand. "He wanted to be cremated. He gave us specific instructions about what to do with the ashes."

"What? When?" The color drained from her face.

Carson sighed. "We've attended quite a few funerals. Afterward, we'd drink and talk. *Really talk.* Ryan wanted Dixie, Nate, and me to each pick a place that reminded us of him and spread some of his ashes. He figured it would force people to think about his life and not his death."

"That's so like Ryan." Trip hung her head, likely to hide her tears.

Carson embraced her from the left and Nate from the right, as she let her emotions come to the surface and run down her face. They held her, sandwiched between them, and stared at each other. Nate didn't care for his boss touching her, but Carson seemed uncharacteristically moved by this woman. Unlike the parade of women who came and went, he might actually care about Trip. *This is going to be trouble.*

"Thank you, Carson, but why did you pay for the funeral?" She stepped from between them.

"Ryan didn't have a pot to piss in, besides your grandmother's house. I didn't want to see you have to sell it to pay for the service." Carson shrugged.

She asked, "And he worked for you, right?"

Nate set his hand on the small of her back, but she pulled away.

"Yeah, he did."

"Running drugs?" Trip's voice grew cold.

"Sometimes, but mostly he worked at the bar. I tried to keep him on the legit side of things." Carson folded his arms.

Nate shot him a warning look. Each piece of the puzzle Trip learned painted another circle around the bullseye on her back. Once a Marine always a Marine, how far would she go to keep Carson's, and his, secrets?

"Nate doesn't want me telling you about the *family* business." Carson winked.

Trip glanced at Nate, then turned back to Carson. "Why *are* you telling me about the family business?"

"Because you have been brushing against this business since you were a kid. You don't remember, do you?"

"Carson, enough." Nate stepped between them.

"Remember what?" Trip ignored Nate.

"You've been here before. I remember you, though you were a skinny little girl then."

Trip squared her shoulders and raised her chin. Any emotion she'd shown disappeared behind her dead-eyed mask.

"Your mother brought you here, which wasn't done. Pops never let his customers on this property, even after my mom passed away. Dixie was heavy into blow back then. She offered you to my dad in exchange for drugs. He had me take you upstairs to my room while he corrected her way of thinking. I bet she never pulled that shit again, did she?"

"No."

Nate's breath caught in his throat. How was this woman remotely sane after her childhood? "Motherfucker."

Trip stared at Carson, and a light came on behind her eyes. "You showed me your Nascar collection."

Carson nodded. "Pops never sold to her again. He banned her from the house and the bar. He threatened to take you and Ryan from her if she didn't clean up."

Bile rose in the back of Nate's throat. "Trip, let's go."

She held up a hand. "How could he take us away from her?"

Carson stared at her, his lips pressed into a thin line, but his eyes remained soft. "I don't know, maybe it was all talk. Pops always had a soft spot for kids, just not the one with his name on the birth certificate."

"Why do I get the feeling there's more to it?"

Carson shrugged. "There usually is."

Trip's voice rose. "Say whatever it is you want me to know, Carson. I'm done with this bullshit."

"There's a real good chance Ryan's my half-brother."

"And me? Is there a good chance I'm your sister?"

Carson exaggerated a cringe. "I've been rock hard for you since Nate threw you over his shoulder. That would be wrong, even for me."

Trip stormed out the door, leaving Nate standing with his mouth hanging open.

"Damn it." Carson sighed as he ran his hand over the back of his neck. "Better go after her."

"You're an asshole." Nate shook his head.

"That I am, that I am."

SEVENTEEN

TRIP STUMBLED OVER A FALLEN BRANCH. Her bare feet stung and her vision blurred. Carson's words ricocheted through her head. *Was he trying to tell me we share a father?* She never knew her father other than his first name, Chip. Chip, Dixie had explained, died in the service, training accident or some shit.

"Trip, hold up," Nate called from behind her.

"I need to be alone." She picked up her pace.

"Dammit." Nate followed a few yards behind but gained ground. He grabbed her arm and spun her around.

"Leave me alone. I can't deal with you right now." She pushed him away. "I can't talk about this."

"You don't have to talk, but you shouldn't be alone." He fell into step beside her.

"He said no one would come on his property."

"I'd rather not take the chance."

"Whatever." She walked toward the garage apartment to find shoes and her purse. Dixie had some serious explaining to do.

Nate followed her without a word. She could only imagine what he must think of her. Damaged goods with a junkie mother. Trip had worked so hard to put her past behind her, but she was up to her elbows in it now.

Trip punched the code into the alarm panel. "Did you know about this?"

"Not a clue."

"Do you believe him?"

Nate nodded. "It makes sense. Ryan pulled a lot of shit, and Carson never turned his back on him. Reminded him of who was in charge from time to time, but never cut him off."

"So, Carson wasn't responsible for Ryan's death?" The words entered her head and fell out of her mouth.

Nate's eyes widened. "No. Ryan was responsible for Ryan's death."

"What was he doing with a backpack full of drugs?"

"I don't know, but my guess is he owed the Trevinos money and planned to sell the heroin."

"Money for what?" Trip shook her head. "On second thought, don't answer that. I don't want to know. Not tonight."

He took her by the shoulders and forced her to face him. "Babe, Ryan was trying to help Marcy and her kid. I think he had a business deal go bad and panicked when he couldn't make good."

"Where *is* Marcy?" She had a feeling Nate knew exactly where the woman was holed up.

Nate hung his head. "Hell, if I know."

"Right." Trip didn't believe him for a second.

"I haven't seen her since the night of Ryan's accident."

"Did he love her?" Trip couldn't imagine her brother trying to make a life with that woman. That bitch waiting so long to call for help had contributed to Ryan's death.

Nate shrugged. "I don't know, but he loved Izzy. Marcy's baby."

Trip's mouth went dry. "Was he the father?"

"I don't know. Marcy claimed she didn't know who was the father but said it could be Ryan."

"There are tests…"

"She refused paternity tests."

Trip pushed the door open and stepped inside. "It's like I woke up in a redneck nightmare. I need to see my mother."

"That's probably not a good idea. Not tonight. Take some time to cool off."

She sighed, exhausted and in need of some sanity. Nate made sense, though he lived in the middle of these lunatics. Once upstairs, she collapsed into a chair and cradled her head in her hands.

Nate turned on his computer, seeming to ignore her. The clicking of keys grated her nerves, but silence would annoy her more. She closed her eyes and forced herself to focus on the facts as she understood them. Unfortunately, for every fact she had five unanswered questions.

"Nate, could you check your Facebook another time?"

"I don't have Facebook."

"What are you doing?" She frowned at her whiney voice.

"We are going away for a few days."

"What? No, no way. I can't run away. I have to…"

"You have to get to your doctor appointments and take care of yourself. You're under too much stress. A few days away will help."

"Carson won't let you go away now. He needs you to clean up his mess, remember?"

Nate flinched. "He'll be okay with it."

"I bet you a thousand bucks, he loses his shit if you try to leave the state."

"Can you afford to throw away a grand?"

"I wouldn't have made the bet if I thought I'd lose." She laughed, surprised she still remembered how.

He moved to her, placing his hands on the arms of the chair. "We are going to honor Ryan's wishes. I plan to take my third to a special place in the mountains, and you're coming with me."

She lowered her head.

"When is your appointment?"

"Tomorrow morning."

"Good. We'll leave after the appointment. Lurch said he'd have the ashes ready."

She couldn't learn about Carson from another state, but that much time alone with Nate could help the mission. He had already proven he trusted her. Perhaps he'd feel chattier away from the drama. A few days to get her head together sounded damned good. "Fine, three days."

"Four. It takes ten hours to get there." He grinned.

"That's what airports are for."

Nate shook his head. "I don't do planes."

She brought her hand to her mouth to cover her smile.

"Are you laughing at me?" Nate climbed into her lap, a knee on either side of her thighs.

His weight crushed her legs, but she laughed. "Get off me."

He kissed her neck and whispered, "Make me."

Her eyes drifted closed as his lips moved over her flesh. She waited until he relaxed, then shifted her weight and pushed him back with all of her strength. He barely budged.

Nate laughed until she changed positions and he toppled backward to the floor. She didn't have enough room to evade his next move. He grabbed her waist, and she fell with him. Trip grinned down at his face, but Nate had other ideas. He held her close and rolled to the side, tucking her beneath him.

"I have a hundred pounds on you, babe."

Her eyes half closed, she lowered her voice and purred. "Maybe I let you win?"

"I think we both won." He sat up and grabbed her wrists, pulling them above her head.

Trip struggled against his grip and ran her tongue over her lips. "Uh-huh."

"I can't tell if you are planning your next move or flirting with me." He laughed and released her arms.

She ran her fingers through his hair. "Both, but I'm not comfortable…"

"Oh damn, babe. I'm an ass." He moved off her and stood. "Sex is probably the last thing you want."

"No, the floor. You had me pinned on something sharp." She pulled out the set of car keys she'd landed on. "Sex is a great diversion." Something about the way he smiled at her made her slide back behind her protective shield. They were getting too close, any closer and things would get even more complicated.

"We've been through a lot today. Can I hold you tonight? I promise not to breathe on you."

She folded her arms. "I'm not into hearts and flowers, Nate. I'm more of a fuck `em and leave `em kind of girl."

He brushed her hair from her face.

She stepped back as if he'd struck her. "Don't look at me like that."

"Like what?"

"I don't need your pity." First, he acted like she walked on water, now he treeated her like something he needed to save.

Nate sighed and bowed his head. When he looked up his eyes glistened. "No, no, you don't. But I could use a little tenderness tonight. It's been a hell-of-a-day, and I'm—"

She interrupted, "Don't you dare…"

"What, darlin'?" He ran his hand down her arm. "Talk to me."

"What Carson said has nothing to do with you not wanting to screw me?"

Nate wrinkled his brow. "You might be his sister? Who cares? Half the town could be related to him."

Trip shook her head. "Not that part."

Nate sighed. "I'm not surprised Dixie did that to you. It makes me want to kill people, but I'm not surprised. I was around that house growing up. Ryan told me horror stories."

"Oh." She met his eyes and frowned. The emotions of the day showed on his face. "Let's get some sleep."

Trip sighed when Nate pulled her close. Despite what he said, she'd seen the look in his eyes and refused to allow him to think of her as a victim, even when a child. The problem with Nate was the thing that drew her to him, familiarity.

EIGHTEEN

"WHAT TIME IS IT?" NATE'S PHONE SCREAMED from the nightstand.

"I don't know, but turn that thing off," Trip mumbled into his chest.

He rolled to his side and stretched his arm wide to grab the phone. "Yeah?"

Carson's voice boomed through the phone. "Get dressed and get to Dixie's. She's partying."

Nate sat upright. "It's four in the morning."

"I know what fucking time it is. Izzy is there. You need to get your ass over there and pick up the kid. Don't take Trip with you." Carson mumbled to someone, and a woman laughed.

"I don't think—"

"I don't pay you to think. Send Trip to the house. She can wait for you in the guest room."

"Christ. On my way." Nate tossed the phone onto the nightstand and crawled out of bed. "I'll be back soon."

"Where are you going?" Trip turned the light on.

"Your mother. She's out of control, and I need to get over there."

"I'm going with you." Trip pulled her jeans on.

Nate didn't have the heart to send her to Carson's when he had company. Not to mention, Nate could use some help with Izzy. If things went south, Trip could hold the baby while he did damage control inside. They dressed and pulled out of the drive five minutes later.

"What the hell is she thinking?" Nate stopped at a traffic light and slammed his palm against the steering wheel several times. "When we get there, you need to stay in the car unless I call you inside."

"She's my mother."

"Exactly. She is your mother. You don't need to see her like this, nor do you have any filters when it comes to her. You need to stay in the damned car."

"You're right." Trip turned to look out the window.

Fucking Carson. Trip had enough on her plate without dealing with this bullshit. They passed by JJ's on the way to Dixie's. Music and laughter spilled out of the packed bar. Nate considered turning into the parking lot for half a second, then the light turned green, and he continued to drive forward.

"Does Carson send you to rescue his customers often?"

"No."

"Then why? I mean, why in the hell would he send you to help my worthless mother?"

"Babe, there's more to it than that."

"Like what?"

He sighed, not wanting to get into this. "Like she is your mother, and he cares about you."

"Yes, but it still doesn't make sense."

"She's supposed to be taking care of a baby."

Trip turned in her seat. "What baby? Izzy?"

"Yes. She means something to Carson." He gripped the steering wheel tighter.

"She's Carson's kid?"

"I didn't say that."

"Then why does he care?"

"Does it matter? Your mother is on a binge while taking care of an infant."

"Right." She folded her arms and stared straight ahead.

"Trip. There are some things I can't tell you."

"Where's the kid's mother?"

"Missing, likely dead." Nate frowned at the road.

She narrowed her eyes. "Dead or likely dead?"

"Marcy's dead." Nate nodded, not daring to look her in the eye.

"Like I give a shit if Carson has a kid with that crack whore."

"Good, then drop it." The woman would come unglued if he told her the truth.

The thirty-minute drive gave him a chance to get his head on straight before he faced Dixie. Nate rolled through the residential area, mindful of the speed limit. He hadn't had enough beer with dinner to be legally drunk but preferred not to speed with alcohol on his breath.

Dixie's little red sports car was in the driveway, along with a blue sedan. She had company. Nate pulled to the curb and cut the engine.

"Stay put."

"Sir, yes, sir." Trip glared at the house.

Nate walked to the front porch, but before he could knock, a leggy blonde wearing little more than a smile opened the door. He recognized her from the bar but had never caught her name.

"You don't look like the pizza guy." Her gaze moved over him as if she couldn't make up her mind whether to slam the door in his face or slam herself against him. "I know you. You're Nate, right?"

"That's me. Where's Dixie?"

"She's occupied at the moment." The blonde glanced over her shoulder, then back to him. "Look, I don't want any trouble."

Nate folded his arms as he debated the best course of action. He could easily push his way inside, but that could end up with him in the backseat of a police car. "You going to invite me in?"

The blonde smiled and shook her head. "I don't think so."

"Why the hell not?" He set his hand on the door, pushing gently.

The blonde pushed back for a split second, then stepped back to give him room. "You need to go before I call the police."

Once inside, Nate glanced around the living room. Bits and pieces of clothing and trash covered the couch. Bottles and glasses littered the coffee table. A small mirror with white lines sat off to one side of an end table. "I doubt that."

Nate picked up a wine bottle and shook it, something rattled inside. He didn't need to look to know it was a syringe. Nate's attention drifted to an empty baby swing in the corner, and his jaw tensed. "Tell Dixie I'm here."

The blonde put her hand on her hip and rolled her eyes. "I told you she's busy."

He turned and walked down the hall with the blonde on his heels.

"Hey, you can't just—"

Nate opened the first door, empty bathroom.

The blonde grabbed at his arm as he opened the next door. Before his eyes could adjust to the darkness, a female inside the room shrieked and let loose a slew of curses.

He recognized the voice. "We need to talk."

"I'm busy." Dixie shoved the man beside her as he struggled to pull on his jeans.

The blonde behind Nate made a pained sound. "I'm sorry. I tried to stop him."

Nate took a step inside the room. "Get dressed, Dixie."

"You're no fun." She pushed her lower lip out and ran her fingers across her sagging breast. "You've fucked the daughter, how about giving the mother a try?"

He took three quick steps toward the bed, pulling her up by her arm. "Where's Izzy?"

Dixie whimpered, and he loosened his grip enough that she pulled her arm free and caught him in the jaw with a wicked right hook. She shouted to her friends, "Call 9-1-1."

Nate rubbed his chin as he worked his jaw. "I wouldn't call the police with all of that coke on the table and an infant in the house. She's in the house, isn't she?"

Dixie glanced at the woman in the hall and shook her head, then turned back to Nate. "It's none of your fucking business. Get out of my house."

"I'm not leaving until we talk." He stared until she fidgeted with the sheets.

"Paul, Sarah, will you guys give us a minute?" Dixie motioned toward the blonde and the half-dressed man.

The guy practically ran to the door, but the blonde hung back until Dixie motioned for her to go.

"Put some clothes on," Nate repeated.

Dixie sighed and rolled her eyes, then climbed from the bed and slid on a silk robe. "Happy now?"

"Hardly. Carson called me."

Her eyes widened before she could smooth her expression. She pulled her robe tighter and sat on the edge of the bed. "How does he know my business? He shouldn't have called you."

"He's worried about you, and the baby."

She narrowed her eyes. "So now you're here to be super dad or something? Neither one of you gives two shits about that baby. Even if she's yours, Marcy left her with me. She's fine."

Someone gasped behind him. Nate turned in time to catch the look of horror on Trip's face before she darted back down the hall. He wanted to go after her but not before he had Izzy. "Where's the kid?"

"Why do you care? You've never had anything to do with Izzy or Marcy because you know that she's Ryan's." Dixie shouted.

"Until someone runs a paternity test, only God knows who her father is. I care because she's an innocent child stuck in the middle of a bad situation." He grabbed her arm and pulled it straight, turning it to expose the inside of her elbow. Small bruises dotted her pale flesh from the crook of her elbow down her forearm. He pushed her arm away as if it was something foul, then stormed out. The second he opened the next door, he knew it was Izzy's nursery. Not because the walls were painted pink, or because a crib sat in the corner…the smell of urine hit him hard enough that he turned his head and covered his mouth. He forced himself to enter the room and look in the crib.

Urine stains covered the pink floral sheets. A blanket and full-sized pillow sat crumpled in the corner, but the crib was otherwise empty. He seethed at the sagging bumper pads and pillow in the crib. That this child had survived her first couple of months was a miracle. Dixie and Marcy didn't have a clue about how to care for an infant.

"Where is she?" He met Dixie in the hall, grabbing her shoulders and shaking until she went limp in his arms.

Dixie threw herself against him and sobbed into his chest. "I need help. I can't do this by myself. It's too hard. Please, Nate, for Ryan, please help me. That baby belongs to him. She's all I have left."

He'd tensed the moment she touched him. Refusing to comfort her, his arms remained at his sides until he couldn't take another second and eased her off of him. "Where is she?"

"She's with Marcy's sister. Jessica came and picked her up right before you got here."

"Will you go to rehab?"

Dixie nodded too quickly, then sighed and shook her head. "I want to, but I will lose my job. I can't miss so much work."

Nate noted every flinch, every shift of her eyes, curl of her lips. "I have thought I should pay you child support for Izzy. If she's my daughter. I need to make sure she is taken care of."

Dixie chewed the inside of her lip as she stared at him. Nate could practically hear the gears turning in her head as she considered her next move. "I need two thousand a month to pay my bills while I'm not working, then a thousand a month when I go back to work."

"I'll have my attorney put it in writing and file it with the court." He sighed and patted her on the shoulder, not knowing where he could touch her without sending her the wrong idea—that he cared.

"I'll find a program next week."

"Mack will pick you up in the morning around ten." He turned and walked toward the front door.

"Wait. I can't tomorrow. I need time. What about Ryan's funeral?" she called after him.

"Screw this up, and I will bury you." Nate walked outside, willing to bet his right arm she'd blow off treatment. He had enough of the games. One way or the other he'd get paternity tests on every guy in town if that's what it took to end this bullshit.

Nineteen

TRIP SAT IN THE CAR FUMING. She'd clearly heard her mother call Nate super dad. Why hadn't he told her the baby was his? Why the cloak and dagger bullshit?

Nate climbed into the driver's seat empty-handed.

"Where's your baby?" Her voice held more sarcasm than she intended.

"She's not my kid, and she's with Marcy's sister." Nate put the car in drive and pulled from the curb.

"Is she safe there?"

"Yeah, Jess is a good mom." Nate glanced in the rearview and sighed.

"So why in the hell did Marcy leave her baby with my mother and not her sister?" Trip couldn't imagine letting any child close to Dixie, let alone a baby.

"Jessica and Marcy weren't on good terms. Jess is married, lives in a nice neighborhood, raising four kids of her own. She can't have her drug addict sister around, ruins her image with the PTA." He checked the rearview again and turned onto a side street.

"Now that Marcy's dead maybe Jessica will adopt Izzy?" Trip checked her side mirror and noted a car following close behind them. "Do we have a tail?"

"Looks that way. Hang on." Nate took a sharp right and hit the gas.

"Any weapons in the car?" She rummaged through the glove box.

"This car is clean." He leaned back. "Reach into my pocket. I have a small nine."

She slid her hand into his pocket and pulled out the subcompact. "This won't do much. It looks like a toy."

"It'll put a hole in someone, and it's all we have." Nate took a sharp left, and the car bounced over the rough pavement.

"Where are we going? Do you have a plan?"

He grinned, made another left, and pulled onto Main Street. "I always have a plan. We're going to the police station."

Trip's mouth hung open. That was the last thing she expected him to say.

Nate squealed into the police station and didn't stop until the car sat three feet from the front door. "Give me that."

Trip handed him the gun. The car that had followed them hadn't turned in. Four uniformed officers and a plain clothed one came out of the building. She had no idea what to say to them, so she stayed in the car. Nate opened his door and put his hands up. The officer in street clothes rapped on her window and motioned to the unlock button.

The door opened, and she stared at a face she'd hoped to never see again, John Daugherty—the man who had knocked her around and knocked her up.

Nate cleared his throat. "Sorry about that, officers. We had a bit of a problem. Someone was following us home tonight."

"Trix, is that you?" John grinned from ear to ear. "I figured you'd be back for Ryan's funeral but never expected you to be hanging out with this trash or involved in a homicide."

Trip glared but remained belted into her seat.

John motioned to Nate. "Go on inside and file a report."

"I didn't see anything other than headlights. Nothing to report."

"Where were you coming from?"

"JJ's."

"Been drinking?" John glanced at Trip. "How about you, did you see anything?"

"No." Trip kept her voice calm, drawing her training to keep from jumping out of the car and beating the shit out of him.

"Step out of the car." John took a step back to give her room.

Trip stared straight ahead. "I don't want to file a report."

John leaned down and reached in, seemingly to unbuckle her seatbelt. In the process, he groped her breast and then between her legs. "Have you missed me, baby?"

Trip grabbed his wrist and twisted, drawing him further into the car, then shoved her elbow into his face.

"You fucking bitch." He pulled back, holding his bleeding nose. "That is assaulting a police officer. Smitty, get her out of the car and book her."

"Actually, I want to press charges for sexual battery. You had no right to touch me, let alone my breast." Trip smiled.

Nate walked to her side of the car.

John held up a hand. "Step aside, Nate, unless you want to join her in lock up."

The officer, she assumed was Smitty, said, "Daugherty, think this through. I hear she's military and pretty high up."

"She's lying." John glared at them.

"I'll make a statement. He grabbed her crotch, too. She's just too much of a lady to say it." Nate folded his arms.

The other officers present glanced from John to Nate.

"Go, but you better watch your step, sweetheart." John spat on the ground and slammed her door closed.

Trip stared straight ahead, neither engaging him nor showing one hint of fear. She had no doubt he would hurt her if given half the chance. He'd done it many times before. However, unlike before, she could fight back. And she would.

Nate sank into the driver's seat and started the car. "Are you okay?"

Trip nodded.

An officer knocked on Nate's window. "Hold up. I was just about to go home. I'll follow you to Carson's to make sure there's no trouble."

"Thanks, Tom. That'd be great. My girl is a little shaken up." He squeezed her hand.

Once Tom walked away, Nate rolled up the window and turned to Trip. "Mind telling me what just happened?"

"John and I dated in high school. Well, I was in high school, and he was in college. He used to use me as his personal punching bag."

Nate gripped the steering wheel. "I'm not surprised. He has a track record of hitting women. One tried to press charges a couple of years ago, but nothing stuck."

She pulled her hand from Nate's and stared at the doors to the station. One day she'd make him pay. "Last time he hit me I was seven months pregnant."

"Damn, Trip. Is that what...?"

"Partially. Dixie owns part of the blame, too."

"No wonder you stayed away from this hell hole so long."

She sighed. "You don't know the half of it."

"No, but I'm here if you need to talk. We have a long drive ahead of us today."

She hung her head, remembering the trip he'd planned. "I'm in no shape to see a shrink today. Can we push the trip off a couple of days?"

"No. We're going home, getting cleaned up, doing the appointment, and getting the hell out of here." The marked cop car followed him out of the parking lot.

"What about Ryan's ashes?" Surely it would take a day or so to get them.

"Lurch will have them at Carson's this morning."

She turned to face him. "If I go within ten feet of a doctor, they're going to lock me up. I'm an emotional mess."

"Babe, your brother just passed away. You are supposed to be a mess."

"All right, but you should stay in the car, keep it running. If I get one hint they are pulling out the straitjackets, I'm out of there." She turned, checking to ensure their police escort followed.

"I'll gladly be your get-away driver." Nate grinned and headed toward Carson's.

TWENTY

NATE WALKED AROUND THE POOL DECK as Carson swam his morning laps. He had to hand it to the guy, other than alcohol Carson took care of himself. "Hey, man, we need to talk."

"Did you take care of Dixie?"

"Izzy wasn't there. She's with Jessica for now. Mack is picking Dixie up this morning and taking her to rehab."

"Why aren't you taking her?"

"If I go, Trip will want to go, and it's not safe." Nate frowned and glanced over the yard. "We picked up a tail coming from Dixie's."

"You lost them?"

"Of course."

Carson swam to the edge and grinned. "Where's Trip? You wear her out?"

"She's getting dressed for her appointment."

"With the shrink?"

Nate nodded. "Did Lurch drop off the ashes?"

Carson narrowed his eyes. "On the desk. Why?"

"I'm going to take Trip to Deals Gap to spread Ryan's ashes on the Tail of the Dragon."

"That's at least a three-day trip." Carson pushed himself from the pool. "I don't like it."

"Four days, and I didn't figure you would."

"She's on board with this?" Carson dried his hair, then wrapped a towel around his waist.

"She needs a break from the drama. A few days away will help her get her head on straight."

"Is that what you want? The quicker she gets her shit together, the quicker she goes back to Lejeune."

Nate laughed through his pain. "If you love them set them free, brother."

"Don't fall in love."

"I know she's passing through. We've been over this." Nate squared his shoulders. "We're leaving after her appointment. The sooner we get out of Crystal Beach, the better."

Trip walked up the path with all three dogs trailing her. "I couldn't agree more."

Carson said, "First you ruin my fixer, now you ruin my dogs? Damn, girl, what's next?"

"I didn't ruin anything. I merely pointed out the flaws in your perception."

"How do you figure?"

"Nate is a fine fixer, but you don't utilize him to his full potential. Loosen the leash, let him do his job without you supervising, and he'll surprise you. Same thing with the dogs." Trip scratched the Basset Hound's belly.

Nate and Carson exchanged a look.

"So, you're saying Nate is like a well-trained dog?" Carson grinned.

Trip rolled her eyes. "Forget it."

Nate ignored the remark. "Ready to roll?"

She stood and settled her bag on her shoulder. "As ready as I'll ever be."

Carson gave Trip a quick hug. "You kids have fun. Don't drink and drive and always use a condom. You never know where's he's stuck that thing."

Despite the banter, the air around them thickened with tension. While Nate understood Carson's reservations, it was time for his boss to spend some time alone. Nate wouldn't be around forever.

Trip's hips swayed from side to side as she walked to the car. Her usually purposeful march had changed into a slow saunter.

"If I didn't know better, I'd swear you were scared." Nate started the car.

Trip shut the door and shrugged. "I'm not a big fan of doctors."

"Want to talk about it?"

"Not much to talk about. I had an incident, drew my weapon on a team member, broke his nose, ended up in the bin for an eval."

"You've been under some serious stress here, and you haven't lost your head."

"I've—" She shook her head. "I've not been myself."

"What do you do, in the Marines? What's your job?"

"I started as an MP, Military Police. Now I train them."

"I should have guessed." He smiled, though something told him she lied. "Ever think of getting out?"

"No, not really. I've spent my entire adult life in the Corps. It's where I belong."

They continued in silence for a while. Nate rolled Carson's words around. He shouldn't fall for this woman, but he was pretty sure he already had.

She curled her legs beneath her. "What about you? What do you plan to do when you leave Carson?"

"I have it all set. I'm going to pick up Sophie and drive out west. I have some property and a little place. I'm half owner of a small garage. I'll work part-time and take care of the munchkin after she gets out of school in the afternoon. Spend our weekends kicking back, being a family."

"Aren't you worried someone will track you down?"

Nate shrugged. "I've been careful. Carson isn't as omniscient as he thinks he is."

"What about the people he works for?"

He managed to keep his face smooth while inside he cringed. The million-dollar question, the one he'd been waiting for Trip to ask. "Carson doesn't work *for* anyone."

"Right, but he works with people. I'm assuming people you can identify. How safe are they going to feel when you up and vanish?"

"Like I said, I've been careful." He gripped the wheel. "What would you have me do? Stay inside until Sophie hates me for abandoning her or until I catch a bullet?"

"No, of course not." She sighed and looked out the window.

"Look. You said it yourself. You're passing through. No sense in telling you all my secrets, unless…"

"What?"

He wiggled his brows. "Unless you plan to come with me. Then I'd need to get you a new identity. Maybe a new face? How do you think you would look as a blonde? We could get you new tits while we're at it."

"No thanks, you can keep the tits and the blonde hair." She shook her head.

"You're right. I like the dark hair, it adds to your mystery, and as for your breasts…I like your little bites."

Trip reached between his legs and squeezed. "I like your itty bitty, too."

The car jumped into the next lane before Nate could correct it. "It's average."

"Sweetie, it's better than average."

"Yeah?" He glanced over and grinned.

Trip laughed as she removed her hand. "Tell me about Marcy and her daughter."

"What do you want to know?" More questions he didn't want to answer.

"Who's the kid's father?"

"I don't know. Marcy claims it could be a couple of guys."

"Such as?"

Nate decided to go for broke and tell her the truth. "She claimed it was either me, Carson, or Ryan."

Trip sat back in her seat. "Damn, did she get around or what? Should I get STD tests?"

"Suit yourself, but I'm clean. It was a one-time thing before she fell off the wagon." Nate checked for traffic and pulled onto the exit ramp.

"Fell off? The damned thing ran her over, backed up and hit her again." Trip fidgeted in her seat.

"That was catty."

She shrugged.

Oh, she's jealous? "Izzy isn't mine. I had a vasectomy."

"Those things can fail."

"Ryan and I offered to have the paternity test, but Marcy refused. Which tells me the kid belongs to Carson."

"I would think Marcy would be on that like a fat kid on ice cream."

"That's rude." Nate gave her a scathing look.

"What? Marcy didn't exactly strike me as the brightest. She could do worse than child support from Carson for the next eighteen years."

"No, I mean the fat kid comment."

Trip wrinkled her brow until a slow smile crossed her face. "Oh yeah, you were pudgy in school, weren't you? What was your nickname again?"

He sighed. "Ham-thanial."

Trip giggled. "That's stupid. I remember it being much funnier when I was a kid. Then again, everything Ryan did was..." She stared out the window. "Are we almost there?

"Five minutes, give or take. Are you okay?"

"Not really. I mean, I haven't had time to grieve him."

"I feel the same way. We'll have time in North Carolina. I promise."

"Thanks, Nate, or should I say, Ham?"

TWENTY-ONE

TRIP STARED AT THE FRAMED CERTIFICATIONS and diplomas hanging on the wall while the good doctor went over her intake forms. She'd played this game before, or at least watched others play it, enough to know what to say, and what not to say, if she wanted to keep her job.

"May I call you by your first name?" The doctor set the file aside.

"I prefer Peyton if you don't mind. It's a military thing, I guess."

He tilted his head. "You can relax, Peyton."

She blew out a sigh and sat back against the chair.

"You noted that you are not experiencing any sort of flashbacks or nightmares. Do you remember the events in Sinaloa?"

"Yes."

"I've read your reports from your time there. I'm surprised you've adjusted as well as you have."

Her shoulders rose and fell. "It sounds more traumatic than it was."

"You were held captive for ninety-three days, beaten, and not provided with proper nourishment. It sounds pretty traumatic to me." He sat back and eyed her.

"If you read my reports, you know I was only beaten when I tried to resist capture. I was given food and water, but this is Mexico we're talking about. The water isn't safe to drink in the major cities, let alone in the country."

"Were you sexually assaulted?"

His question surprised her. "No, sir."

"Did you develop friendships with your captors?"

"Yes, one or two of the women. Mostly I stayed close with the wives and other females in the camp."

He nodded and wrote something in her file. "Tell me about the incident with Sergeant Rodriguez."

"It was my first week back on duty. I wasn't used to overnights after three months of sleeping ten to twelve hours a night. I was drinking a lot of coffee and pretty jittery. I didn't put it in my report, but I fell asleep twice that night. Rodriguez must have found me sleeping and tried to wake me."

"How did he wake you?"

Trip lowered her head and feigned embarrassment. "I woke up with his arms wrapped around my waist and him kissing my neck."

"Is this usual behavior between the two of you?"

"No, sir. We dated a couple of years ago, but it ended when I outranked him. The Corps frowns on fraternization. We are good friends, but there is nothing sexual between us."

"Other than kissing your neck?"

She shook her head. "He jokes around a lot. He startled me, and I reacted."

"Have you reacted in such a way again?"

If she said nothing else had happened, she'd appear resistant. However, Trip couldn't tell him anything related to the case. *I have to make something up.* "My first night home, my brother took me out for drinks. This guy kept staring at me. Next thing I know he is moving my shirt down my shoulder to look at my tattoo. I pinned him to the bar."

"Did it frighten you? A stranger touching you?"

She laughed. "No. I wasn't in the mood for touchy drunks. I figured I'd end it before it started."

"So, it wasn't a reflex?"

"I guess it was a reflex. It happened before I had time to think it through, but I didn't feel threatened."

He steepled his hands under his chin. "Tell me why Sergeant Major McGuire and the doctors ordered a PTSD evaluation."

"My heart rate was elevated, and I was short of breath. They checked for blood clots, thyroid issues, diabetes, you name it. When nothing came up, they decided I had anxiety and blamed it on the stuff in Sinaloa. Put me on meds."

He flipped through her chart. "I don't see a mention of medication here."

"Evidently, there was a mix-up, and the discharging doctor forgot to give me meds. He called my commanding officer with the prescription." She dug in her bag and pulled out her prescription bottle. "Levoxyl. I take two of these a day."

"May I see the bottle?"

Trip shrugged and handed it to him.

He turned to his computer, typing furiously. After taking a moment to read the screen, he opened the bottle and dumped a pill into his palm. His brow furrowed as he turned the medication over and made some notes in her file.

"Something wrong?" Trip didn't care for the way his brows knitted together.

"This medication is for thyroid disorder. Not to mention, this is twice the standard dosage for a woman your size."

"I don't have thyroid problems."

He nodded. "It must have been a medication error. They happen more often than you might think. Stop taking these immediately. At this dose, they can cause heart palpitations, rapid heart rate, and anxiety, as well as other symptoms."

Trip sat back in her chair. "Is it possible the meds are causing all of my symptoms?"

"After everything you have been through, I'm going to say no. They're most likely exasperating your underlying PTSD." He flipped through her chart again. "Did they do a tox screen to rule out chemical exposure?"

"Yes. When I returned to the states, I was hospitalized for a week. They ran a lot of tests."

He nodded. "I'll get those results before our next appointment."

Trip smiled. "You might want to go through McGuire for those. Our missions are classified, as in they didn't happen."

"Noted." He stood. "I'd like to see you back in three days. That'll give me time to get the records if they exist."

"I'll be out of the state for a few days. My brother passed away, and I'm going to spread his ashes in the mountains."

The doctor sat. "Your brother died since you have been in Florida?"

What the hell was that supposed to mean? Trip took a moment to gather her wits. "Yes, he was in a motorcycle accident."

"How are you coping with the loss?"

"It's difficult, but I'm glad I was able to see him before he died."

"Peyton, therapy, even medication, will only work if you want it to work. It involves time and trust."

She nodded. "I believe that, but I also know myself better than anyone. I'm coping pretty well. Yes, I'm more jittery than before, but not because I'm traumatized."

He motioned for her to continue.

"Because I let my team down. I was cocky, thought I had it under control. When my cover was blown, I made sure everyone was safe… everyone but myself. I guess being taken, and my brother's death have reminded me that I'm human."

He smiled and offered his hand. "Welcome to the club. Now you can begin to forgive yourself for not being perfect."

"I'm far from perfect, sir." She laughed.

"I was in the service for twenty years. I know what stress they put on young people to be all they can be."

"Forgive me, sir, but that's the Army."

"They have the best slogans, though." He chuckled and motioned to the door. "Schedule an appointment for next week and call me if you have any issues. Night or day, my service will know how to reach me."

"Thank you."

Trip walked into the Florida sun, feeling as if her feet left a lighter imprint in the sand. For the first time in a while, she didn't feel broken. Chipped? Maybe. Bruised? Definitely, but not broken.

Nate stood when she entered the coffee shop. "How did it go?"

"Better than I expected." She stole his coffee and knocked back the remainder of the cup. "Seems they gave me the wrong medication. The crap I've been taking can actually cause a racing heart and shortness of breath."

"Are you kidding me? You don't have PTSD?"

"He says I do, but the meds are making it worse."

"That sounds like a lawsuit waiting to happen."

"Marines can't sue the government. It's in our contracts."

"That's almost as screwed up as being given the wrong meds." He shook his head. "Want some coffee for the road?"

"No, if you insist on driving, I insist on a book on tape and sleep."

"We need to get rolling, babe. I don't have a library card, and I haven't seen an actual bookstore in years."

"No worries, *babe*. I have a couple on my Kindle."

He furrowed his brow. "Do you have headphones? I'm not listening to some cheeseball romance all the way to North Carolina."

"They aren't all cheesy. Some are quite erotic." She feigned indignation.

"Uh huh. You don't need anything to make you hornier. I barely escaped with my life in that hot tub."

"Oh, my God, you're the girl in this relationship."

"We're in a relationship?" His brows rose.

"Fuck-buddies counts as a relationship. We should hit the road." She turned for the door. *Keep your head on straight, Marine. It's an act. Keep your heart out of it.*

TWENTY-TWO

NATE NEARLY RAN OFF THE ROAD TWICE while stealing glances at the woman sleeping in the passenger's seat. The first couple hours she'd listened to her book. The story didn't completely suck, but he enjoyed her reactions more than the words. Trip had laughed, bitten her lip, and sighed. Once or twice she reached for his hand and smiled. *Yeah, I could watch her listen to audiobooks for hours.*

Trip stirred, stretched her arms, and glanced out the window. "Where are we?"

"A little north of Atlanta. We have about two and a half hours to go. You hungry?"

She shrugged. "Not really. I just want to get out of this car. I'm feeling claustrophobic in here."

"You've slept most of the time."

"I'm not sleeping now, though." She thumbed through her Kindle, then tossed it in the backseat. "Battery's dead."

"I have chargers in the glovebox."

She took her hair down and shook it out. "I'm bored with it. Where are we staying when we get there?"

"With my folks."

"What? No. I don't do well with parents." She squirmed in her seat.

Nate locked the doors. "In case you thought about jumping out."

"Funny. I'm not jumping out, but I can't stay with your family and your daughter. It's not good to introduce kids to people who are temporary."

"You're not temporary." Nate tugged her hand to his mouth and kissed her palm. "We'll still be friends even when you return to Lejeune."

"What about sex? We can't have sex with your parents and daughter around."

"If the mood hits, we'll find a way. Relax. I don't see Sophia very often. I can't come all the way up here and not stay with her."

Trip sighed. "I'm sorry, that was really selfish of me. Of course, you should see your daughter but leave me at the nearest hotel."

"Not happening."

"You can't possibly believe someone followed us all the way up here."

He set his jaw. "No, but I'm not taking any chances. Besides, it'll do you good to spend time with a normal family."

"Can we at least stop and clean up before I meet your parents?"

"You look beautiful. I mean, maybe change into a T-shirt that doesn't have ketchup down the front and run a brush through your hair."

She punched his arm.

He laughed, rubbing the sore muscle. "What?"

"I'd like to stop and wash my face before I meet your mother, please."

"Why are you so nervous? You're a Marine." He enjoyed her freak out more than he should, but damn, she was cute when she squirmed.

"I don't have to deal with mothers in the Marines."

They passed a sign for a hotel at the next exit. "I'll get us a room for the night. It's getting late, and it'll be past Sophia's bed time anyway. I'll let them know we will be there for a late breakfast."

"No, it's okay. I don't want to keep you from your kid even for one night."

"*And I* want to spend a few hours making you scream my name before we are sent to separate bedrooms." Nate merged into the right lane and took the exit ramp off the highway.

The room looked like any other interstate hotel room, mostly clean, nondescript, and basic. Nate dropped her bag on the extra bed, turned the AC on full blast, and pulled both layers of curtains closed.

"Food, shower, sex?" Trip wandered into the bathroom.

"How about sex, shower, food, sex?" He moved to the door as she washed her face.

She reached behind her and turned the shower on. "Sex in the shower, food, and more sex."

Nate shook his head. "Anyone ever tell you that you're a serious pain in the ass."

She ran her hands up his chest. "Every day, twice a day."

He curled his fingers around her stained T-shirt and pulled it over her head. "You went to see a shrink without a bra?"

She pressed her chest against his. "No, I took it off at that rest area in Florida."

Nate tugged his shirt over his head and kicked off his shoes. "How did I miss that?"

"You were arguing with Carson." She opened his belt and popped the buttons on his jeans.

"Right." He followed her lead and lowered her zipper. To his surprise, he managed to remove her skinny jeans while she stood. He stepped out of his pants and into the shower.

Trip followed him in and pulled the curtain closed behind her. He leaned against the wall as the water sluiced over her body. Her natural beauty stole his breath. She had what most women spent hours trying, and failing, to achieve.

Trip opened her eyes and grinned. "Why are you looking at me like that?"

He pulled her to his chest. "You're beautiful."

"You're crazy, I'm—"

Before she could say another word, he covered her mouth with his and snaked his arm around her waist. She rose to her tiptoes as she wrapped her arms around his neck, returning his kiss. The way her body slid against him, the feel of her soft skin, the fierceness of her kiss, all of it drew something from deep inside him. His desire for her went far beyond the physical, he wanted so much more.

Nate released her. "Turn around."

Her eyes widened as she turned to face the wall.

Nate unwrapped the miniature soap and wet the washcloth, wondering what she'd seen in his expression that startled her. He ran the washcloth over her back in slow circles, then lifted one arm above her head and washed from fingertip to shoulder.

"Why wash me when we're going to get dirty again?" She started to turn, but he pulled her against him.

"So I can do it all over again."

"But—"

"No arguments." He smacked her perfect, heart-shaped, ass.

She gasped and tensed as if she might try to take charge. In their short time together, he'd learned she liked to have control. However, she surprised him once again. Trip placed her hands on the wall above her head and lowered her chin. It took him a moment to recognize she'd given in without a fight.

Nate took his time washing her back, then squatted and ran the cloth up her legs. A pink impression of his hand on her cheek brought out a primal need to mark her as his. He pressed his lips to her hip and drew her flesh between his teeth, sucking and biting until she moaned in protest.

He stood, admiring the purple mark on her skin. "Turn around."

She turned to face him. Though she kept her eyes low, he caught a hint of a smile on her lips.

Nate put more soap on the rag, then squeezed it over her chest. "I love your breasts."

She reached for him, but he took her wrists in one hand and pulled her arms over her head. Nate ran the soapy cloth down the center of her body and back up again. Once finished, he moved to the side and eased her forward under the water. His chest pressed to her back, he held her while the soap rinsed away.

"Good girl. Get out and dry yourself off. I'll be out in a minute."

"But, Nate—"

He tugged her hair hard enough to get her attention, then whispered into her ear. "No arguments. Do you understand?"

Trip trembled in his arms. "Let me touch you."

He turned her to face him and cupped her chin, forcing her to meet his gaze. "If you touch me right now, I'm going to explode. I need a minute."

"I want you to, all over my chest."

The look in her eyes undid him. Her cockiness had faded into something he couldn't put his finger on. Not vulnerability, not Trip, but something softer and needful. "Why can't I ever say no to you?"

She dropped to her knees and took him in her hand. Her firm grip drew all the blood from his brain, and he set his hand on the wall for support. The feel of her lips around him caused his knees to wobble. *Oh, God, that thing she did with her tongue.*

Nate curled his fingers in her long, dark hair and held her head in place. Unfortunately, he couldn't still her tongue. He pulled his hips back, then thrust into her open mouth.

Trip moaned around him, sending another shudder through his body. Nate forced himself to think of golf. The world's most boring sport. *Those stupid little balls, Oh, God, what is she doing to my balls? Golf, men in preppy clothes, driving those dumb carts around.* His lower abdomen tightened, and he twitched in her throat.

"Babe, stop. I'm close."

Trip didn't stop, in fact, she sucked harder and faster. He tugged her head back a split second before he came. She held him in her hand as he coated her chest, then took him back into her mouth when he'd finished.

"No...sweetheart...no." He pulled away and sank to his knees.

Trip smiled as she smeared the evidence of his pleasure over her breasts. "Anyone ever tell you how hot you are when you moan?"

"I want to taste you." Nate lowered his head, transfixed by her hand moving down her body.

She ran her finger between her folds. "I want you inside me."

"Yeah?" He reached for her, but she slapped his hand away.

"Get yourself hard."

Nate swallowed, his throat dry and palms sweaty. He stroked himself, never taking his eyes off her fingers.

"Stand up." Her hand moved to her right breast.

Nate stood and helped her to her feet.

Trip pressed her back to the wall and set her foot on the soap dish. He stepped in front of her, and she took his shaft in one hand and his shoulder in the other. The height difference between them made this impossible without an adjustment. He wrapped his hands under her thighs and lifted as he pressed forward.

Trip wrapped her legs around his waist and guided him to her entrance. The twinkle in her eye told him he'd been played. She'd stolen the control with one look. She owned him, and they both knew it. "Fuck me, Nate."

He thrust inside her, pinning her to the wall. Her entire body tensed around him. When her thighs relaxed, Nate pulled his hips back and pushed inside again, slower and deeper this time. Her heat and arousal threatened to push him too hard, too fast. He tilted his hips forward, grinding his pubic bone into her.

Trip's eyes closed, and she moaned into the steamy air, her nails clawing into his shoulders. Over and over again Nate inched back and pushed forward, grinding more than thrusting until her body became taut as a bow string. Still holding her upper thighs, he slid his fingers between her cheeks.

Trip's eyes flew open, and she shook her head, but he pushed his index finger into her tight ass. Nate held her gaze as he circled and stretched the opening. Her eyes fluttered shut.

He whispered, "Do you like that?"

"Uh huh."

Nate thrust his length and finger deeper. Trip bucked so hard that he nearly lost his balance. Her fingernails tore down his back as she moaned incoherently, though he heard his name in there somewhere.

"You okay?" Nate removed his hand but otherwise stayed in place.

Trip's heart raced as the aftershocks coursed through her body. "Uh huh. You?"

"Off the charts, but next time I'm going to tie you down."

Trip giggled. "It won't help. You are *such* my bitch."

TWENTY-THREE

EACH MILE CLOSER TO THE BENZ HOMESTEAD brought Trip closer to a nervous breakdown. This. This is how she knew she didn't have heavy-duty PTSD. Sure, the moisture had left her mouth and now coated her palms and pits, but her pulse remained steady.

"Nate, this is silly. There's no reason I should meet your family. I'm a temp-fuck."

Nate narrowed his eyes and stiffened his spine. "If that's all you are, then this is no big deal. Suck it up for forty-eight hours. You don't need to worry if they like you. You're not going to be around."

Right. I'm not going to be around, but then why did his words sting? "I don't do well with mothers."

"Besides your own, how many mothers have you met? I got the impression you weren't much of a serious dater."

"I'm not. It's near impossible to date in the Corps. I'm deployed more often than not, and they have fraternization rules."

"So, how do you know you don't get along with mothers?"

"I don't know." She turned to the window. Only one guy had taken her home to meet his family. John Daugherty had waited until her belly swelled to the size of a watermelon before he introduced her to his mother. Needless to say, the woman hadn't reacted well. "Maybe you're right."

Nate squeezed her hand without taking his eyes off the road. "I'm always right, besides you've met my folks before."

Trip's stomach lurched as he made his way up the twisted mountain road, two narrow lanes with nothing but a pitiful guardrail between her and sudden death. "I have?"

"You tagged along with Ryan to my house a few times. I know you were at my twelfth birthday party."

She remembered following Ryan everywhere, but the five-year age difference meant she was seven at Nate's party. "I don't remember much of my childhood."

"You caught us looking at my dad's porn mag."

A grin tugged at the corner of her mouth. "How can you remember that?"

"Because you ratted us out. I ended up grounded for a month."

Trip furrowed her brow, shaking her head. "I don't remember that at all. Are you sure it was me?"

"Oh, I'm sure." He winked and turned onto a gravel drive.

In the distance sat a white two-story house, surrounded by flowers. The yard had a gentle slope, surprising considering the elevation. A dark haired little girl waved from the porch, then ran toward the car.

Nate cut the engine and met the girl in the middle, scooping her into his arms and holding her tight. The child squirmed and giggled, but Nate refused to loosen his grip. His shoulders shook with emotion, and the little girl pulled back. She took her father's face in her hands, smiled, and kissed his nose.

Trip pretended to rummage through her bag to give the two some privacy and to give herself a moment to gather her wits. She'd never had a father, let alone one who held her like Nate held Sophia.

Trip forced a smile and opened the door as they approached the car.

"Sophie, this is Trip. My friend. Trip, this is my daughter, Sophia." Nate beamed at the two of them.

"Trip? Cool name. Nice to meet you." Sophia grinned, revealing the absence of at least two teeth. "Are you Daddy's girlfriend?"

Nate laughed and messed her hair. "She's a girl, and she's my friend."

"So, she is your girlfriend." Sophia squealed and ran for the porch. "Nana, guess what? Daddy brought his girlfriend."

"Seriously?" Trip mumbled as she slung her bag over her shoulder. "What happened to no big deal."

"Relax, babe." He took her bag.

"I can carry my—"

He covered her mouth with his, right there in front of his mother, daughter, God, and everyone. He freaking kissed her.

"See, Nana? I told you." Sophia bounced on the balls of her feet.

Nate walked toward the porch, leaving Trip had no choice but to follow. She kept her eyes low until he stopped at the bottom of the porch. Nate's smile lit her entire face. Trip could spot a fake smile from twenty yards, but a genuine one made her nervous.

"Momma, this is Trip Peyton. Do you remember her?"

"Heavens, yes, of course, I remember her." Momma Benz came down the steps and wrapped Trip in a hug before she could stop her. "Please, call me Lynette. I'm so sorry to hear about your brother. How are you holding up? I was worried when Nate said you had to stop for the night."

"I'm all right." A blush crept into Trip's cheeks. *What the hell? I'm blushing?*

Nate ran his hand over the back of his neck. "Momma, do you have breakfast on? We're starving."

"You're always hungry." She turned and hugged her son.

Travis, Nate's father, came in through the back door with an armful of firewood. He set the logs down and embraced his son. Trip shifted her weight from one foot to the other as her stomach roiled. She'd seen parents hugging their children after boot camp graduations, or when returning from deployment, but this was too close, too personal. *I'm intruding.*

The men parted with slaps on the back. Nate turned to her and smiled. "Pops, do you remember Ryan Peyton's baby sister?"

Travis studied her for a moment. "Isn't she the little squirt that tattled on you and Ryan for looking at my girlie magazines?"

Lynette swatted his arm. "Don't bring that up in front of Sophie."

"What?" As if on cue Sophia popped up.

Trip took a step back and stumbled over a chair. Her pulse pounded in her ears, drowning out the concerned voices of Nate and his parents. Her chest constricted, leaving her fighting for her next breath. She imagined what she must look like, what they must think of her. Her pulse increased until she thought she'd stroke out in the middle of their living room.

Nate lifted Trip from the floor as Lynette placed a cold washcloth on her forehead. Sophia's shrill voice filled her ears, followed by the baritone voice of Nate's father. Trip closed her eyes, surprised by the hot tears that ran down her cheeks. She hadn't cried since boot camp, one trip home and she leaked like a damned rusted spigot.

"I'm sorry. I must have—"

"Easy, babe." Nate drew her closer.

"Let's get her upstairs. Poor thing, she's probably exhausted."

Nate followed Lynette into a small bedroom. He set Trip on a bed, and Lynette pulled a blanket over her. With the two of them standing side by side, it was easy to see the resemblance. Not to mention, they wore the same concerned expression.

"When's the last time she ate?" Lynette whispered.

"Last night. I told you we were starving."

Lynette's voice lowered again. "Pregnant?"

"No." Trip and Nate said at the same time.

"I'm sorry. No. I mean, no. I'm definitely not pregnant. Dehydrated maybe." Trip sighed and shut up.

"Stay with her. I'll get her some juice." Lynette hustled to the door.

"I'm okay." Trip eased to her elbow, but Nate put his arm on her shoulder and pushed her back.

"Take it easy." He ran his hand through her hair. "I couldn't have knocked you up, but are you sure you didn't come home that way?"

"Pregnant?"

He canted his head. "Don't play coy."

"I'm absolutely sure."

"Are you on the pill?" He furrowed his brow.

"Nate, relax. I'm not pregnant. I no longer have a uterus."

Lynette gasped from the doorway.

Sophia grinned ear to ear. "What's a uterus?"

TWENTY-FOUR

NATE SAT ON THE PORCH THINKING. He couldn't wrap his brain around Trip's change in mood. Since they'd pulled into his parent's driveway, all rational thought had abandoned her, leaving a lunatic behind. He'd fed her, rubbed her shoulders, joked around, but nothing brightened her mood.

He moved the swing with his foot. "Why don't we go for a walk?"

"When are we going to the Dragon's whatever to scatter Ryan's ashes?"

Is that the problem? She's finally grieving? "I thought we could go tomorrow. Say our goodbyes, then head into town for dinner."

She gave him a chilly look and shrugged.

"Trip, what is going on? You've been on edge since we got here."

"I can't. I can't do this. I can't deal with these fucking emotions."

"What emotions? Talk to me." He took her hands.

"Everything. Losing Ry, my mother, you…"

Nate stood, tugging her to her feet. "All right, that's it. We're getting out for a while. You have too much energy to burn off if you're lumping me together with your mother and losing Ryan."

Trip groaned. "That's not what I meant."

"Go change into jeans, boots, and grab a jacket."

"What? No. I don't—"

He swatted her ass. "I didn't ask. Go."

She narrowed her eyes but turned and walked inside. He could take her dirty looks, but couldn't handle the lost look in her eyes. Nate went inside and pulled an old quilt and basket from the closet.

"Going on a picnic?" Lynette smiled when Nate came into the kitchen.

"Yes, ma'am. Trip and I need to talk. I think it finally hit her we're saying goodbye to Ryan." He rummaged through the fridge unsure of exactly what he should pack.

"Oh, for heaven's sake. Let me. You're letting all the cold air out." She pushed him out of the way. "I have some left-over ham and potato salad."

"Sounds great." He ran his hand over his chin. "Does Pops still have wine in the cellar?"

"Yes, if it hasn't turned to vinegar by now. You're welcome to it." Lynette arched a brow. "You like this girl."

"I need to shave." He made scraping sounds with his stubble for the sole purpose of irritating his mother.

"Stop doing that." She frowned. "You always did like the birds with broken wings."

"Ma, she's not broken. She's grieving."

His mother gave him a patient look, then shook her head and made their sandwiches.

Nate went to the cellar for the wine and returned with a plan. He'd take her to his favorite spot, talk, watch the sun go down, light a few candles, pry until she opened up, and make love. By the time he finished with her, she'd sleep like a baby.

Nate tucked the bottle into the basket. Lynette smiled and gave him a half hug. She'd said her piece. Thankfully, his mother didn't nag.

He walked upstairs to find Trip. She sat on the windowsill staring out over the back pasture with her hand pressed to the glass. So much had happened since she returned home, he could only imagine what thoughts danced behind her stormy eyes.

Nate cleared his throat. "Ready to go?"

She shrugged and followed him downstairs. "Exactly, where are we going?"

"A hike to my favorite spot." Nate tied a ribbon around the handle of the basket to keep it closed.

Trip eyed it, then Nate. "Are we going on a hike or a picnic?"

"Both. Ready?" He couldn't help but smile. She made his old flannel sexy.

"I borrowed your shirt."

"I see that." Nate grinned and motioned for the door.

Sophia and Lynette sat on the porch swing, both wearing secret-keeping smiles. Nate had a pretty good idea about their secret. He'd never brought a woman here, or anyone for that matter. They had to know he had feelings for Trip. Feelings that could go nowhere.

"Sophie, we'll be back before bedtime." Nate braced himself for her protests.

"All right, Daddy." She waved. "Bye, Trip. I hope you're feeling better."

"Thanks, I am. Do you want to come along?" Trip glanced at Nate.

"Can I?"

Nate set the basket in the bed of the truck. "Next time, baby. Trip and I have some grown up things to discuss."

Sophia rolled her eyes. "It's called kissing, dad."

Trip climbed into the passengers. "She's got your number."

"She is growing up too damned fast." He put the truck in gear and followed the dirt path toward the back of the property.

"Where are you taking me?"

"It's a surprise." He ran his thumb over the back of her hand.

They rode in a comfortable silence for the remainder of the drive. The sun still sat high in the sky. His timing couldn't have been more perfect. He pulled off the dirt path and walked around front to open her door.

Trip climbed out and stared toward the next mountain. "Your folks own all this land?"

"Technically, it's half mine." He took her hand.

"I'd never leave. It's so peaceful like there's not another soul for miles."

"It's deceiving. There's a little town down in the valley, about ten minutes away."

They walked hand in hand for a country mile. Her lost in her private thoughts, while Nate thought of her. He couldn't decide which version of

Trip he liked more, the no-nonsense Marine or the fragile woman who walked beside him now. He wished he could have them both, but the mixture of the two ate her alive. Clouds snaked across the sky in a variety of colors when they reached the tree stand.

Nate motioned to the ladder. "Ladies first."

She eyed the wooden structure with a dubious grin. "How high up is that?"

"Twenty feet, but don't worry. It's safe. Pops and I built it a couple years ago." They'd built it for hunting, and for the views.

Trip slung the blanket over her shoulder and ascended the ladder with Nate following behind her. She reached the top and gasped.

"Afraid of heights?" He set the basket down and wrapped his arms around her.

"No, this is…this is just breathtaking. I haven't seen a sunset like that in years."

Nate spread the quilt over the rough wood and motioned for her to join him. "My mom says angels paint the sunset clouds with their wings."

She sighed. "Pretty to think so."

Nate uncorked the wine and poured two glasses. "Talk to me."

Trip took a quick sip. "When I'm busy working, I can ignore most everything except the mission. Everything falls into place, and I forget or pretend to forget, the past. Since I've been home, I'm drowning in it."

"Your mother?"

She nodded. "Some of it is her. Some is just being in Crystal Beach, too many bad memories."

"I've seen the way she acts around you. It's like she's a different person."

"She's always hated me." Trip drew her knees to her chest.

"I doubt that."

She shrugged. "It makes Mother's Day interesting. Try buying a card for the bitch who gave birth to you but never loved you. She loved Ryan all right, he walked on fucking water. No matter how bad he treated her, or how bad he screwed up, she loved him and made excuses for him. Me? I rolled my eyes once and ended up with a concussion. Of course, she'd never admit I had a concussion. She said I was looking for attention, never bothered to take me to the doctor."

Nate had grown up around the Peyton household. He believed her, but it hurt him to hear her say it.

"The sad thing is, she doesn't care enough about me to even bother with hate. I'm like the can of asparagus in the back of the pantry she bought thinking it might be good but never bothered to open and find out."

"You're not asparagus."

She shrugged. "Do you know what I'm most afraid of? That I'm just like her."

"You are nothing like her. You're strong."

"Yep. Strong. Tough as nails. I follow orders. I do as I'm told. Hell, I kill without remorse. I hate weakness. I hate tears. Crying never got anyone anywhere, plus when you cry you mark yourself as a victim. I'm not a victim." She studied his face.

"There's nothing wrong with tears. Especially when you lose someone close to you."

"I'm so angry at Ryan."

Nate sighed. "Me, too."

"He had no business driving. The docs said his blood alcohol was four times the legal limit. And the drugs? He died because of the drugs, and because that bitch didn't call…"

"Trip, we can speculate, but we may never know what happened that night." Nate hesitated to tell her the truth.

"That's just it. I don't know, and I need to. I need to make sense of this. Why would he pull that kind of shit the night I came home?"

"You can't be blaming yourself for this."

"No, but …I just got him back. I wanted to know him, and now it's too late." She turned to face Nate. "What's going to happen to Izzy? What if she is really my niece?"

Nate ran his hand through his hair. He didn't want to discuss Izzy or Marcy. "She's Ryan's or Carson's. My money is on Carson."

"What the fuck is it with men, creating babies and not sticking around to raise them?"

"I don't know why Carson is so stubborn about it. Maybe now that Ryan and Marcy are gone—"

"What happened to Marcy?"

He hesitated, debating on telling her the truth. One look in her eyes and his conscience took over for his brain. "Carson killed Marcy the night Ryan died."

"Were you there?" Trip scrambled away from him.

He nodded. "I tried to talk him out of it. She was off the rails."

"Of course, she was, she'd just seen her boyfriend bleeding to death on the side of the road." Trip wrapped her arms around her middle as if she might be sick.

"Trip, her car has a dent on the hood and damage on the bumper. Yellow paint—"

"Are you saying she caused the accident?"

"It's a strong possibility. There's more. She had Izzy with her that night. She left her in the car while she partied at the bar."

She shook her head. "I believe you, but that doesn't give Carson the right to kill her."

"I should have realized what he was doing, but I was preoccupied."

"With Ryan?"

"Yes, and with you. Babe, Carson would have killed you had you gone to the police."

"I gave you the drugs." Her eyes widened. "That child is without a mother because of me?"

He shook his head. "No, because her mother was a coke whore who would have ended up dead sooner than later. At least Izzy has a fighting chance at a normal life now."

She moved a few feet from him. "I guess… Damn it, Nate. I can't believe this."

Not liking where the conversation had gone, he panicked. "Why you choose the Marines?"

She snapped back to reality. "What?"

Nate sat beside her. "Why the Marines?"

"Because I'm a number, a safe, faceless number. Nobody is looking at *me* saying I'm not good enough. They're looking at my record, what some fuck wrote about me. Never me, they don't know the real me. If they did, they'd throw me out. They may anyway if I can't get my head together."

"I think you're selling yourself short. From what I know, you've made quite the career for yourself."

She sighed and grabbed the wine bottle. "Enough of the pity party."

"Feel better?" He ran his hand down her arm, and she pulled away.

"I'm numb. You confess to killing a woman, then change the subject? I'm fucking numb."

"I can't change the past."

Trip's voice rose. "I can't feel anything anymore, and when I do feel, I don't trust it. I'm angry, but not angry enough to do anything about it. I'm hurt, but what else is new? I need to get back to work, back to where things make sense. I can't be around you, your lifestyle, the drugs, the murders. I can't do this."

"Trip, you can't run away every time someone or something hurts you."

"You don't know me well enough to make that kind of call."

"I want to know you. The real you." He stood and pulled her to her feet. His touch melted her heart, and it drained through her eyes. Slowly at first, then in wracking sobs. She clung to him like a child, crying away a lifetime of tears. "Let it out, babe."

"I used to pray things would get better, my life would get better, but after so long I've come to the conclusion that nothing changes except the scenery."

"What would it be like if it changed?" He smoothed her hair back from her face.

She stared at him as if trying to understand his question. "It won't change. The pain stays. The doubt stays. The rejection, the humiliation, the fury. It all fucking stays. It eats at me like a cancer until there's nothing left."

"Bullshit." He grabbed her shoulders. "What do you want your life to be like?"

"I don't know."

"Yes, you do."

"You wouldn't be a murderer or drug dealer."

"This isn't about me. How would *your* life be different?"

"I'd ride a bike with no helmet, no regs telling me I can't feel the wind on my face. I'd smile more and remember what it feels like to really laugh. I'd be strong, proud of myself, and believe I'm invincible like I did when I was a kid." She wiped her tears away.

"What's stopping you?" He offered her a slight smile.

"I guess I am."

Nate nodded. "I remember you told me one time you studied so much so you could go to college and leave Crystal Beach. You had big plans."

"I got pregnant, remember?"

"Yes, but you did leave. You worked your ass off and have every reason to be proud of yourself."

"Why can't my mom be proud of me?"

Nate had a sense of how deep that question had cut. "Would you be disappointed in her if she had brain cancer or Alzheimer's and forgot who you were?"

"No, of course not."

"Your mom is sick, a different kind of sick. She isn't able to give you what she doesn't have. She loves the drugs, babe. She treated Ryan different because he fed her addiction. You …you remind her of what she could have been."

Trip stared blank-faced, for so long he thought she might have checked out. Had he pushed her too far? Where the hell had those words even come from? He knew, he'd had a similar conversation with Ryan, with Carson, and countless others. Nate had won the birth lottery, with two normal parents, but none of his friends had.

Trip whispered, "Izzy would have grown up the same way if Carson hadn't killed Marcy."

Nate nodded.

"I wouldn't wish that on anyone." She hung her head. "I…I don't know what happened to me, to that girl I was. I don't know her anymore."

"I saw her the other night, flirting with me at the bar. I saw her hold it together when Carlos had you cornered, and every time you handle Carson."

"That's me pretending." She dipped her chin.

"That's bullshit, and you know it. She's in there beneath the layers of garbage, fighting to keep from suffocating under the weight of it."

TWENTY-FIVE

THE LAST OF THE SUNLIGHT DISAPPEARED behind the horizon. Trip didn't know how to respond to Nate. No one had ever spoken to her like that. Part of her wanted him to put the macho mask back on and stop getting into her head, but the other part loved that he'd seen her. Actually seen her.

Nate wrapped his arm around her shoulder and drew her to his side. She turned her face toward his, and he took the hint. His lips moved over hers as he cupped the back of her head. Kissing him was a safer bet than continuing the conversation.

Trip pulled back and tugged her borrowed shirt over her head. She met his eyes and stilled. "What's that look for?"

"I'm surprised, I guess. Are you sure this is what you want?"

"I don't want to think for a while. Remind me that some things don't hurt."

"I can do that." He leaned forward and nuzzled into her chest.

She closed her eyes and allowed the weight of Nate's body to push her onto the quilt. He explored her chest with his hands and mouth, but she struggled to get her head in the game. Thoughts of her childhood and a little girl without a mother wouldn't let her relax into his touch.

"Babe? Are you with me?" Nate propped himself on his elbow.

"I am now." She shifted her weight and rolled over, pinning him down. Unlike his slow, methodical touch, she bit and tugged.

He pulled her pants over her hips as she fumbled with his belt. They kicked and yanked until her pants hung from one ankle and his were around his thighs. Trip grabbed his shaft, hard enough to elicit a moan, and came to her knees. She sank back, taking him into her core in one motion. The pain, mingled with pleasure, cleared the troublesome memories from her head. Her focus zeroed in on a singular goal—to fuck it all away.

Nate ran his hands up her body to her shoulders and pulled her to his chest. He embraced her in his iron grip, making it difficult to move more than her hips. "Where did you go?"

A lump formed in her throat and her chest tightened. "I'm right here."

"No, babe, you're not." He stroked her hair. "Just let me hold you a while.

Trip didn't trust her voice enough to argue. Her need to fight fled, leaving her with nothing but a ball of emotions. She hated him for not allowing her to forget but loved him for seeing through her bullshit. The tears started again, but Nate held her firm.

After she'd exhausted herself, he loosened his grip and moved her to lie beside him. She didn't dare look at his face for fear of seeing the one thing she hated more than anything, pity. He pulled the quilt over her and tucked her head against his chest.

Trip woke some time later with nothing but the quilt to beat back the night air. She opened her eyes to find Nate sitting beside her staring at the stars. "Hi."

He turned and smiled. "Hey, sleeping beauty."

"Sorry about that."

"Don't worry about it."

"Are you hungry?" Nate motioned to the basket.

"A little."

He pulled sandwiches, and God only knew what else from the basket. "Looks like my mom cleaned out the fridge."

"Answer a question for me." She sat up and drew the quilt around her shoulders.

"What's on your mind?"

She opened a baggie of grapes and tossed one into her mouth. "Who does Carson work for?"

"Carson works for Carson." Nate took a bite from his sandwich.

"That doesn't add up. Carson is small potatoes in the larger picture, but you keep Sophia hidden. His reach can't be that far."

"Don't underestimate him."

"I'm not, but you are overestimating him."

"Carson's smart and well connected. The good-old-boy charm suits him. He knows where some influential people hide their bodies. His greatest gift is getting people to trust him, feel comfortable enough to spill their secrets, and using the info to push his agenda."

She shook her head. "What is his agenda?"

"He likes his lifestyle, his toys, his power. He'll do what he needs to do to keep it." Nate filled his cup and handed her the bottle of wine.

"So Carson is the bogeyman. Where do the drugs come from?"

"Trip."

She took a sip of wine. "I'm trying to wrap my head around why you're so afraid of Carson."

"I've seen what happens to people who cross him." Nate tossed his half-eaten sandwich aside. "He'll see my leaving as a betrayal."

Trip sighed. She needed information but had to tread carefully with Nate. "You have cash and property without a paper trail. What's stopping you from leaving now?"

"Carson has influence. Cops, judges, politicians. I have to make sure everything's in place."

"In other words, you know too much about too many people to walk away without someone looking for you?"

"Something like that." He ran his hand through his hair. "We should get back to the house."

"Now?" She scooted closer. "You have candles in the basket, and an extra blanket."

He glanced at his watch, then slung his arm around her shoulders. "We have another hour before Sophie's bedtime. Let's not waste it talking about Carson. I'd like to talk about what happened earlier."

"I have one more question."

Nate's jaw tightened as he nodded.

"What's the deal with the Trevinos?"

"Local Mexican gang."

"Uh huh. Again, this is Crystal Beach, not Sinaloa."

He sighed. "Funny you should mention that."

Trip's stomach sank. "They're involved with the cartels?"

"What do you know about drug cartels?"

"I spent some time on Kingsville Air Station, and at Laughlin. It's hard to be that close to the border and not know about them."

"Rumor has it the Trevinos still have close ties to their Mexican cousins."

"…And that's where the drugs come from." Trip finished the wine in one swig. Her heart galloped, and she broke out in a cold sweat. "That explains why they ransacked Ryan's house. Carson isn't the only bogeyman you're worried about, is he?"

Nate took her by the shoulders. "Drop this, now."

"Who tipped them off that Ryan had the drugs? He killed the guy in the bar. That's what you were doing with the cleaning crew, isn't it?"

Nate nodded. "Yes. Ryan shot a Trevino enforcer at JJ's."

"Did Carson send them to Ryan's house to look for the drugs? How did they know he took off? How did they know to search his house? I'm guessing he shot the guy before he had a chance to call his boss."

"I don't know, but it wasn't Carson."

"Then who? Marcy?"

"Drop it!" He grabbed her arms until she cried out.

"Yes, sir." She pulled away from him as the pieces fell into place. *The night at JJ's, Carson's meeting, Nate rushing her out of the bar. Someone in the bar had tipped off the Trevinos. Could Ryan have known? Is that why he flew out of there in such a hurry?* "Let's go."

"Babe. Don't get in the middle of this."

"Too late." Trip turned and climbed down the ladder. As soon as she had a moment of privacy, she needed to call in a request for intel on the Trevinos. *Did they visit Mexico, how often, and which part?* This information would paint a clearer picture. Memories of her time in Sinaloa flooded her. Weeks of fearing each day would be her last.

Nate caught up and led the way back to the truck. From the set of his shoulders, she could tell he didn't want to talk any more than she did. Trip stumbled on a tree root and fell in step behind him on the path. Her chest tightened making it difficult to catch her breath. She wouldn't have an anxiety attack, not here, not now.

He set the basket in the bed of the truck and patted his jeans, his shirt pocket, and his jeans again.

"What's the matter?" Trip focused on her breathing to force herself to calm down.

He rummaged through the basket, then opened the door and looked inside the truck. "Misplaced the key."

"Are you kidding me?" She ripped the passenger's side door open and dug around the console. "Was it on a keyring?"

"Single, silver key. I used the spare." Nate checked both visors, then used his phone as a flashlight and searched the perimeter of the truck. "It has to be here somewhere."

Her hand trembled as she felt beneath the front seat. She grasped the door frame and tried to slow her breathing as her pulse thundered in her ears.

"Trip?" He placed his hand between her shoulder blades. "What is it?"

"My heart. It feels like it's going to explode."

He lifted her into the truck and eased her seat back. "Close your eyes, try to breathe slowly."

"Don't you think I am?" Frustrated, she leaned forward and closed her eyes.

Nate rubbed her shoulders as her body waged war against her brain. The more she fought to catch her breath, the more she panicked. Tears stung her eyes, and she gave up the fight to hold them in.

Nate remained blessedly quiet, offering his support through a gentle touch and his constant presence. Exhaustion that only a good cry could bring overtook her, and she sat back.

"Feel better?" He brushed her hair from her eyes.

"I'm losing my mind."

"No, you aren't. You're letting go of an ass-load of pent up emotions. You're only human."

"I have to get a handle on this."

"You will, but it takes time."

"Find the key, please." She forced a smile as she patted his scruffy cheek.

Twenty-Six

NATE'S CELL HAD DIED BEFORE HE FOUND THE KEY. They had no choice but to sleep in the tree stand and wait until the sun rose to find it. Wood planks squeaked when he moved and nails poked into his back, but the woman in his arms made it seem like the Ritz.

Nate nodded off only to wake to Trip crying out in her sleep.

Unless he'd dreamt it, she had spoken in Spanish. "Trip, baby, wake up."

Her hand shot to his throat, fingers digging into his skin. She shifted her weight and sank her knee into his groin. Nate groaned, resisting the urge to curl into the fetal position as his eyes watered. She reached behind her, as if going for a weapon, and wrinkled her brow when she found none. Recognition dawned on her expression, and she eased back with her hands covering her mouth. As soon as her weight lifted, Nate folded in on himself.

"Oh, my God. Nate, are you okay? I'm sorry. I was having a nightmare." She looked around. "It's so dark."

Nate nodded, trying to catch his breath as his testicles emerged from his abdominal cavity. Nauseated, he didn't dare try to sit upright. He rolled to his back and closed his eyes.

She pulled her knees to her chest and rested her head on her arms.

"What's going on?"

"Nothing, just a nightmare."

He turned his head toward her. "I didn't know you spoke Spanish."

"I told you, I was stationed in Texas. I was offered the opportunity to participate in a language intensive, and I took it. Came in handy working along the border." She moved closer. "Are you all right?"

"My balls feel three sizes too big."

"Let me see. They could be ruptured."

"Uh, no. I just need to lay here until my head stops spinning."

She reached for his belt, but he swatted her away.

"No touching. I'll be fine. Just need a minute." He took her hand. "Talk to me."

"I can't give details."

"Tell me what you can. I want to help you sort through this shit."

"I was working in Brownsville, near the border. My unit ran into some issues. A couple of the guys were killed. I was taken to Mexico with two others."

"What do you mean *taken?*"

"Kidnapped and held for ransom. It happens more often than you think."

He propped himself on his elbow. "United States Marines kidnapped and held in Mexico? How the hell did you get out?"

"I'm the only one who survived. A spec ops team rescued me after a few weeks."

Nate sat too quickly, causing nausea to return. "Were you hurt?"

"A little in the escape, but I'm fine now."

"Physically, maybe, but you aren't fine. How long ago was this?"

"A year or so."

Even in the dim light, he caught the shift in her eyes. She'd lied. "This is what caused the PTSD?"

Trip nodded and scooted closer to him. "How are the jewels?"

He wrapped his arms around her. She obviously didn't want to talk about her ordeal, yet he had questions. Nate didn't believe the how of her story. Sure, he'd heard of kidnappings and murders along the border, but a unit of Marines? What had they done to her? It seemed just as unlikely they held her for weeks and didn't tortured or raped her.

"Is that why you freaked out earlier? Was it members of a cartel that took you?"

Trip shrugged. "They were drug runners working for someone. They saw an opportunity to make some money and took it. We weren't anything other than a paycheck."

"Why did they kill the other prisoners?"

"Because they ran."

Trip tensed in his arms. *Had she seen her friends killed? There was more to the story.* She'd warned him she couldn't tell him everything, but what else had happened?

"Nate, I'm telling the truth. They didn't hurt me." She turned her face up toward his. "I mostly stayed with the women in the house. The señoras didn't want me near their men."

He stared into her stormy eyes and couldn't form a single thought other than he would never let anything happen to her again. He'd protect her or die trying.

Trip whispered, "What's that look about?"

"You never cease to amaze me."

"Don't." She frowned, burying her face in his chest.

"Don't what?" He pulled back to look at her. "Admire you? Not many could come out the other side of something like that relatively unscathed."

"Maybe I should thank Dixie for raising me to be a survivor." Her crooked grin broke his heart.

"Come with me. Leave the Corps and run away with Sophie and me."

She stared at him as if he had lost his mind, and maybe he had. Her entire body stiffened, and her heart thudded against his chest. He waited, expecting her to pull away or crack a joke. Instead, she sighed and closed her eyes.

"Think about it." He rubbed her back, praying she'd agree.

"I'm not mom material or even girlfriend material."

"I disagree, but we don't need to argue about it. The offer stands."

"You hardly know me. Not to mention, I can't take care of another human being. What if I turn out like my mother?"

"Again. You're nothing like your mother." He lifted her chin, forcing her to meet his gaze.

"I can't walk away from my entire life, Nate. It's a pretty thought, but I'd hate it. I belong in the Corps."

He nodded and brushed his lips across hers. "I've never met anyone like you."

She poked his side. "You need to get out of Crystal Beach to find a woman. Nothing there but beach bunnies and bar whores."

"And if I told you I'm falling in love with you?"

She pulled away. "I'd tell you it was lust. We've only known each other a few days."

"I've known you since you were a kid."

"You know what I mean. Don't ruin this. Don't put me on a pedestal. I'll just disappoint you."

He grinned. "I'm not ruining anything. You're passing through. I get it, but that doesn't mean I can't try to change your mind or enjoy your company while I have it."

"How're you feeling?" She ran her hand down his chest.

"I think I'm out of commission for the night."

She kissed the corner of his mouth. "Thanks for the talk and the offer. You're pretty amazing."

"You kids all right up there?" Travis announced his presence before he came close enough to see anything improper.

Nate stood, a little slower than he would have liked, and moved to the railing. "Yeah, we're up here. I dropped the key to the truck, figured we were stuck till the sun came up."

"Nathanial, that old trick didn't work when you were sixteen. It isn't going to work now."

Nate cringed when Trip laughed behind him. "I honestly lost the key."

"Your mother sent me to get you. Sophie has a fever."

"Is she okay?"

"Your mother is your mother, she worries. I'm sure Soph will survive. I have church in the morning, and she didn't want to be stuck at home with a sick child and no transportation."

Nate climbed down and waited for Trip to follow.

Travis narrowed his eyes and shook his head. "I bet you haven't set foot in the Lord's house since last time you were here. Come and bring your girlfriend."

Trip wrapped the blanket around her shoulders. "I'm not much of a church-goer, Mr. Benz."

Nate took her hand. "We have to scatter Ryan's ashes tomorrow."

Travis' gaze dropped to their joined hands. "I can't have my son in town and not attend services. How am I supposed to get other folks to bring their kids if the preacher's son doesn't show up on Sunday?"

"Yes, sir." Nate led the way down the path to the truck.

Travis grinned. "Trip. Why don't you ride back to the house with me? Keep an old man company."

TWENTY-SEVEN

TRIP SAT UP STRAIGHT AS TRAVIS BENZ, preacher at a local Baptist church, drove her back to his house with Nate following in the second truck. She wanted to throttle the younger Benz for failing to mention his father was a preacher.

"Nate tells me you're a Marine."

"Yes, sir."

"Not planning to get out soon, are you?"

She drew a deep breath. "No, sir, I'm not. I'm going to return to duty as soon as I'm cleared."

He nodded and glanced in the review mirror. "You've told Nate this?"

"I have, many times."

Travis sighed. "He hears what he wants to hear and is as stubborn as the day is long."

"I care about him, but we have no future together." She turned to face Travis. "I don't want to hurt Nate, but I'm afraid it's inevitable."

"I figured as much. I saw how he looked at you."

"I have a couple favors to ask." Trip hesitated. "I need to make a private phone call and a ride to the closest airport."

Travis handed her his phone. "Nate will be busy dealing with his momma when we get to the house. Make your call. I'll take you to the airport when you're done."

"Is it close? I don't want to be the cause of your missing church."

"I'll get someone else to preach. This seems more important."

Trip nodded, unsure if he wanted her out of his house or if he picked up on her need to get to McGuire. The idea he might be helping her to keep her out of Nate's life stung, but she couldn't blame a father for looking out for his son.

Travis nodded to her as he closed the door, leaving her alone in the truck. Nate walked to his father, glancing back at Trip with a concerned expression. She held her breath and waited for him to come for her, but Lynette appeared on the porch, and they went inside.

Trip dialed the secure line and entered her information. She chewed her nails, waiting for McGuire to answer. *What am I doing? This is ridiculous. I can't share the information on Carson without risking Nate. How can I turn Carson in, when he might be family?* "Damn it."

"Peyton?" McGuire's voice pulled her out of her head. "Report."

"Requesting permission to return to my duty station, sir."

"Denied. Report."

Trip rested her head on the window. "I have unconfirmed intelligence that Juan Trevino, Sr., Juan Trevino, Jr., Carlos Trevino, and a known associate nicknamed Domino—all living in or around Crystal Beach, Florida—are connected to at least one Mexican cartel. I need all intel on the Trevino family and their known associates."

"Source?"

Trip chewed her lip. "Carson James."

"Continue."

Trip went on to describe the incident in the hospital with Carlos.

"Police Department and case number?"

"None. Reporting the incident to the authorities would compromise my cover."

McGuire sighed. "Continue."

"I've established residence in the personal home of Carson James."

"Anything else?" McGuire didn't sound pleased.

Only a million things. "My life was threatened twice. With no backup, I no longer feel confident in my ability to perform this mission."

"Is your current health status, or anything else, interfering with your duty?"

Trip closed her eyes. She couldn't answer the question truthfully without compromising her career. "No, sir."

"Tell me about the incident with Detective John Daugherty."

Her heart skipped a beat. *How did he find out about John?* "Nathanial Benz pulled into the Crystal Beach Police Department seeking assistance. We were being followed and feared for our safety. Detective Daugherty groped my crotch and breast in front of witnesses. We have a personal history."

"Describe the history."

"I was involved in a sexual relationship with him beginning at age fifteen. I became pregnant at sixteen. Daugherty assaulted me throughout the relationship, resulting in the pre-term birth and death of our child."

"God dammit, Peyton. How is this not in your records?"

"I was a minor—"

"You signed sworn statements regarding previous incidents involving criminal behavior."

"I was the victim, not the perp. The forms don't require—"

He cut her off again. "You never filed a complaint against him?"

"No, sir."

"Detective Daugherty has requested copies of your service records in relation to possible assault charges."

"I stopped him from touching my person, sir."

"Basic information will be sent, per protocol. Peyton, what's going on with you? I need you to complete this mission. We have reason to believe that Crystal Beach is an active entry point for the Gulf Cartel."

"How long have you had that intelligence, sir?" Something clicked in her brain.

"That information is above your pay grade."

"Sir, with all due respect. I'm on medical leave. I have not been cleared to return to active duty."

"Consider yourself cleared, Gunny. I expect timely reports on your findings. Have you replaced your cell phone?"

"No, sir. I'm on a borrowed cell."

"Get a phone. Give me six hours to pull the requested information."

"Yes, sir."

"I'm counting on you, Peyton." He disconnected the call.

She let her head fall back against the seat, her mind reeling. Had McGuire sent her to Crystal Beach knowing she'd be in the middle of an organized crime syndicate? Better question. Why had he forced her to stay? She remembered the medication mix-up. McGuire had handed her the prescription. Would he poison her to make her think she needed treatment for PTSD?

Travis knocked on the window, startling her.

"Ready to head out?" His bloodshot eyes told her he needed sleep.

Trip opened the door. "Change of plans. I hope you don't mind if I stay one more night."

"Of course, not." He opened his thermos, and the scent of strong coffee warmed the air. "I hope I didn't give you the impression you weren't welcome here."

"I know you're worried about Nate."

"Nate's a grown man. He'll make his own decisions. Come inside and warm up. You look frozen."

Trip handed him his phone and climbed out of the truck. "Thank you."

He slid his arm around her shoulders. "Promise me something?"

"If I can." She didn't like to make promises she couldn't keep. Nor did she feel particularly trusting. The only father figure in her life had probably set her up.

"Take your time before you make any decisions. I saw the way Nate looks at you. I also saw the way you react to him when you're not thinking about it."

"I can do that." She smiled.

Travis gave her shoulder a squeeze. "The Lord does work in mysterious ways."

TWENTY-EIGHT

NATE STOOD IN SOPHIA'S DARKENED WINDOW as Trip spoke on the phone below. Her posture straightened she wiped her eyes and nodded. When the call ended, she put her head in her hands. What the hell is that about?

Travis walked to the passenger's side with his travel thermos. Were they leaving? Trip's shoulders slumped when she exited the truck. Her secrets weighed heavy on her tonight.

He moved to Sophia and pulled her quilt to her chin and kissed her brow. "I love you, sweetheart."

"Love you too, Daddy." She rolled over and went back to sleep.

Nate walked downstairs to find Trip sitting in front of the fire with a fresh cup of coffee. Her hands shook as she brought the mug to her lips.

"Hey." Nate motioned to the spot beside her. "Want some company?"

"Sure." She smiled, but it didn't reach her eyes.

"I didn't lose the key on purpose."

"I know. I mean, you don't have to trick me to get into my pants."

He sighed at her attempt to lighten the situation. "About what I said earlier…"

"Which part?" She grinned.

"Leaving with me, my feelings, all of it."

She shook her head. "Nate, it's okay."

"I didn't mean to make you uncomfortable."

"Listen to me. I'm in no position for a relationship. I'm a mess, and I have nothing to offer you."

"I disagree, but will back off." He ran his hand over her cheek.

"I'm seeing someone. We...we are engaged. I called him tonight."

Engaged? She certainly didn't act like someone in a committed relationship. Was she lying to push him away, or was she not who he thought she was? Did it matter? "That explains a lot."

She turned to the fire. "I'm sorry."

"Don't be." He stood and stretched. "I'm going to catch an hour or two of sleep. Do you need anything?"

She shook her head, still avoiding looking him in the eye.

He went to his room but couldn't get her out of his mind. Try as he might, he couldn't reconcile the woman he'd fallen for with someone who would screw around on her fiancé. She'd warned him not to fall in love, told him she was passing through, but he'd refused to listen. He couldn't decide which pissed him off more, her using him to cheat on another guy, or her lying about being engaged to end their relationship.

The floorboards outside his door squeaked as someone walked by. He strained to listen but couldn't hear anything. A shadow swayed in the crack between his door and the floor. It had to be Sophia standing outside his bedroom.

Nate opened the door to find Trip in the hall. "Yes?"

"Can I come in?" She'd washed her face and brushed her hair out. It hung over her shoulders in soft waves. Her cheeks flushed pink, and her eyes, her stormy gray eyes, sucked his soul out of his body.

"I don't think it's a good idea."

She nodded but pushed into the room. "How's Sophie?"

"Her fever is down."

"Lock the door." Her gaze lingered on his low-slung pajama bottoms.

The door locked with a click, and something broke inside him. This woman, this fucking woman, had worn his balls around her neck since that night at JJ's. She snapped, he jumped. He pulled, she pushed instead and insisted he did things her way. Carson was right, she had him whipped.

She started to speak, but he pulled her into his arms. She tilted her face to his as if waiting for him to kiss her, but he tangled his fingers in her hair, pulled her head to the side, and whispered into her ear. "Don't say another word."

178 KATHRYN M. HEARST

She nodded.

He tugged her hair again, forcing her chin to rise. He scraped his teeth over her earlobe while untying his pajama pants with his free hand. "Is this what you came for?"

"Yes." She wrapped her fingers around his length and leaned in to kiss his chest.

"Don't." Nate set his hand on her shoulder and pushed down until she got the message.

Trip met his eyes. He expected to see confusion, uncertainty, anything but that fucking grin.

This woman is so used to being treated like trash, she doesn't notice the difference. He wanted to turn her away. He wanted to pull her into his arms and love her until she realized her worth. Mostly, he wanted the world to make sense again.

Trip sank to her knees without a word. Nate sucked in a breath when she took him into her mouth. Her tongue worked magic, but that's all there was to it—sex. He locked his heart away to protect it, but she hadn't noticed. *Sex. That's all she's wanted since the first night.*

He closed his eyes and tightened his grip on her hair. She eased back, but he held her in place, both fighting for dominance. For the first time, Nate refused to back down. He set the pace, keeping her where he wanted her. Every time he opened his eyes, he found her staring up at him with her damned sad eyes.

In no mood for teasing, he wanted to get it over with. "Stand up."

Trip smiled as she stood. "How are your balls?"

Nate grabbed her waist and turned her back to him. With one arm around her middle, he walked her to the bed. "Bend over."

"Let me take these off."

He pushed her hand away and tugged her sweats and panties down to her thighs. *God, she's beautiful.* Nate shook his head and positioned himself at her entrance. He couldn't think about her, not about anything but getting off. Nate drove into her and lost himself in the feel of her body. Each stroke harder than the last, until he stopped thinking of her as anything more than a hole. He came, and while physically satisfying, it killed a piece of his soul.

Nate left her in a gasping heap on his bed. The sun would rise soon, no sense in trying to sleep. They had things to do and a long drive ahead of them. Trip watched him as he pulled on a pair of jeans and sat to lace his boots.

His voice as raw as his emotions. "You should get dressed. I plan to leave early."

She hugged herself, her expression crestfallen as she moved to the door. "That was a dick thing to do."

"Far be it from me to turn down a blowjob and piece of ass." He stood and stuffed his pajama bottoms into his bag.

She left the room as quietly as she'd come.

TWENTY-NINE

THE ACHE BETWEEN TRIP'S LEGS did nothing to improve her mood. Usually, rough sex didn't bother her, but this was something different. Nate hadn't bothered to kiss her, let alone make sure she enjoyed herself. He'd fucked her and tossed her out. Sure, she deserved it, but it stung.

Nate took up all of the oxygen in the car as he drove. His eyes fixed straight ahead, his hands gripped the wheel. Trip couldn't bear to look at him, but the silence ate away at her with each passing mile."

The views along US Highway 129 took her breath away. The morning mist clung to the mountains creating an ethereal feel. She couldn't imagine traveling this road on a bike.

Nate tapped the screen on his cell. "Hey, Bud. Yeah, we'll be there in twenty. Everything all set?" He paused, chuckled, and said, "Yeah, man. See you soon."

Curiosity got the better of her. "Are we meeting someone?"

"A few people want to pay their respects." Nate dropped his phone in his lap and turned his head as if trying to work kinks out of his neck.

"Did Ryan come here a lot?" Those were the first words Nate had spoken to her since he threw her out of his bedroom. Trip wanted to keep him talking.

"We came here once or twice a year for the last decade, I guess." He pushed a button on the nav screen and music filled the car.

Trip folded her arms and stared out the window. They traveled uphill, or up-mountain, and the views changed from beautiful to terrifying. She hated heights. The steep cliffs along her side of the road made her heart race.

Nate slowed and turned into a parking lot. The place looked like a motorcycle dealership with its rows of bikes. The building itself resembled many they'd passed along the drive, wooden and worn. Nate hopped out of the car and greeted a handful of guys. Some wore old leather while others wore more modern riding gear. Two of the men had long beards, while the rest were young. They each hugged Nate and patted his back like old friends. Nate pointed to her, then turned back to the men.

"Oh, for fuck's sake." Trip slammed the door and strode to the gathering.

Nate ignored her, but one of the older guys held out his hand. "I'm Pete. I'm sorry to hear about your brother, good guy."

"Thanks. I'm Trip." She refused to cower as the wind cut through her.

"Can you handle three hundred and eighteen curves in eleven miles on the back of a bike?" A blond guy winked.

"I can handle that on my *own* bike. I wouldn't risk it as a passenger."

Nate set his hand on her arm as if to shut her up. "No, she's following me down with the car."

"I am?" She'd had about as much as she could handle.

Nate shot her a hard look, then spoke to the guys. "How is this done?"

Pete clamped his hand on Nate's shoulder. "A little along the way, and the rest at the bottom over the river. The little lady won't want to follow too close, or she'll get a lungful of ashes."

"The little lady is right here."

They all looked at her as if she'd materialized out of thin air.

"How close is too close?"

"Close enough no one cuts in front of you, but far enough back that the ashes don't hit the car." The blond chuckled. "Ruins the mojo."

She locked her knees to keep them from going out from beneath her. *This is what Nate planned to do with her brother's ashes? Dump them on the road from the back of a bike?* Her stomach roiled at the thought. "Nate, can I talk to you?"

Nate nodded and led her away from the group. "What is it?"

"I don't want Ryan's ashes dumped on a highway."

He glanced off into the distance, then back to her. "Trip, this is what Ryan wanted. We had a pact. If you don't want to follow the procession, then you can go first and meet us at the bottom."

What's wrong with me? Nate knew Ryan better than I ever did. "I'll bring up the rear."

Nate handed her the keys, and she went to the car as they divvied up the ashes. The sight of her brother's remains being poured into coffee cans tore her to shreds.

The bikes lined up with Nate leading. She put the car in drive and followed the last bike out.

Trip's attention waffled between the road, the bike ahead of her, and the speed limit. They didn't exaggerate when they said this stretch of road had a lot of curves. She caught sight of Nate now and then before he disappeared around the next corner. He set the pace, one incredibly unsafe for this road pace. She hit forty-five on the speedometer and slowed. Trip estimated the bikes pushed sixty miles per hour. They could flirt with disaster all they wanted, but she wouldn't follow them off the cliff—literally.

A fine haze filled the air as the bikers turned the cans upside down. Someone had punched holes in the plastic lids, creating a salt shaker effect. Trip eased off the gas to allow more time for the air to clear. Her vision blurred, but she couldn't think of Ryan until they reached the bottom. She hated this ritual. It served no purpose other than to give them an excuse to ride like idiots.

She rounded the corner and slowed. Their group, as well as dozens more bikers, had gathered at a scenic overlook. A river meandered in the valley below, stretching into the distance. Nate stood alone, his head bowed and his shoulders shaking.

Trip walked to the edge of the overlook and let her thoughts drift to her brother. Bits and pieces of memories from their childhood crossed her mind, but the years void of memories threatened to drown her. Years of not speaking, hurt feelings, running away. Years of life that she'd missed. Ryan had grown from a skinny punk kid to a man, and she'd missed it. She'd never get that time back.

She turned as Nate opened his can and poured the remaining ashes onto the breeze. The other men in the group did the same. Strangers knew and loved her brother. *No, I'm the stranger, the outsider of the group. These men earned their place here today through time and memories shared.*

Trip hugged herself and bent at the waist, trying desperately to hold herself in one piece. Arms wrapped around her from behind. She turned, expecting Nate, but it was Pete who offered comfort.

THIRTY

THE WIND PICKED UP AS THE LAST OF THE ASHES disappeared in the valley below. Nate couldn't have hurt more if he'd been run down by a semi-truck. He'd wrapped himself up in Trip since Ryan's death, using her to avoid dealing with the loss. *I used her as much as she used me.*

Nate searched the parking area for *her*. She'd parked beside a line of bikes, but the car sat empty. A sea of grim faces turned to him. Some people waved, others dipped their heads. He'd attended enough of these things to know they were each lost in their own fears. Anyone who straddled a motorcycle took their lives into their hands every time they cranked it up. Moments like these reminded them of their mortality.

Pete stood near the railing, rocking back and forth. It took Nate a moment to realize Pete held Trip. She must be struggling if she allowed a stranger to comfort her. Nate walked to them and tapped Pete's shoulder. The burly man nodded and released Trip.

"I got you." Nate pulled her against his chest as he mouthed "thank you" to Pete.

She tensed as if to pull away, then collapsed against him. He closed his eyes and prayed for peace and strength. Trip's demons outweighed his. She'd lost her brother, and God only knew what else.

"I'm all right." Trip wiped her eyes as she pulled away.

Nate wanted to reach for her, but she turned and walked toward the car before he worked up the nerve. He'd dug himself quite the hole. "Trip, wait up."

She leaned her hip against the car. "Are we through or is there more?"

He paused. *Are we done? How can there be more between us?* "I don't know."

Her voice rose. "What do you mean, you don't know? Is there a wake or something or can we go?"

Smooth, Nate, real smooth. "The guys have food set out back at the lodge, but we don't have to stay."

She opened the back door and grabbed her bag. "I'll get a ride."

"Trip, get in the car. Someone needs to drive the bike back."

"I need some air. Give me the keys."

"I don't think you should be—"

"I don't care what you think, give me the keys."

He fished the bike keys out of his pocket and tossed them to her.

"Car keys are in the ignition." She stormed away.

"Hey, darlin', where you going?" Pete jogged over to her as she climbed onto the Harley. They exchanged words, then Pete squeezed her shoulder. He motioned to his bike, and she nodded. A moment later Trip followed him onto the road.

Nate sank into the driver's seat. Pete would keep an eye on Trip, and her speed. Of course, going up was less hazardous than coming down, but the switchbacks were tricky. Nate's eyes stung both from his emotions and exhaustion. He didn't look forward to the nine-hour drive on no sleep. Making that drive with a pissed off woman seemed like the expression of a death wish.

Nate took the opportunity to check in with Carson.

"Yeah?" Carson breathed heavily into the phone.

"Bad time?"

"No, just finishing a workout. Hang on." Muffled coughing and the sound of water running filled the phone. "What's up?"

"You okay? You sound like hell."

"I love you, too, buttercup. Now, why are you calling?"

"Checking in. I need to catch some shut-eye, then we'll be heading out."

"I had the sit-down with Juan Sr. last night. He denies putting a hit on Trip. Said he'd call the boys in." Carson wheezed, then the phone went quiet.

Nate sighed. "Do you believe him?"

Carson unmuted the line. "No. He's also cut me off. Said cops have been investigating the murders. Wasn't a good time to move product."

"I wondered when that was going to happen."

"How's Trip?"

"How bad are your lungs?"

Carson ignored the question. "That good, huh? What did you do?"

"Well, she's fucking engaged."

"To who?" Carson's laugh devolved into a coughing fit.

"Hell, if I know. Probably some jarhead at Lejeune. Listen, we need to be careful around her. She nearly removed my balls last night when I woke her."

"What did you expect? She has PTSD."

Nate sighed. "There's more. She was kidnapped in Brownsville and taken somewhere, probably Juarez."

"So? The likelihood of anyone recognizing her or vice versa is nil."

"No, but there's something off with her story. Why is an MP doing border patrol in Brownsville? She's hiding something."

"Marines don't handle drug shit. That's what ATF and the DEA are for."

"Maybe she's not just a Marine."

Carson coughed into the phone until he could hit the mute button. When he came back, he whispered. "I doubt it, but get your ass home."

"Will do." Nate pulled into the lodge and rested his head on the steering wheel. Last time Carson sounded this bad, he ended up in the hospital for weeks.

Nate walked into the bar to find Trip surrounded by men. No surprise, but it pissed him off nonetheless. "Trip, we need to hit the road."

She knocked back a shot and shook her head. "Let's stick around a while. I'm learning all sorts of things about my brother."

Nate ran his hand down his face. "Something urgent came up. I'm needed back home."

"I can drop you off on my way home." A guy Nate had met once or twice grinned at Trip.

She smiled and set some cash on the table. "Thanks for the offer, but I should get going."

Nate slid her bag onto his shoulder and turned for the door. It took another hour for him to say his goodbyes but, eventually, he and Trip made it to the car.

She stopped him before he started the engine. "What's going on? I thought you were too tired to drive?"

"Carson's sick."

"Sick how?"

"He's wheezing. Could be a cold, could be side effects from his last chemo. Hard to say."

"We can take turns driving, while the other sleeps."

"Sounds good." He pulled onto the highway, racking his brain for something to say. "Look, I'm sorry about last night."

"I should have told you about Scott sooner. We've been on and off, and I wanted to have some fun while I was home. It all just got out of hand."

Scott. His name is Scott? Why does having a name make her story more believable? "You told me you were passing through. Ryan dying messed with my head more than I thought."

"Friends?" She smiled.

"Friends." Nate turned his attention back to the road. *What kind of name was Scott?*

THIRTY-ONE

TRIP HADN'T LEFT CARSON'S SIDE since she returned from scattering Ryan's ashes. On the third day of Trip's vigil, he woke in one hell of a mood. He complained of hunger, but nothing tasted right. He ached, but nothing could make him comfortable. He wanted company but didn't want to talk. Trip understood his restless need to get out of bed when his body worked so hard to keep him there.

"Where's Nate?" Carson fidgeted with the oxygen tubes in his nose.

"He went to talk to the folks at my mom's rehab facility. Seems she tried to break out."

Carson shook his head. "I don't know what to do with that woman."

"Why is it your problem to do anything with her?" Trip couldn't wrap her head around why Carson and Nate insisted on getting Dixie help, especially when she fought them at every turn.

"She's family, and I take care of my family." He must have seen the look in Trip's eye, because he added, "Not all family is blood. She's your mother, Ryan's mother, possibly Izzy's grandmother. She deserves the chance to get clean."

Trip pressed her lips together. It took all of her strength not to throttle him. *Where was his compassion when he killed Marcy? How can he want anyone clean when he sits on top of the local drug trade?* She folded her arms and stared.

"What?" Carson coughed until his lips took on a peculiar shade of blue.

Trip helped him sit upright and rubbed his back as he gasped for air. "Why don't you close your eyes and get some sleep?"

Carson needed rest but insisted on arguing. "I'll sleep when I'm dead. Tell me what that look was about."

"I can't figure you out. You sell drugs and then worry when people become addicts?"

The corner of his mouth turned up. "What can I say? I'm complicated."

She ignored his lopsided grin and stood. Outside the window, the world went on as usual, while hers disintegrated. Carson wouldn't tell her what the doctors had said, but she assumed the worse. He'd be lucky to see Christmas.

"Trip, come stretch out beside me. If I have to be in bed, might as well be with a woman."

She squared her shoulders and turned from the window. Carson held one arm out toward her, but his eyes were what drew her in. Pain and fear creased the corners. This man lived on borrowed time and didn't want to spend it alone.

Trip curled against him and sighed.

"There's some things you need to know." Carson wrapped his arm around her.

"I'm listening."

"Izzy is my daughter."

She pulled back and studied his expression.

"I thought Ryan would make better daddy material, plus he had a thing for Marcy. I thought if I could get her to clean up they'd make a nice little family unit." Carson's cough rattled deep in his chest. "But Ryan was stubborn."

"What's going to happen to her now? Are you going to claim her?" Trip hadn't met Marcy's sister, but she sounded like a stand-up kind of woman, a better parent than any of the other choices.

"I want you to raise her."

Trip's laughter died when she caught the look in his eyes. "You can't be serious."

"As a heart attack." He ran his hand down her cheek.

"That can't happen. I'm always on assignment, never home. Not to mention the courts won't just turn over custody of a kid. If Marcy's sister fights it, I'll lose." At least she hoped Jess would fight to keep her niece, the only thing left of her sister.

"I had my attorneys file the paperwork to legally claim her as my daughter. I can name whoever I damn well please as her guardian."

"Carson, I'm flattered, but no." She sat upright.

He grabbed her jaw and turned her head toward him. "Trip, we share the same father. You and Izzy are the last of the James' blood line. You two are the only family I have left."

She stared until he released her face. "You don't know that for sure."

"I stole a piece of long brown hair out of Nate's bed while you two were gone."

The idea that Macon James had an affair with her mother, one that evidently spanned many years, made her stomach hurt. How different would her life have turned out if he'd claimed her as his daughter? How much pain would she and Ryan have avoided if he'd manned up and taken care of his kids?

"Why me? Why not leave her with her aunt?" Trip stood and paced the floor.

"When I claim her, she'll have a target on her back." He eased his feet to the floor and gripped the edge of the bed. "I'm not going to make it this time."

Trip wanted to go to him, to tell him he would live long enough to be a father to his daughter, but she didn't believe in false sentiments. She didn't have to go to medical school to know the gravity of Carson's condition. In the few short days, she and Nate were out of town, his skin and eyes had taken on a yellowish tinge. His liver couldn't handle the stress. Each breath sounded as if pebbles rolled around in his lungs. "I'm not mother material, Carson."

"You take pretty good care of Nate and me. I think you'll be a great mom."

"I already lost one baby."

"Nate said something about that. What happened?"

"John Daugherty used me for a punching bag when I was six months pregnant. I went home for help, only Dixie didn't think it was so bad. I had these pains, but she was too busy getting high to drive me to the ER."

"You were in labor?" Carson frowned.

Trip wrapped her arms around her midsection. "By the time she took me to the hospital, it was too late."

Carson sighed. "Come here."

She shook her head. If he touched her, she'd break down. "I can't have kids. When my daughter was born, my insides were messed up. I ended up with a C-section and hysterectomy at the same time. It was the only way to stop the bleeding."

"Oh, hon. I'm sorry. Maybe you were meant to raise Izzy."

"I can't take care of another human being. What if I turn out like my mom?"

"You're nothing like her."

She should have known better than to argue with Carson. He had his mind made up, and she couldn't change it. "What are the doctor's saying?"

"Weeks, months at the most. It's been coming for a while now."

The confession stunned her. Trip had just lost one brother, now she'd lose another? It didn't matter she'd only known him a short while, his loss would sting. "You looked healthy before we left. I don't understand what changed so fast."

"The meds could start working again tomorrow, and I would *look* a little better, but my body is shutting down." He pushed to his feet.

Trip rushed to him as he took his first step. "Carson, get back in bed."

"Agree to raise Izzy." He clutched her hips. "Promise me you'll keep her safe."

She slid her arms around him, partly to keep him from falling but mostly because she needed to feel close to the brother she didn't know she had. "On one condition."

"What's that?" Carson rested his brow on her shoulder.

"Make things right for Nate. Let him go before he ends up dead or in prison."

"It's not that easy." Carson's weight shifted as if his knees came out from under him. Trip tightened her grip and eased him back into bed.

"It *is* that easy. If you expect me to give up my career and raise a kid, the least you can do is allow Nate to do the same." As soon as the words came out of her mouth, she regretted them.

Carson tilted his head, studying her expression. "You're that serious about him?"

She closed her eyes and drew a breath. She'd meant allow him to raise Sophia, but Carson hadn't caught on to her slip. She couldn't tell him the truth, not when it meant betraying Nate's confidence. "If it wasn't for his profession, yes, I could see myself building a life with Nate."

"You'll take care of Izzy if I get Nate out free and clear?"

The glint of hope in his eyes chipped another piece off her heart. "I need some time to think about it. But…please, do this for Nate."

Thirty-Two

NATE SAT ON HIS COUCH STARING AT A BLANK television screen as his world unraveled around him. Usually, in situations like this, he'd call Ryan and talk it out over a beer. With Ryan gone, he didn't quite know how to cope. He'd gone and fallen in love with Trip despite the warnings. Nate wanted to beat the shit out of this Scott person for asking her to marry him.

"Nate?" Trip knocked on the front door.

"Damn it." He sighed and pushed himself to his feet. He didn't want to see her and couldn't imagine his life without her. He opened the door and took in her tear stained face. "Is Carson all right?"

She shrugged. "He's weak but as full of it as ever."

Nate's hand tightened on the door. He wanted to shut it in her face as a matter of principle, but they'd agreed to remain friends. *What sort of friend shut a door in a crying woman's face? The same kind who wanted to kill the competition. The pissed off kind.* "Do you need something?"

She glanced over the yard and sighed. "No, I guess not."

Had he witnessed a friend of his in this situation he'd have railed on the guy. She obviously wanted to come inside, and he wanted her there despite her fiancé, her lies, her using him. Nate hung his pride on the coat rack and opened the door. "Come in."

She looked as if she might refuse, then shook her head and walked past him into the hall. "Can we talk?"

"Talk or did you need a screw?"

Her shoulders tensed, but she kept walking to the living room.

Nate plopped down on his couch and motioned to the chair on the other side of the room. The further away from him, the better.

"I lied to you in North Carolina." She turned to face him.

"Could you be more specific? Seems to me you've lied about quite a bit."

"I'm not engaged, there is no Scott, or anyone else." She drew a breath. "I panicked."

Nate ran his hand over the back of his neck and laughed. "You panicked?"

"You...we..." She motioned between them. "I can't do this. I have to go back to my unit. My job...It's not the sort of thing you can just give two-weeks' notice and quit."

"I know that." He leaned forward and rested his elbows on his knees. "You made up a fiancé, why exactly?"

Trip paced and wrung her hands. "You freak me out. I care about you more than I should. I tried to keep you at arm's length, but you kept pushing."

She put this on him? "I kept pushing?"

Trip nodded. "You got into my head, and it scared me."

"You don't think it scared me? You've said you were passing through since the day you walked into JJ's." Nate's head spun. She'd lied. Trip didn't have someone waiting for her. On some level, her story had always felt off, but he couldn't wrap his brain around it.

Trip stopped pacing and turned to him. "Carson's really sick. Ryan's gone. Nothing is keeping you here. Why don't you and Sophie come to Lejeune?"

"You know it isn't that simple."

"What if it was? What if you could walk away from all of this free and clear? Would you do it?" She met his gaze and didn't look away.

No. Say no. Going with her isn't part of the deal. Nate planned to leave, He'd set the wheels in motion when they got back from North Carolina. It couldn't work, he'd be in the open with Sophie. "If it were a perfect world, yes."

Trip smiled.

He stood and moved to her. "It's not a perfect world. I don't think I could ever stop looking over my shoulder living in the open with you. We wouldn't be safe."

She threw herself into his arms and wrapped her arms around his neck. "But there's hope? Right?"

He hid his face in her neck and prayed. "There's always hope, babe."

"I should get back to Carson." She started to pull away, but he held on.

"Stay with me, just a little while." Nate didn't trust her, not yet, but he didn't want to be alone. Trip had laid her heart out to him, or at least given him a glimpse of her feelings. Their time together would end sooner rather than later, he didn't want to miss a minute.

"All right."

Nate grabbed her face and pressed his forehead to hers and closed his eyes. "Don't ever lie to me again."

Her breath quickened. "There's things I can't tell you, about work."

"I'm not talking about work. I understand that." He pulled back enough to look into her eyes. "I need to know I can trust you."

Trip looked away. "Nate, we aren't the kind of people who will ever share everything."

"I know."

"Is it enough that you have my heart?"

Nate wanted to argue, to tell her he wouldn't settle for anything less than a relationship like the one his parents had. *But I'm not my father, and Trip isn't like my mom. She's right. We aren't the kind of people who go to church every Sunday and share the details of our day over dinner. We never will be, but we could be happy.*

"It's more than enough." He reached down and grabbed her thighs, lifting her off her feet.

"What are you doing? I have to get back to Carson." She laughed and wrapped her legs around his waist.

"You owe me some serious make-up sex."

THIRTY-THREE

"IS THAT RIGHT?" TRIP NIBBLED HIS EARLOBE as he carried her upstairs. She'd not come here expecting sex, but they needed this. They needed to put the ugliness behind them as much as they could.

Nate set her on her feet in the bedroom and went to his computer. The images on the screen sent a shock of fear down her spine. Several small windows, each showing a different security camera angle, filled the monitor. Days had passed since her last report. Trip needed to call in before McGuire got squirrely and yanked her out or sent someone else in.

Nate turned off the monitor and pulled her close. His kiss felt different, softer, yet more possessive. He took a step forward, forcing Trip to step back until they reached the bed.

He tilted his head. "Where'd you go?"

"Sorry, I was thinking about Carson."

Nate pulled her shirt over her head, breaking the kiss long enough to toss it to the side. His stubble scratched her cheek as he whispered, "I need your full attention right now."

She nodded. "I'm all yours."

"I love you, Trip Peyton."

Trip eased back enough to look into his eyes as she ran her hands down his chest and unbuttoned his shirt. His words hung in the air like living things—sucking her feelings from her mouth. Trip couldn't return them. Not until she could stop living a lie. Not until the investigation closed and Nate was free. "Kiss me."

Nate obliged, this time his kiss turned demanding. If she wouldn't say the words, then he'd pull her love out of her mouth manually.

Trip slid his shirt off his shoulders and down his arms. She took a step back and reached to unclasp her bra. The half-drowsy look on his face made her grin. She took her time peeling the thin lace from her chest.

He took a step back and licked his lips. "Take your jeans off."

Trip opened her jeans one button at a time and slid them over her hips as she turned her back to him. She bent at the waist and lowered them to the floor, along with her panties. As she stood, he grabbed her waist and yanked her against his chest. Nate's lips crashed down onto hers, his tongue invading her mouth. He lowered his zipper as he hitched her thigh around his waist.

Nate slid his hand under her other leg and lifted her. Once again, Trip wrapped her legs around his waist. Her body spread wide-open, he moved his hips until he pressed against her slick entrance. Nate closed his eyes and eased her down. They exhaled as he filled her so slowly that she thought she'd come unglued if he didn't move things along.

Trip whimpered and rocked her hips, but he dug his fingers into her ass and held her exactly where he wanted her. "Nate, please."

"Be still."

Her muscles tensed around his shaft. "I can't."

Nate eased her hips back and forth a few inches, enough to drive her out of her mind, but not enough to give her what she needed. "You will."

She rested her brow on his shoulder and watched as his length disappeared inside her body. He thrust forward, sinking in as deep as he could, then pressed her against him, forcing her sex to grind against his pubic bone. The friction hit her in just the right spot to steal her breath. A moment later she cried out as the orgasm tore through her.

"That's it, baby, come for me," Nate whispered.

When she finally relaxed against his chest, he laid her on the bed and removed his jeans. Sure her legs wouldn't cooperate if she tried to move, she rolled her head to the side and watched as he pulled the comforter down.

"My legs are rubber."

"No?" Nate stretched out just out of reach and began stroking himself.

"Oh, that's not fair." Trip couldn't tear her eyes away from his hand moving up and down his shaft.

Nate drew a breath. His stomach muscles clenched, and he flexed his feet. It dawned on her that he had to be close, he hadn't come when she had. Trip rolled to her hands and knees and crawled toward him.

"I thought you couldn't move?" He grabbed her hips as she straddled him.

"I got my second wind." She took his hands from her hips and pulled them over his head.

Nate raised his head and licked the side of her breast. He tried to pull his hand free, but she held it tighter.

"Turnabout is fair play." Trip entwined her fingers with his and eased herself down his body, dragging her chest across his. She moved her hips until she had him where she wanted him, then sank back onto his length. "Keep your hands where I put them."

"Yes, ma'am." Nate grinned.

Trip sat up, slowly raking her nails from his shoulders to the little V-shape below his naval. Her chin dipped to her chest as she rose to her knees, then eased herself down until he filled her completely. She ran her hands over her breasts and set a quick pace.

Nate pulled Trip forward and kissed her. He didn't follow orders, but she'd let it slide. Their eyes met, and for once, she didn't look away. The expression on his face told her he enjoyed her body, but more than that, he cherished her.

Nate's back arched, and he grabbed her hips, thrusting deeper still. He held her gaze as his warmth filled her. His expression softened. "Kiss me."

Trip leaned down, brushing her lips across his. Nate's arms encased her against his chest. As his tongue slid into her mouth, he rolled over and tucked her beneath him. Still joined, Nate continued to rock his hips. Trip lost herself in him. His hand supporting her head, fingers tangled in her hair, tongue exploring her mouth, and the feel of him filling her core.

Trip prayed to whoever listened that Carson would work a miracle. The thought of losing Nate brought tears to her eyes. This man loved her as much as she loved him. For the first time in fourteen years, she didn't care about the mission. Trip didn't care about anything but saving the man in her arms.

"Babe, are you all right?" Nate eased off her.

She wiped her eyes as she laughed. "You've turned me into a weepy girl."

"Is that a bad thing?" He brushed her hair from her face.

"It depends." She climbed out of bed.

"Where are you going?" Nate lunged for her, but she dodged.

"To clean up. I have to go check on Carson." Trip headed for the bathroom.

"What does it depend on?"

Trip called from the other room. "My teammates will never let me live it down if I cry in uniform, but in private I guess it's okay."

"Why do you call them teammates? I've never heard that expression from another Marine."

"My team has been together for over ten years. Unlike most Marines who bounce between different units, we stick together." She pulled on her jeans.

"I thought you said you trained MPs?" Nate furrowed his brow.

"I do." She turned her back to him as she fastened her bra. When she turned back, she plastered a smile on her face. "It's complicated. I'll explain it to you, but right now I should go make sure Carson hasn't called in the hookers or burned the house down."

THIRTY-FOUR

NATE SAT AT HIS DESK STARING AT THE COMPUTER screen. He clicked between camera views as Trip walked out Carson's sliding glass door. Something about her story didn't add up. He'd scrolled through the call history on the burner phone he'd loaned her, but found nothing. He'd seen her on the phone, so she must have erased the call history, but why?

Trip walked past the pool toward the hot tub. He switched from the security camera on the side of the house to the hidden camera in the control panel. Nate had installed secondary cameras for exactly this reason. Anyone with half a brain would notice the cameras mounted to the awning, but only he and Carson knew to avoid the web of hidden cameras around the property.

He turned the audio volume to max and waited as she dialed. His stomach turned at the thought of spying on her, but something in his soul told him she kept secrets from him. "Who are you calling, sweetheart?"

"Tango, zero, alpha, lemur, five, niner, seven, niner." Trip glanced back toward the house. "I need to give report."

Nate froze, unwilling or unable to comprehend what he'd heard. He'd suspected she'd lied about her job, but seeing her in action left him stunned. He leaned closer to the screen and pressed his hand over the earbud.

"Yes, I realize I'm breaking protocol." She listened to the person on the other end of the call. "Correction of former report. As per Carson James, Nathanial Benz is not involved in the criminal activities. Benz is an employee at Jessie James's bar and resides on Carson James' compound."

"What are you doing?" His mouth went dry. She betrayed Carson after he'd warned her of the consequences. Why did she stand there and give false information? To protect him and Sophie, or something else? Nate had told her he loved her, and he did, or so he thought. The longer he stared at the monitor, the more he realized he didn't know this woman.

"James won't be an issue." She hugged herself and bowed her head. "Yes, I'm certain."

Certain of what? Carson didn't look good, but he'd looked worse over the years. He'd bounce back to his ornery self in a week or two like he always did. *Does she plan to kill Carson or turn him in?* Nate's mind raced.

"Arrest warrant? When?" She sank into a deck chair. "No, sir…Yes, sir…Roger that."

Nate pressed his hand against his ear until he drove it into his brain. He needed more information. She said "arrest warrant" loud and clear, but who, and when?

"Thanks, McGuire. No. I understand. I can handle it. Did you send the medical records to the shrink?" She wiped her eyes on the back of her hand. "I appreciate it. Out."

Nate pushed his chair from the desk when she stuffed the phone back into her pocket. His mind spun like a roulette machine. The first thought that solidified—*she's DEA or ATF*. He had gone with her to the psychiatrist, hell, he'd witnessed her in the throes of PTSD. If they hadn't sent her here to investigate Carson, then what? *Could it have all be a coincidence? No. No coincidences, she's here to infiltrate the organization and got caught up in more than she bargained for. That's it. Why else would she lie about my involvement?*

The front door opened. Whatever had happened, Nate couldn't let her know that he knew. He hit the button to close the security feed and opened his email. He recognized the sound of Trip's feet on the stairs, the pattern of her footsteps as she moved. *What the hell am I supposed to do? Risk my life by betraying Carson, or do my job and kill the woman I may or may not love?*

Trip dropped onto the bed and sighed. "Carson's awake. You might want to go talk to him."

Nate couldn't look at her. He thought he heard the concern in her voice, but then again, she'd played the part. How far did that go? Had Trip played the part the first night he'd brought her here? Was flirting with him at the bar part of the deal? Did spending time with his family help her weasel into the organization? What about that afternoon when they'd made love? *Fuck.*

"Nate? Are you okay?" Trip's stormy eyes bore into him, her lying mouth frowned.

He wanted to pick her up and shake her until she told him the truth. "Just thinking about Carson. You staying here?"

Trip reached for him, but he dodged her hand. "Yeah, sure. I'll be here when you get back. Unless you want me to—"

"No. Stay. You've been with him night and day. Stay here and relax." He hated Trip for putting him in this position and hated himself for caring. He kissed her forehead. "I'll be back soon."

Nate hit the kill button on the computer, locking it down in case she decided to snoop. The walk to the main house felt like miles. He couldn't decide how to handle the situation. He had to warn Carson, but that would mean a death sentence for Trip. A punishment he'd have to carry out.

Carson sat in the chair near the window when Nate entered the room. Likely, he'd seen Trip make her phone call. Nate had watched Carson battle cancer for years, but he'd never seen him look so old. What a difference a few days and IVs full of poison could make.

"Hey, we need to talk." Nate stuffed his hands in his pockets.

"Did Trip tell you?"

Nate pulled a chair closer and sat. "She told me you were awake. What's up?"

Carson studied his expression, then shook his head. "Nothing. What do you need to tell me?"

"You know how I said something didn't add up with her?" Nate couldn't keep the secret, not when it could blow up in his face. All Carson had to do was look at the footage, and he'd hear her conversation. Nate could delete it, of course, but even that would leave a hole he would have to explain. "She's either DEA or ATF. I caught her on the security cameras near the hot tub giving report."

"Son of a bitch." Carson bowed his head and sucked air between his teeth. "What did you hear?"

"From the sound of it, this wasn't her first report. She mentioned something about an arrest warrant."

"Whose? Mine?" Carson's laughter turned into a coughing jag.

"Not sure, she seemed surprised. Maybe concerned. She told them I wasn't involved in the business. For whatever reason, she's trying to get me off the hook."

Carson spit pink sputum into his handkerchief. "She's in love with you."

"Yeah, well, sucks to be her." Nate ran his hand over his head. "What do you want me to do?"

Carson turned his face to the window. He stared so intently Nate wondered if Trip had decided to take another walk by the pool. "I want you to arrange for her to overhear a conversation. Let's use her to our advantage."

Nate exhaled. "That's it?"

Carson hung his head. "Are you sure you heard what you think you heard?"

Nate was sure, as sure as the sun would rise in the morning. He hadn't seen Carson so dejected since his father passed away. If Carson was short on time, he didn't need to leave the world with a broken heart. "I'll go back over the tapes. See if I can find anything else."

Carson frowned. "I know when you're lying. Get her over here. Let's set her up with everything she needs to bring down my organization."

THIRTY-FIVE

EVERY FIBER OF TRIP'S BEING SCREAMED for her to get in the car and drive until she passed through the gates at Camp Lejeune. She'd screwed up with Nate and gone too far too soon. Her emotions had clouded her judgment. As Nate had said, *in a perfect world they would be together...* A world that didn't exist. A world where she wasn't a Marine, and he didn't work for a drug dealer.

The cops would come and take her to jail for manslaughter, murder, or whatever other bullshit charge they could throw at her for killing Juan Trevino. The case would never make it to court. McGuire assured her he'd see to her bail and the investigation would end long before a criminal trial would compromise her cover. None of that concerned her, but the idea of being locked up again made her stomach turn. Not to mention John would have access to her twenty-four seven.

She walked into the house on a mission. Trip needed to come clean with Carson about the investigation. If he knew the truth, he could help her set things up so Nate would walk free. They may not live in a perfect world, but she'd do her best to make sure Sophia grew up with a father, even if that meant saying goodbye to the man she loved.

Carson's voice echoed through the hall. "That's right. The old barn out on Highway 46. I don't give a rat's ass about funerals. I want the entire fucking Trevino family front and center tomorrow. We have things to discuss."

Carson's voice cracked, lost in his worsening cough.

Nate must have taken the phone. His voice boomed over Carson's wheezing. "This is Benz. Carson plans to discuss a change in leadership."

Trip's heart skipped a beat. Carson had followed through on his promise to get Nate out of the organization. Did the change have to do with letting *Nate walk away? But hadn't Nate said he knew too many secrets? No, it couldn't be that easy.*

Nate continued, "I'll be assuming control of the organization, effective immediately. Yes, assure Juan Senior that I intend to make things right. I intend to meet his terms at the sit-down, but I want double the order. Yes, double, and I'll take delivery at the meeting."

Her hand tensed on the handrail. What terms? The only demands from the Trevinos she knew about involved her dead and buried.

"That matter is not open for discussion. I'll take care of any problems with my people. I suggest you do the same…Good. Yes, we're bringing everyone. I expect you to do the same."

Trip turned to go back downstairs when Nate appeared in the doorway.

"Babe, I didn't realize you were here. Come in." He glanced over his shoulder with wide eyes.

Trip forced a smile and walked into Carson's room. Her new brother sat in a recliner near the window. At first, she thought he'd fallen asleep, but she caught a slight nod. *Has he grown so weak he can't lift his head?*

"There she is." Carson wheezed each breath as he lifted his hand in her direction.

Trip took a step back from the two of them, jail looked better with each passing moment. She couldn't stand the idea of watching another person die, not even someone who'd broken his promises. Nate's words had trampled her spirit. How could he agree to such a thing? She couldn't help but feel he'd lied about wanting out.

"I can't stay." She took Carson's hand, resisting the urge to squeeze until his knuckles ground together. "There's an arrest warrant for me. I have to turn myself in."

Nate and Carson exchanged a look she couldn't decipher.

"The warrant is for you?" Nate furrowed his brow.

Trip puzzled over his words. *The* warrant, not *a* warrant? Did he already know? Of course, he knew, he had friends on the force. "My commander told me about the warrant a little while ago. I was hoping to have a chance to speak to Carson before I go."

"Let me call my attorney. From what you and Nate said, the assault on John Daugherty was self-defense."

"No, this has to do with my shooting Juan Trevino at Ryan's. My commander is aware of the details. The Marines will send representation." Trip kissed Carson's forehead. "But thanks."

Nate reached for her arm. "Let me go with you."

She jerked away from him. "I'm sure you have other things to do that are more pressing than escorting me to jail. I'll take the rental car."

Nate glared and opened his mouth to speak, but Carson held up a hand. Trip couldn't get over the change in them. *No, they haven't changed, I have. I allowed them to suck me into their world until I believed the lies.*

Her head high and shoulders squared, Trip walked from the room and out the front door. She couldn't pinpoint the moment hope had sprouted inside her, hope for a normal life, hope for a child, hope for a future with Nate, but she would never forget the second it died.

Trip drove her car to the end of the drive and went through the protocols to reach McGuire on the secured line. When he answered, she put the car in drive and headed toward the police station. She relayed the information about the meeting with the Trevinos, though she couldn't bring herself to mention Nate's involvement. "There'll be enough narcotics on site to wrap up the investigation."

"How many will be there?" McGuire's tone remained steady, all business.

"It's a formal sit-down. All the major players and sufficient muscle from both organizations. What did Intel say on the numbers?"

"I'd say forty to fifty on each side. Local law enforcement is compromised. I'll call in higher level back up. Good job, Peyton. I knew you could do it."

She frowned. Usually those words would put a smile on her face, but today they rang hollow. "I'm on my way to the Crystal Beach P.D. to turn myself in."

"Negative. Go straight to MacDill. I'll call you back with the contact name and number. I want you on lockdown until this is over."

Sirens filled the rearview mirror. She glanced over her shoulder. "I'm being pulled over by local PD."

"Damn it." McGuire sighed. "Follow procedure. I'll have your walking papers before they finish processing you."

The call disconnected as Trip eased the car onto the side of the road. She would have preferred to stop in a more well-lit area, but the country roads didn't have many street lights. She reached for the rental car agreement in the glove box.

"Step out of the car with your hands on your head."

"Are you kidding me?" Trip muttered as she opened the door and slowly exited the car.

"On the ground, now." The beam of a high-powered flashlight blinded her.

"Officer?" Trip shielded her eyes.

A fist landed in her gut. The air left her lungs, and bile filled her throat as she hit her knees. The *pop* and *crackle* of the Taser filled her ears before the probes embedded into her back. Her muscles cramped as the electricity flowed through her body. Trip's cheek hit the pavement, cracking a tooth. Her brain screamed "run," but her rigid body refused to move.

"Stupid bitch." A male boot came down on her face.

THIRTY-SIX

"I WANT YOU TO CALL TOM and make sure she's treated right when she gets to the station." Carson drummed his fingers on the bedside table. "What the fuck are they thinking arresting her?"

"Maybe forensics came back with contradictory information." Nate had seen how cold she behaved that night. She certainly hadn't acted like a woman who just killed a man in self-defense. Then again, what did he know? Trip deserved a gold medal for the way she'd worked him over earlier in the bedroom.

"More likely John Daugherty had something to do with this. He's had a hard-on for her since she got back into town."

"You're right." Nate sighed. "I'll call Tom."

"Of course, I'm right." Carson stood and walked to the bathroom on shaky legs. "She bought the phone call. The Trevinos won't know what hit them."

Nate ran his hands over his head unable to comprehend the previous couple of hours. He still couldn't believe she'd come here to bring Carson down. It didn't make sense, one female sent to infiltrate the largest crime syndicate in the southeast? Of course, this particular woman had family ties to the area and the organization. How could he have been so stupid?

Carson returned to the room with color in his cheeks. He'd put on one hell of a show for Trip. Whatever he'd told her, she bought hook, line, and sinker. "She'll make the call. They'll storm the castle, and take care of the Trevino problem in one shot."

"You don't think they'll have surveillance on the building to make sure we're all there before they bust in?"

"Not your problem. Sit down. We need to talk."

"Famous last words." Nate took a seat and prepared himself for one of Carson's lectures. He hadn't screwed up on this level in years. "Look, I know I fucked up by inviting Trip into the house. I let my guard down because of the shit with Ryan."

Carson pressed his lips into a line. "Are you finished? Can I talk now, or do you need to continue unburdening your soul?"

Nate sat back and motioned for him to speak.

"Yeah, you messed up. We both did. I didn't see it coming either, but here's the thing. That woman loves you."

Nate chuckled. "Loves me?"

"She made a deal with me to get you out of the business, and I intend to keep it."

Nate's mouth fell open. How in the hell could he keep that promise when the two of them had convinced her Nate would take over the business an hour earlier? "She heard me tell Juan's guy I was stepping up."

"You're going to have to trust me on this one if you want out. That is what you want, isn't it?" Carson held his gaze until Nate looked away.

"What I want and what I can have are two different things." Nate's world came down to this one moment, this conversation. The talk he'd avoided having for so long that he planned to run like a coward rather than face his boss.

"I get why you never told me about Sophie. That's why I never pushed the issue when you sent Kelly away after you knocked her up. This is no life for a kid." Carson coughed into the handkerchief.

"You knew?" Nate had spent the last five years away from his daughter for nothing. He leaned forward and rested his elbows on his knees.

"Kelly told me, made me swear to keep it secret. I figured you'd get around to telling me when you were ready."

Nate drew every ounce of courage he had and met Carson's eyes. "Yes, I want out."

"You have an exit plan?"

"I do."

"Good. Get Trip the hell out of jail, pick up Izzy, and go." Carson poured several pills into his palm, popped them into his mouth, and washed them down.

"Trip and I are through, and why would I take Izzy?"

Carson shook his head. "You never were the sharpest tool in the shed, were you?"

The pieces of the puzzle snapped into place, leaving Nate with information overload. "You've known Izzy is yours."

"Yep."

"And Trip? She's an informant. Where does she fit in?" He needed to hear the words.

"My sister. I had two DNA tests run, one for Izzy and one for Trip. My attorneys are hard at work drawing up the documents."

"When?" Nate thought back to the night he killed Marcy. Had Carson known then he ordered the mother of his child murdered?

"A while ago, and don't give me that look. You know as well as I do that Marcy would have ended up pulling the same shit with Izzy that Dixie pulled with Trip. No one deserves that kind of life, no one."

Nate conceded. While he didn't agree with Carson's tactics, he couldn't imagine sitting by and allowing that sort of thing to happen to an innocent baby. "What about Dixie? She loves that little girl."

"She's still in rehab. I trust Trip to make the decisions when, and if, Dixie can see Izzy." Carson sank into his chair. What little color had returned to his face had faded.

"I'm not running with Trip. She could lead the feds right to us."

"You need to have a conversation with her. Give her the option to come clean. If she doesn't, then go alone."

Nate mulled over Carson's words. "I think it's safer for me to get the girls and run alone. I don't think I'll ever trust her."

Carson bowed his head. "I'm sure she could say the same about you. If she's willing to tie herself to you with all the shit you've done, who are you to take the high road?"

"You have a point." Nate frowned. "You honestly think she wants me?"

"Yeah, I know she wants you. Now, are you going to get the girls or are we still playing twenty questions?"

"I'll go after you tell me what you intend to do. The feds will be watching the building. You can't go in there. It'll be a bloodbath."

"I'm not going near the place." Carson winked. "The less you know, the better. You want out, get out. You can't have it both ways."

"What did the docs say, Carson?"

"They said I wouldn't live to see twenty, remember?" He laughed until he doubled over gasping for breath.

Nate pulled the oxygen tank to the chair and helped adjust the nasal cannula on Carson's face. "I can't leave you like this. I'll stay until you're back on your feet."

"There's no time."

"What happens to you when the shit hits the fan?"

Carson grinned. "I'll be here, sitting in front of the television with a beer."

"Come with us. I know you have enough money hidden in the Caymans to last three lifetimes. We can all go together." He couldn't leave Carson to take the fall alone. Over the years, they'd participated in enough bad shit that they both deserved to rot in a cell or Hell, whichever the jury decided.

Carson rubbed the stubble on his chin. "I would like to see my kid grow up."

Nate grinned, imagining Carson raising a daughter. Karma would bite him in the ass when she hit her teen years. "It'll take some time to get Trip out, and the custody papers for Izzy finalized."

"Tomorrow. The papers will be ready first thing in the morning." Carson grew serious. "You have to go before the sit-down."

"We'll leave before the meeting, and you're coming with. Meet us at the marina at noon."

Carson stood and gave Nate a half hug, followed by a slap on the shoulder. "I love you, like a brother."

Nate chuckled. "Evidentially, I'm the only person not related to you."

"I've been meaning to tell you…"

His brows rose.

Carson grinned. "I'm screwing with you. Now go."

THIRTY-SEVEN

ROPES BIT INTO HER ANKLES AND WRISTS as Trip woke. Her face throbbed, and it tasted like something died on her tongue. The Taser, her shoulders quivered at the thought. A cop had pulled her over, but she never got a look at his face. His voice though? She glanced around the room and spotted a gym bag with the initials J.D.D. Johnathon Dean Daugherty. That son-of-a-bitch.

John had taken her. John, her ex, the father of her dead child, had knocked her out and taken her somewhere. She swallowed her fear and surveyed her surroundings—a bedroom cluttered with boxes and covered with a layer of dust. The floral quilt and throw pillows led her to believe a woman had decorated the room. Did John have a girlfriend or wife? Surely, he hadn't brought her to his home. No, he wouldn't risk it.

Trip tugged at her bindings. From the rough feel, she surmised he'd hog tied her with rope. Her muscles screamed with the slightest movement, reminding her again of the Taser. She didn't recall seeing another cop in the car when he pulled her over, but who knew? It had all happened so fast.

The adrenaline in her system lessened, and pain took its place. Her face ached with each breath. She ran her parched tongue over her lower lip, noting an abrasion and swelling. Trip's vision remained unobstructed, a good sign. She moved each of her limbs as far as her restraints would allow. Her ankles and wrists rotated without pain. Nothing broken.

Trip stilled and closed her eyes as footsteps approached the door. She swallowed air fast, too fast for someone supposedly out cold. *Breathe in, two, three…out, two, three.* Despite her heart racing, she managed to slow her breaths as she waited for the doorknob to turn.

"You shouldn't have brought her here," a female said.

"Relax, she'll be gone within the hour. Go in and make sure she's still out," John said.

Trip recognized his voice. How had she missed it before? Nate and Carson had her so distracted she wouldn't have known her mother on the side of the road.

"You do it. I don't want any part of this." Something slammed against the door. When the female spoke again, her voice trembled. "I have to get to work, my shift starts at ten."

No sunlight shone through the window. Ten o'clock at night meant the woman worked the graveyard shift, but where? A hospital? Crystal Beach, assuming John hadn't taken Trip out of town, didn't have any factories. Not many other places someone would go in at this hour, except JJ's.

"Do what you need to do, but keep your mouth shut."

The door opened, and Trip maintained the slow, steady breathing as he came closer. The air around her took on a sinister feel. Her heart slammed against her sternum, but she didn't flinch when John ran his hand up her arm. His touch soft, too soft, almost tender. Bile rose in her throat. What would he do to her after the woman went to work?

John left, closing the door behind him, but his loathsome touch lingered on her skin. He'd told the woman Trip would be out of her house within an hour. Did he plan to take her someplace, or would someone pick her up? McGuire told her more than once local law was compromised.

Trip turned her head but stilled. Two shadows split the light filtering beneath the door. She should turn her head back in case he returned, but she couldn't tear her gaze away.

"I have the goods," John said.

She froze, waiting for a reply. When he spoke again, she assumed he'd made a call.

"That wasn't part of the deal." His voice rose. "I'll take care—"

Tension rolling off him, and she imagined him flexing his fingers before he made a fist. The conversation involved her, it had to. *What deal? What had changed?*

"Yes. I understand."

He moved away from the door. Trip exhaled a breath and closed her eyes. It occurred to her she should be having flashbacks, or hyperventilating. The situation mirrored her first day in Sinaloa, yet she had no symptoms of PTSD now. Before she could puzzle it out, John stormed into the room.

"I thought you'd never wake up." He loomed over her.

Her chest tightened. Trip refused to flinch, to give him the satisfaction of seeing her react. Instead, she focused on keeping her breathing even and her eyes on him.

He grabbed her shoulder and shoved her to her side. "Open up."

"What is that?"

"Something to keep you contained." John grabbed her hair, yanked her head back. "Open your mouth."

She pressed her lips together and shook her head.

"Open your damned mouth, or I'll open it for you." He gripped her chin and turned her face up. "Damn, girl. Your nose is a fucking mess."

Trip met his eyes and refused to break the stare. She hated John for beating her when he claimed to love her, for the way he'd messed with her head, and for his part in their daughter's death. One day, she'd pay him back for the pain he'd caused.

He pried her mouth open and leaned close. "Take the pills, baby. It'll make it more fun when I fuck you later."

Trip made a sound, an involuntary reflex, half gag, half cry. He shoved the pills into her mouth and held her jaw closed.

"Swallow them."

The bitter taste of medicine dissolving on her tongue caused her salivary glands to kick in. She gagged on her own spit until she had no choice but to cough. John held her jaw closed as she struggled. Trip swallowed the remnants of the pills, choking between sobs. He had her. If she passed out again, he could do whatever he pleased. Then again, if she passed out, she wouldn't have to feel John's hands on her body.

As if he'd read her mind, he reached between her legs and cupped her sex. John squeezed her until she cried out in pain, then rubbed his fingers over the seam of her jeans. "Tell me, Trix, is your pussy as tight as I remember, or has Nate stretched it out?"

Trip buried her face in the mattress. Pain shot through her nose, clearing her head enough to bring her back to the moment. "I imagine any cock would make it too loose for that little prick of yours."

The blow came fast and hard on the side of her head, leaving her dizzy. Trip forced a smile and closed her eyes. Between the drugs and the possible concussion, she had little hope of staying conscious.

Thirty-Eight

NATE GAVE UP CALLING TRIP AFTER THE THIRD message. If she wanted him, she'd return his call. Carson seemed so sure of her feelings, but Nate didn't trust her. She'd played them both, but she'd played him harder. Nate thought back over their time together. *She's like two people, one distant and cold, and the other? The other is too perfect for words.*

Why hadn't she taken off in North Carolina? She had every opportunity to go. Nate recalled her face while she sat in the truck on the phone. "Fiancé, my ass, she called to give report."

He pressed the alarm code and slammed the keypad shut. How could he be so fucking stupid? He'd bought every bit of her act. She'd lied up until the last second. Trip never made it to the police station. Nate figured she'd made it halfway to Lejeune by now. How could Carson expected Nate to run away with her after everything she'd done? *The hell with that.*

"Hey, Dad. It's time." Nate had imagined making this call a million times over the past five years. Now that he could see an end to this life, he second guessed himself. He had to get Carson out, too, or he'd never be able to look himself in the mirror. Whatever time Carson had left, he didn't need to spend it inside a prison cell.

"I'll let your mother know. When?" His father's voice, normally so certain, trembled with the question.

"Now. Drive all night if you have to. I'll meet you at the place. I won't have time for a long goodbye, but I'll send word when we're safe." Nate hated the idea of taking Sophia away from the only life she'd ever known, but this was always the plan.

"Be careful, son. I'll call you when we are an hour out."

"I love you, Dad. Thanks." Nate disconnected and pulled his duffle bag from the closet. He'd rehearsed this so many times over the years he knew exactly what he needed to pack. Bare necessities, the new ID cards, birth certificates, and passports he had made after Sophia was born. He stashed bank records and receipts from the accounts he'd set up under his new name in the bottom of the bag. Nate packed or destroyed anything that provided a clue to his plan, but left everything else, including a fat balance in his existing bank account. To the world, Nathaniel Benz would be another statistic, a missing person presumed dead.

"Trip, damn it. I need to speak to you." Nate shoved his phone in his pocket and tossed the bag into the trunk. He couldn't sit around and wait for her to return his call. He had a shift to pull at the bar if he planned to keep up appearances.

Nate walked to his car and called Trip one more time before he drove to the bar. A handful of cars sat in the parking lot, slow even for a weeknight. He walked in the back door and headed straight for the bar. A drink would help calm his nerves, but more importantly, this is what he always did. Nate would drink a beer and catch up with the bartenders. Then he'd go into the office to go through the day's receipts.

"Hey, Celia," Nate claimed a stool.

She turned to Nate with wide eyes. "Hi."

He grinned, though he had the feeling he caught her with her hand in the cash drawer. "Everything okay?"

"Yep. Everything's good." She nodded and skittered to the other side of the bar.

He made a mental note to double check her receipts. Celia had worked at JJ's for a couple of years and never given him any trouble, but something felt off tonight. She hadn't even asked if he wanted a drink. Nate slid behind the bar and pulled a beer from the cooler, watching her from the corner of his eye.

Celia glanced over her shoulder a couple of times, before she grabbed a rag and wiped down the prep area, a job usually handled by the barmaids. Nate shook his head and went back to his stool.

"Hey, man, what's up?" Mack slapped Nate's shoulder.

"Not much. Something happen in here earlier? Celia seems out of sorts."

Mack sat beside him. "She's been out of it since she started dating Daugherty."

Nate prided himself on keeping tabs on the local gossip, especially when it involved an employee dating a crooked cop. "When did that happen?"

"A few months ago. They're keeping it quiet, but I caught her doing the walk of shame one morning."

"Huh." He tipped his beer back. Celia had worked the night that Ryan brought Trip in, the night Domino took one to the chest. Come to think of it, she'd seemed skittish that night as well. "Mack, do you remember if Daugherty was in the evening Domino was shot?"

Mack scratched the back of his head. "Yeah, he was. He gave me a ticket for parking my truck in the fire lane. Cost me a hundred bucks."

"You sure it was the same night?" Nate's gut rolled over. Something didn't sit right. He paid attention to who came and went from JJ's. How could he have missed that prick in the bar? Simple. He'd been too wrapped up in a woman to do his job.

Regardless, someone had tipped off the Trevinos that night. Someone with something to lose. He'd heard rumors that John Daugherty was up to his neck with the Mexicans, but John wasn't stupid. If he involved himself in a drug deal gone bad, he had to have a reason.

Mack pulled a crumpled piece of paper from his wallet. "March twenty-first?"

"That's the night." Nate finished his beer and stood. "Cover the bar for a minute?"

"Sure."

"Hey, Celia, can I have a word with you?" Nate motioned to the office.

The color drained from the woman's face. She glanced from him to the office and the exit. "I need to use the ladies room."

"Now." If he had any doubt she knew something he needed to know, it vanished with that look.

Celia nodded and headed for the office. Nate turned to follow, but before he could reach the door, Tom walked in still in uniform. He caught Nate's eye and shook his head. Tom, the one cop he could trust, pressed his lips together in a grim line. Not a good sign.

"Tom, what can I do for you?" Nate stood between Celia and the exit.

"I'll go take a break." Celia side-stepped him.

Nate grabbed her arm and shook his head. "Wait for me in the office."

She pulled her arm free. "I'm taking my break, or I quit."

Tom watched the exchange with cop eyes. "Celia. I need to ask you a few questions. I suggest you stay put."

She burst into tears and ran into the office with Nate and Tom on her heels.

Nate shut the door and folded his arms. "What's going on?"

"I found Sergeant Peyton's rental car out on Route Ten." Tom glanced at Celia, then turned to Nate. "There were AFID tags on the ground. Her purse and cell phone were inside."

"What's an AFID tag?" Celia wiped her eyes.

Tom said, "Anti-felon identification tags. They look like confetti, but they contain serial numbers of the Taser that deployed them."

Celia hung her head. "I had nothing to do with it."

"You had nothing to do with what?" Nate growled.

"Nothing. I didn't do anything. I quit. I'm leaving. You, you can't keep me here against my will. That's kidnapping." Celia looked to Tom for help.

The word kidnapping fell from her lips, and alarm bells went off in Nate's brain. She knew what happened to Trip, or she knew who had her. Nate grabbed her shoulders. "Where is she?"

"Easy, Benz." Tom tugged Nate away from her. "Celia, I suggest you start talking."

Her makeup ran in black streaks down her red cheeks. "John brought her to my house. I didn't know what it was about. He said she'd be gone within the hour."

"Gone where?" Nate's hands balled into fists. "Was she hurt?"

Celia shrugged. "Her face was a mess, and she was unconscious."

Tom unclipped his radio and called for backup. "Celia, you are under arrest. Anything you say…"

Nate turned for the door, ignoring Tom calling his name. He had to get to Trip.

THIRTY-NINE

"DID YOU MISS ME, BABY?" John ran his hand down Trip's arm.

"Why are you doing this?" The drugs made her head too heavy to lift. Her arms and legs ached, still tied behind her back. Trip struggled to stay awake and keep him talking.

"You never should have come back here."

"Believe me, I know." Her throat felt as though she'd gargled sand. "Can I have some water?"

He leaned close, putting his face in her site line. "You thirsty, baby?"

"Yes." She attempted a smile.

"I got something else you can put in your mouth."

It hurt when she laughed, though Trip tried to hide it. "That might be more fun if my mouth wasn't so dry."

He ran his hand over her ass. "I bet something else is wet."

"Maybe, but it's going to be a challenge to get these jeans off when you have me strung up like a prize pig." His hand on her made her want to vomit, but she'd play along in hopes he would untie her.

John slid his hand between her legs. "I like you this way, so helpless. You're right, though. I should have stripped you before I tied you up."

Trip pressed her crotch against his hand. "I've missed you, John."

He shot to his feet and yanked the rope binding her wrists to her ankles, lifting her off the bed. Her shoulders screamed at the unnatural angle. Trip bit back a cry of pain and fought to keep her muscles engaged, so her shoulders didn't dislocate.

"Don't fucking lie to me." John laughed and dropped her to the bed. "Then again, you can't help it, can you? You come from a long line of liars."

"I guess I do. Why are you doing this? It can't be for a piece of ass." She rolled her shoulders forward as far as the ties would allow.

"Some people are willing to pay a lot of money for you." John turned for the door.

"I bet Carson James would pay more. You should call and ask him."

"You think because you're screwing Nate, you're worth something to Carson?" John chuckled.

"No. I think Carson will pay because I'm his sister." Trip hoped she hadn't made a mistake by playing the sister-card, but she had no other leverage. She surmised he planned to turn her over to the Trevinos for cash. Perhaps, he'd sell her to the highest bidder.

"You expect me to believe you're Carson's sister?"

"Half-sister." Her voice cracked, leaving her coughing. "Remember how Dixie paid for her drugs? Seems old Macon was a regular customer."

"No shit?"

"I was just as shocked."

"I doubt he'd pay. Carson had Ryan killed over a backpack full of drugs."

Trip craned her neck to get a look at him. "You believe Carson did that?"

John's expression darkened. "I was at the bar. I caught Ryan and Domino making the transaction. I was about to bust them when Domino went for his gun."

"You shot Domino?"

"Self-defense. Your *real* brother clocked me and took off with the merchandise. Carson doesn't suffer people who steal from him."

It all made sense, but Ryan didn't steal from Carson. He took the heroin to keep from going to jail. No wonder he drove off in such a hurry. John might not have caused the accident, but he certainly played a role in Ryan's death.

John walked out and returned with a glass of water. "Let's get that mouth nice and wet."

Trip nodded, but her thoughts remained on Ryan.

John rolled her to her side and made a half-assed effort to get the water into her mouth. She managed to swallow a couple of mouthfuls, while the rest spilled onto the bed. He set the glass aside and unzipped his jeans.

"John, not to be a downer, but I'm not breathing through my nose. You stick that in my mouth, and I won't be worth as much."

He lifted her chin and inspected his handiwork, turning her head from side to side. "You're not so pretty to look at anyway. Now that you mention it, I can see the resemblance to Carson."

"You should call him." Trip pulled her chin from his hand and glared. He wouldn't call Carson. He'd already told the Trevinos he had her. Trip's training taught her to keep him talking, play nice, but not too nice. Too nice and they caught on.

"I'll think about it." John reached behind him and pulled a huge buck knife from his belt.

How had she missed the knife? Trip noted he didn't wear his service revolver, nor did his jeans bulge with an ankle holster. He hadn't turned his back to her since he returned with the water. His eyes narrowed when he saw her flinch and noticed the fear in her eyes. He made no effort to hide that he liked it.

"Be still." John lifted her T-shirt from between her bound hands and sliced through the fabric from hem to neck, followed by each sleeve. He ran his free hand over her side, then reached beneath her to squeeze her breast.

Trip turned her head and closed her eyes. She had to shut him out. If this continued, she needed to turn her brain off and go somewhere else for a while.

John yanked on the rope again, this time she hadn't anticipated it. Trip groaned before she could stop herself. Her deltoids burned, and something deeper threatened to tear. The rope split in two, releasing her from the awkward position. She tested the bindings on her wrists and ankles, both remained secure. While she had more freedom of movement, John had easier access to the parts of her she didn't want him to access.

He shoved her head against the bed. "You try anything, and I will gut you."

Trip couldn't nod and didn't trust herself to speak.

John released her head to tug her jeans from her hips. She didn't outright struggle, but she didn't make it easy for him. If he dropped the knife, she'd act fast. He didn't drop the knife.

"I have to pee." Trip begged when the air hit her bare ass.

"Too bad." He ran the cold blade between her cheeks.

"You don't want whatshername to come home to a wet bed. She probably won't be happy that we had sex. Let me pee and get a towel." Trip had chosen her words carefully, having sex sounded much less threatening than accusing him of rape.

"God, damn it." John used her hair to pull her upright, and jammed the knife against her throat. "She won't notice the cum or the piss with all the blood."

Trip didn't dare swallow. Her throat stung where the blade had already broken the skin. John chest pressed against her arms, leaving her hands close to his erection. She eased her fingers over him, in hopes of coaxing him into moving the knife.

"Dirty little whore." John chuckled and pulled the blade back a fraction of an inch. He fumbled with his zipper behind her back, then shoved her upper body to the bed.

Trip closed her eyes and let her mind go numb. Her body became nothing more to her than a skin suit, her soul safe from his assault. She imagined killing John, taking her time slicing bits off his body until he begged for death. Lost in the daydream, she didn't hear the door open.

The gunshot and splash of hot blood over her body pulled her back to reality. John tumbled on top of her before she could make sense of what had happened. He hadn't penetrated her, but she couldn't breathe, not yet. Trip couldn't see her savior. For all she knew, one of the Trevinos had saved her so they could kill her later.

FORTY

NATE FOLLOWED THE SOUND OF JOHN'S VOICE toward the bedroom and peeked inside. *Trip, no.* A switch flipped inside him. Without thought or consciousness, the gun appeared in his hand, and the trigger pulled itself. That son of a bitch put his hands, and God knows what else, on his woman. He'd killed before but never like that, and never a cop.

Trip didn't make a sound, nor had she moved. Had John killed her in his rage? Nate couldn't bring himself to check. His hands shook, and his chest tightened. *Why isn't she moving?*

Her foot twitched, then her shoulders shook. Trip tried to lift her head, but John's body pinned her to the bed.

"Trip?" Nate shoved John off her. "Babe, are you okay?"

The sound she made reminded him of a wounded animal, guttural and raw.

"It's okay. I got you." Nate ran his hand over her body, trying to determine if any of the blood belonged to her. He grabbed the discarded knife. "Hang on. Don't move."

She gasped for breath and fought against the restraints.

Nate couldn't think about what she'd endured in the past few hours. He had to focus on getting her out of here. "Be still, sweetheart."

She turned her head toward the sound of his voice. "Nate?"

He forced himself not to turn away. Nate had seen plenty of carnage, but her battered face brought him to his knees. "Yes, it's me. Hold still so I can cut the ropes."

Trip turned her head and went slack.

Nate sliced through the rope around her wrists and ankles.

She drew her arms to her chest and rolled into the fetal position.

Nate brushed her bloody hair from her face. "We need to go. Can you walk?"

"I think so." Trip allowed him to help her sit upright. Her eyes widened at the sight of John's body. The shaking started in her hands and traveled through her. She leaned forward and put her head between her knees, hyperventilating.

Nate positioned himself between her and John to block her view. He rubbed her shoulder as he spoke. "You're safe now. I won't let anything happen to you. Breathe, nice and slow."

Trip pulled herself together before his eyes. One moment she sat shaking on the verge of a breakdown, the next she snapped to grid and surveyed the situation. "I need a shirt."

Nate offered his hand, but she stood on her own and tugged her jeans over her hips. Nate had never seen someone divorce themselves from their emotions in the blink of an eye. It reminded him of his mother's assessment of Trip—a bird with a broken wing.

Trip ignored him as she rummaged through Celia's closet and tugged a black shirt over her head. "Let's go before the neighbors call the cops."

Trip had a point, firing a .45 caliber in a residential area would set the good neighbors into action. He noted her bare feet, and sighed.

He set a gun in her hand. "This way."

The gun didn't faze her. She tucked it into the waistband of her jeans like second nature.

"I parked in the old make-out spot near the river. It's close but wooded. Are you going to be okay without shoes?"

Trip glanced at her feet and back to him. The mask of composure slipped, giving him a glimpse of the turmoil inside her. "Shoes?"

Shit. Hold it together, sweetheart. "I'll carry you when we leave the pavement. Ready?"

She nodded.

Nate lead her through Celia's backyard. The way she moved through the darkness impressed and terrified him. The way she crept along the fence line and avoided the light, spoke of years of training.

He stopped when they reached the edge of the woods, but she continued forward. His footsteps echoed through the night, while she hardly snapped a twig.

He unlocked the car manually and slid into the driver's seat.

Trip stared out the windshield.

"Are you all right? Do you need to go to the hospital?" He started the car.

"He didn't rape me."

Nate glanced at her out of the corner of his eye as he put the car in drive and eased down the dirt path. "Your nose is broken."

"John killed Domino."

He hit the brakes. "What?"

"John was in the bar that night. He walked in on the transaction. Things went south, and he shot Domino. Ryan took off to get rid of the evidence."

"Damn." Nate let the information sink in. Not much he could do about it now, he'd taken care of the problem when he shot John.

"I need to get my car and my ID."

Nate reached for Trip's hand, but she snatched it away before he touched her. "Babe, the police found your purse and cell in the rental car. It's locked in evidence."

"Dammit." She ran her trembling hands through her hair and shifted in her seat. "Stop the car."

"Trip?"

She yanked on the door handle, hit the unlock button, and threw the door open. With her upper body hanging out of the car, she vomited.

Nate set his hand on her back, hating the way she flinched and shrank away from his touch. "You need to see a doctor."

Trip flopped back in her seat and wiped her mouth. "How do I explain wearing John's blood? I don't have time to deal with emergency room bullshit."

Nate handed her a bottle of water. "It's been in the car for hours, but it'll help."

"Thanks." She rinsed her mouth and closed the door. "I have to get to MacDill. It's urgent."

"I'm sure your commanding officer will want your next report." Nate pulled forward until he reached a side street and headed toward Carson's.

"I have to tell him what happened."

"Cut the shit, Trip. What are you? ATF? DEA?" He hated that this conversation had to happen under these circumstances. *Now or never.*

She sank deeper into her seat. "Something like that."

"You've been working against Carson and me the entire time?" His hands tightened on the steering wheel. "What about us? Was that all a lie too?"

"No. I came home to take care of my shit. When Ryan…The incident at Ryan's shook me up. I had to know what was going on, and you weren't talking. I asked to be put on the investigation when I called it in."

Nate couldn't bring himself to look at her. "And us? Was fucking me part of the investigation?"

"At first, but then I—" Trip reached for his arm, but her hand fell short. "I'm sorry."

"Then you what?" He turned onto a dirt road that led to the back of Carson's property. Nate had no idea if the police had staked out the main entrance, but he'd killed a cop less than an hour ago and didn't want to take any chances.

"Then I fell in love with you. I've been trying to get you out of this. I talked to Carson. He agreed to cut you lose." Her voice shook.

"I know. I spoke to him earlier." Nate cut the engine and turned to face her. "Tell me who you work for and what they know."

"I can't, but I'll fix it, so you don't go to jail."

"And Carson?"

"I'll try, but he's…" Tears brimmed in her eyes.

"Run away with me. Carson wants us to take Izzy and Sophie and disappear." Nate didn't know where the words had come from. They sure as hell didn't come from the rational part of his brain. Then again, he'd never been rational when it came to this woman.

"I can't."

"Bullshit. So what? I drop you at MacDill and never see you again? I thought you promised Carson you'd raise Izzy, or was that another lie?"

The sun peeked over the horizon. He didn't have time to debate her. The girls and Carson counted on him to get them safely aboard a boat before all hell broke loose.

"I didn't promise, I said I needed time to think it over. I can't just go AWOL."

"Get out." Nate reached across her and opened the door.

"What?"

The fear in her eyes almost stopped him. *Almost.* "I have things I have to do. Follow the path to the house. Get a shower and change clothes. You can borrow one of Carson's cars to do what you have to do. Call me if and when you make up your mind. I'm leaving at noon."

"I don't have a phone or your number." Trip's voice cracked.

He opened the glove box and dropped another burner phone in her lap. "Problem solved, now go."

"Nate, please."

"Please what? Please tell you that you're right? That you did what you had to do? That I forgive you?" Nate wanted to shake her but didn't know where to grab her without hurting her. *What's wrong with me? I should want to hurt her. I should want to put a fucking bullet in her head.*

Trip stared at him. "I'm sorry."

"Me, too. Sorry I fucking love you."

She hung her head and whispered, "I'm not sorry I love you."

As much as he wanted to hold onto his anger, the lost look on her face drew him in. Nate's brain told him she'd played him, but his heart won the battle. He leaned forward, and Trip met him halfway. Their lips touched, and she gasped. Nate pulled back thinking he'd hurt her split lip, but she curled her fingers in his hair and pulled him back to her mouth. The blood-tinged kiss spoke of promise, a promise of more—of hope.

"That didn't feel like goodbye," he murmured against her ear.

"I want to come with you. Where should I meet you?" Trip met his gaze."

"I'll have two children and a terminally ill man with me. Can I trust you not to turn us in?"

"No. Don't tell me until I need to know." She pulled away and dipped her chin. "I should go."

Nate grabbed her arm and pulled her back to him. "Say it again. I need to hear it."

Trip furrowed her brow. "I want to come with you?"

He shook his head. "No, the other part."

A slow grin crossed her lips. Trip eased closer and whispered into his ear. "I love you."

Nate closed his eyes and hoped she meant it. "Call me when you're on your way, and I'll give you the address."

"I will."

FORTY-ONE

WEEKDAY TRAFFIC GAVE TRIP PLENTY OF TIME to mull over the mess she'd made of her life. She should never have come back to Crystal Beach, but if she hadn't, she wouldn't have reconnected with Nate. Trip couldn't deny her feelings for him, any more than she could deny her fondness for Carson. However, the Marine hated that she'd fallen for the bad guy.

Trip couldn't blame Nate for holding back on the details of his escape plan. He had two little girls counting on him, even if they didn't know it. The idea of being a mother to two daughters made her heart ache for a family. She wanted to try, wanted the life that Nate promised. *I can do this, but I can't go AWOL.*

Trip had a plan. Her PTSD diagnosis gave her what she needed to request a discharge. Given the pending murder charges, she doubted any of the brass would raise a brow. McGuire maybe, but he'd sign off, eventually. Once discharged, she'd go to North Carolina and wait for Nate to contact his parents.

Trip put the car in park at the guard station and prepared for a hassle. The uniformed airman approached with a smile. "Good morning, ID please."

"I'm Gunnery Sergeant Trip Peyton. My identification card was stolen along with my purse. My commanding officer called ahead, I'm here to see Major Patrick Meyers."

He flipped through a few pages on his clipboard. "Security code?"

Trip spat out the code McGuire had given her that morning.

"Proceed to building four hundred and check in at the desk on the first floor."

Well, that was easy. She nodded to acknowledge his salute and pulled the car forward. As Trip approached the parking lot, she spotted a gathering of Marines, one, in particular, drew her attention. McGuire.

Trip exited the car and approached with a hefty dose of trepidation. She'd spoken with him an hour before, and he hadn't mentioned he would meet her. She saluted. "Sir."

He replied with a nod, then motioned for her to follow. Once out of earshot, he gave her a once over. "Are you all right?"

"Yes, sir. Surprised to see you here."

He ran his hand over his jaw. "I'm in charge of this operation. Given the potential loss of civilian life, I thought it best that I come."

"Yes, sir."

"I spoke with your psychiatrist this morning. I understand you haven't returned since your initial appointment?" He narrowed his eyes, silently appraising her response.

"The mission did not allow time to follow up." The formality of the conversation set Trip on edge. When she called earlier in the day, she reported the kidnapping but fudged on the details of her escape. Not fudged, outright lied.

"Are you certain you didn't get a look at the individual who shot Officer Daugherty?"

"As I stated in my report, Officer Daugherty was in the process of sexually assaulting me when he was shot. He weighed approximately two-hundred and twenty pounds, and his body landed on top of mine. By the time, I was able to get him off me, the shooter was gone." Trip enunciated each word with precision, despite the tremor in her voice.

Judging by McGuire's expression, he didn't buy her story. "You need to report to medical immediately. You may be a suspect in a *second* murder. A confirmed sexual assault will go a long way in proving self-defense."

"With all due respect, I'd like to be a part of the operation."

"Absolutely not. We'll have a couple of the guys wired with cameras. You can watch with me after you're cleared by medical. Now go."

"Sir, yes sir." Trip saluted her commanding officer and turned toward the building. She had no idea where to go. Behind her, McGuire shouted for one of the marines to accompany her to medical. Her guide grinned when he saluted her, but Trip couldn't bring herself to return the favor. He looked young. *Too* young and too eager.

"Gunny, Sergeant Major McGuire asked me to accompany you to medical, then return you to the unit. I'm Fiorelli." He motioned to the name sewn on his uniform.

Trip canted her head. "Peyton."

"You're the one who volunteered to go in alone? That's either brave or stupid. These guys are ruthless," he prattled on. "We've been trying to infiltrate them for over a year. How'd you do it?"

Trip stopped walking. "Over a year?"

Her question didn't dull his enthusiasm. "James and the Trevinos, a match made in Hell. Between the two organizations, they have racked up quite the body count, not to mention the amount of narcotics on the street. I have to tell you, you've earned quite the reputation with my team."

Trip turned and continued walking. She wondered what they would say if they learned she'd slept with one and was related to another. The fact that they had attempted to infiltrate the organization for so long bothered her. McGuire acted as if he had no knowledge of the organization before she requested permission to investigate. Come to think of it, the approval for her request had come back fast—too fast. Until that moment she didn't want to believe her commander had given her the wrong medication and orchestrated everything to put her in the middle of an active investigation.

"Ma'am, are you all right?" Fiorelli grabbed her elbow to keep her upright.

"Yes, just need some food." She smiled. "Who's in charge of your team? I wasn't aware we had SOH teams in Florida."

"We're stationed out of Lejeune under McGuire." He tightened his grip on her arm when she stumbled for the second time. "Ma'am, I think we should get you to medical."

"Thank you." Trip had trusted McGuire, thought of him as a surrogate father figure. In return, he'd played her. Her belief system shattered. It had chipped when she ran into her mother, cracked when Donnie hugged her, splintered when Ryan died, and broken when John put his hands on her.

McGuire's betrayal annihilated Trip's values and erased the line between right and wrong. Justice, like beauty, came down to a matter of perspective.

Fiorelli did his part in assisting her to medical, and Trip used the escort to her advantage, leaning on him for feigned support. He approached the first desk. "I need help. She's been assaulted. She hasn't eaten and nearly passed out."

The triage nurse took one look at Trip and hurried them into a private waiting room in the back. "What happened?"

Trip hung her head and mumbled. "I suffer from PTSD and was sexually assaulted last night. I already showered, so I doubt there's forensic evidence."

The nurse went wide eyed before she smoothed her face. "I'll need to get you to complete some paperwork. Would you like a female doctor?"

Trip nodded, betting her life that female doctors were in short supply. She had to get out of here and call Nate.

"All right. I'll have to call someone in. Let's get you some food." The nurse put herself between Trip and Fiorelli, who the woman deemed the enemy simply because he had a penis. "You should go."

He shook his head. "I was told to—"

"You will leave my clinic this moment, or I'll have you escorted out."

Trip whispered, "Thanks for walking me over, Fiorelli. I owe you one."

FORTY-TWO

AFTER A QUICK STOP AT CARSON'S ATTORNEY'S office, Nate had papers giving himself and Trip custody of Izzy. A second set of papers granted access to Carson's offshore accounts under Nate's new name. The final envelope contained a birth certificate for a baby girl born to his and Trip's new identities. Nate had become a father for the second time in a matter of minutes.

Jessica, Marcy's sister, met him at the door with the baby. She'd packed all of her things into two grocery bags. Nate hesitated before he reached for Izzy. Jessica looked so much like her sister it stole his breath. The image of Marcy's face when Carson knocked her overboard still haunted him. Of all the terrible things he'd participated in, Marcy's murder topped the list. He would raise her child but dreaded the day he saw her mother in her eyes.

"I'm glad he finally claimed her." Jessica set her hands on her hips. "Why the change of heart?"

Nate adjusted Izzy in his arms and grabbed the bags. "Who knows why Carson does the things he does."

Mabelle, the Basset Hound, brayed from the front seat. Nate hadn't planned on bringing her along, but he couldn't stand to leave her behind. What was one more female condemning him with a sad look and sniff?

"You can't have that dog around the baby."

"Mabelle's great with kids."

Jessica didn't look convinced as she followed him with the car seat. "Do you know how these work?"

"I'm sure I can figure it out." Nate had installed plenty of infant seats when Sophia was first born. Now he'd have two girls to look after, but would he do it alone? The look Trip had given him that morning, not to mention the kiss, gave him hope.

"Nate?" Jessica looked annoyed.

"Yeah, I got it." He pushed past her and settled Izzy into the seat, then fastened the straps and double-checked the seatbelt. "When will she eat again?"

"I fed her right before you got here, so three or four hours. I wrote out instructions for Carson. They're in the bag." Her eyes filled with unshed tears.

"Hey, none of that. She'll be in good hands. I promise." Nate added another lie to his long list of sins.

"When can I see her?" Jessica leaned in and kissed the baby.

"Soon, just give Carson a call." Nate closed the door and hurried to the driver's side. "Sorry to cut this short, but Carson's waiting."

She turned and walked up the drive without looking back.

Nate pulled out of the driveway and headed toward the beach. Taking Izzy from Jessica would be a cake walk compared to taking Sophie from his parents. He checked his phone, hoping he'd missed a call from Trip. No such luck.

"All right, little one. Let's give your daddy a call." Nate punched in Carson's number and waited until the call went to voicemail.

When the phone rang, he assumed Carson returned his call. "Benz."

"Nate, this is Tom. I need you to come down to the station to answer a few questions."

He glanced in the rearview at the infant seat. "Sure, what about?"

"Celia's neighbors reported gunshots early this morning. They found John Daugherty shot in the head at close range. Sergeant Peyton wasn't there. We found her clothing."

Nate took a deep breath to keep his voice calm. "She showed up at the house this morning saying something about needing to get to MacDill. She took one of Carson's cars. You think she shot him in self-defense?"

"Could be. John had his pants around his ankles. Ropes on the bed like he had someone tied up. Are you telling me you had nothing to do with it?" Tom sounded tired. "Off the record."

"On or off the record, I'm telling you I had nothing to do with it."

"You left JJ's right around the time…Damn it, Nate. Just come in. I need a statement from you and the girl."

"I'll be in around one. I have Marcy's baby in the car with me right now. Let me get her to Carson." Nate crossed the county line and blew a sigh of relief. Another few minutes and he'd be lost in traffic. Just another commuter heading into Tampa.

"You're taking her to Carson?" Tom chuckled.

"He made it official."

"Well, damn. Good for him. I'll see you at one. Don't skip town."

Nate smiled and ticked another mark on the sin list. "I wouldn't dream of it."

By the time, he reached the marina, he'd all but given up hope that Carson or Trip would return his call. Izzy had worked herself into a fit in the backseat, her shrill cries like an icepick to his temple. He caught sight of his mother's tear-stained face and damned near put the car in reverse.

"Daddy!" Sophie wrapped her arms around him before he could get out of the car.

"Hey, baby girl." Nate scooped her into his arms.

Izzy's screams drew his mother to the backseat. Within seconds she had the baby in her arms. "Whose child is this?"

"Carson's, but she's coming with Soph and me." As soon as the words left his mouth, he realized his error.

His mother's eyebrows climbed into her hairline. "You're going off alone with two children?"

"Trip is meeting us." Another tick mark in the lie column. At this rate, he'd have a full scholarship to Hell.

Sophie bounced and clapped, pleased as punch to hear that Trip was coming along. Nate prayed he hadn't lied to his daughter. He could do a lot of things, but breaking her heart wasn't one of them.

His mother opened her mouth and snapped it shut when his phone rang. He grinned and set Sophie down before pressing the phone to his ear.

"You need to come back." Carson wheezed into the phone. "I want to see my kid one last time."

FORTY-THREE

TRIP EXITED THE BUILDING THROUGH THE EMPLOYEE ACCESS Door before the doctor arrived. On the off chance Fiorelli waited in the lobby, she didn't want him to see her slip out. She tucked her hair under her hat and slumped her shoulders as she walked toward the parking lot. Thankfully, McGuire and the others had cleared out.

Trip pulled Nate's phone from her pocket and dialed the only number stored in memory as she walked toward the car. When Nate didn't answer, she disconnected and hit redial. She had to reach him to find out exactly where to meet. In hindsight, Trip should have demanded the information before she got out of his car that morning. The man had a way of making her IQ plummet along with her panties.

"Peyton." McGuire came out of an adjacent building and waved her over. "Finished in medical?"

Trip slid the phone back into her pocket and waved. A smile graced her lips to hide her frustration. "Yeah, everything checked out. The doc said my vagina—"

"Whoa, enough said." He put his hands up to stop her. "The guys are in position. Come join me. It'll be good for you to see how the operations work from a leadership perspective. You'll be calling the shots soon."

Oh, right. She'd forgotten about the promotion. How strange that something that had meant so much to her now meant nothing. "Sounds good."

"We had to call Fiorelli back. It took longer than we anticipated in medical." He watched her from the corner of his eye.

"Yeah, that happens when they have to do a rape kit."

He grimaced.

Years in the Corps taught Trip a lot about men, including their aversion to talking about anything related to female bodily functions that didn't involve having sex. "Fiorelli let it slip this is an ongoing investigation. Why did you lie? You could've told me the truth going in."

McGuire stopped walking and leaned close. "Be careful throwing around that sort of accusation. Protocol doesn't allow for sending in a single asset."

"The PTSD, is it real? Did you give me the bogus prescription to make me sicker than I am?"

"You had an incident that warranted evaluation. I'm not a physician. I don't have the authority to prescribe medication."

"Regardless, I feel worlds better since I stopped taking unneeded thyroid medication. In fact, I've been through worse since, without incident." *Mostly without incident.* Trip didn't want to believe he'd compromised her mental status to create a reason to send her into an active mission blind, but not wanting to believe didn't make it any less true.

"I see no reason why the psychiatrist would prevent you from returning to duty, or why any of it needs to go on your record." McGuire gave her a hard look.

As long as she kept her mouth shut, it would all go away. She'd get her promotion. Trip's stomach turned, but she pasted on a smile. "Thank you, sir. That's good news."

Trip followed him into a conference room. She tried to wrap her brain around McGuire poisoning her to get her to Crystal Beach. Trip accepted the diagnosis. She'd more than likely live with the PSTD for years to come, but he'd exploited it. Trip could have suffered a heart attack as a result of the high dosage of the medication. Yet, there he sat as if he had done nothing wrong. *Mission before Marine.*

A small group of men sat in front of a large whiteboard with three grainy video feeds. The audio feed squealed and chirped like an old cell with bad reception. A technician with headphones sat at a laptop punching buttons until the feed cleared.

"It's almost show time." McGuire motioned for her to take a seat beside him. "Each camera is mounted to a different team member. Ideally, one in the front, middle, and rear."

Trip nodded and leaned closer to the board. The men, at least she assumed they were men, all looked the same. In the field, she could tell her teammates apart by their physical build. These men were strangers to her, or so she thought. Fiorelli's chuckle blasted through the audio feed.

The tech grumbled into the mic, "Hey, Fee. Cut the chatter will ya?"

"Sorry, got it." The goofball cleaned the camera lens.

"Don't touch the camera, forget it's there." The tech shook his head.

"Rookie, first mission," McGuire whispered.

The body mounts disappeared and a long-range view, of the barn where the meeting would take place and an access road, flashed on the whiteboard. Trip could see. Several vehicles were parked outside. Trip leaned forward in her chair, searching for anything familiar.

"Do you recognize any of the vehicles?" McGuire asked.

"Can you zoom in on the large, black SUV on the right?"

The camera angle changed, focusing on the vehicle she specified.

"License plate?" Trip squinted until the letters and numbers came into view. She'd seen Lurch's plates at the bar. That the first three letters were DCK struck her as humorous. She didn't find them funny now. "That belongs to Daniel Sievers. His father runs the mortuary in town. He cremates casualties from time to time."

Trip had grown up a few years behind Daniel in school and had crossed paths with him since she returned home. She knew his sister. Her stomach sank. She couldn't sit here and rat out people she'd known her entire life. *Who else would show up at the sit-down? Who else will I send to prison?*

A black, newer model, BMW eased its way down the access road. The driver drove slower than the others had as if trying not to chip the paint. Trip bit the inside of her cheek and sent up a silent prayer. *Please, God, don't let that be Carson.*

"Zoom in on the Beemer." Trip's hand shook as she wiped the sweat from her brow.

The images went wide, then zeroed in on the driver's side door of the car. Dark windows, it could be anyone. Carson wouldn't be stupid enough to show up. If Nate knew she worked for the Feds, Carson knew.

The door opened, and Trip's heart stopped beating. Nate stepped out of the car. Nate with his hair hanging loose over his broad shoulders. Nate with his low-slung jeans and little boy smile. *Why? Why's he there?*

"Who is that?" McGuire's voice sliced through her.

"Nathaniel Benz."

"I thought he wasn't part of the illegal activities?" McGuire punched the keys of his laptop, likely searching for additional intel on Nate.

"He isn't."

Nate moved to the passenger side and opened the door. He leaned in and assisted Carson to his feet. *Oh, God. No. No. No.*

"Peyton?"

"That's Carson James. He has terminal leukemia. My guess is he's too weak to drive." She swallowed bile. Carson had promised her he'd get Nate out. *Where are the girls? What the hell had happened? Come on, Nate, turn around and drive away.*

Carson straightened and strode toward the building like a leading man taking the stage. He certainly didn't walk like a man too weak to drive. Trip sat back in her chair and watched as Carson turned and scanned the sky as if looking for the cameras. "That son of a bitch."

"He doesn't look like he's knocking on death's door," McGuire said.

"No, he sure as hell doesn't." Trip stood and wandered closer to the whiteboard. "Is Juan Trevino, Sr. already inside?"

"Yes, we're still waiting on Carlos, and then they'll start," a nameless Marine answered.

"Carlos Trevino is dead." Trip folded her arms over her chest, doubting everything Carson had told her. She hadn't seen the DNA results. For all she knew, he'd lied about that, too. Still, he knew they were watching, didn't he?

Her cell phone buzzed in her pocket, and several heads turned. "Let me turn this off."

Trip glanced at the screen. The caller ID read "Contact 1." Nate. She squeezed the phone, struggling to do what she had to. Trip trusted him to get out of there. She believed he'd understand she couldn't answer when it might jeopardize their escape.

Trip sighed and powered down the phone. How could he possibly call her now, when he'd walked into a barn full of criminals? *He feels comfortable making a call in a barn full of criminals because half of them are his people. Our people?*

The wide-angle camera vanished, and the body cams flickered to life. A split-second later gunfire erupted from inside the building and shot through her. Her heart raced, stealing her breath. *Get out of there, Nate.*

Trip couldn't pull her eyes away from the screen. The SOH team members stood at the ready, with weapons drawn. How many good people will die today?

"Seems the bad guys are doing our jobs for us." McGuire chuckled. "Hold position. Shoot any armed suspects that leave the building."

"How will they know if they're unarmed?" Trip balled her hands into fists. Her nails dug into her palms, easing her temper.

"You've been where they are, Peyton. They'll take down anyone they perceive as a threat." McGuire leaned toward the screen. "Move into secondary position. Cover the back exit."

Her chest tightened as the men surrounded the building. Trip knew what came next before McGuire spoke the order for tear gas. Canisters shattered the side windows and smoke billowed out. A handful of men ran outside but were shot before they reached their cars. Trip hadn't noticed a gun in any of their hands.

More shots rang out. At first, Trip thought the people inside the building shot each other, then one of the body cams picked up a Marine taking a bullet to the head.

"Cover and move in," McGuire shouted.

The Marines returned a volley of fire, and the shots from inside the building stopped. Trip watched transfixed as the cameras inched closer and closer to the barn. She'd done the same countless times before, but watching from a distance proved worse. With a gun in her hand, surrounded by her men, she could control the situation. Here, she could do nothing but watch it unfold.

The back half of the barn exploded, sending burning debris and Marines flying. The second explosion took out the front and ignited the cars parked adjacent to the building, including Carson's BMW. *Carson. Nate. Oh, God. No, please, not Nate.*

Trip grabbed the edge of the table to keep from toppling over. Carson and Nate were inside or bleeding outside. The third explosion surprised her. It came from the same area as the first. One of the body cams jostled violently and went dark. Screaming filled the room as light filled the camera.

The concerned face of a Marine filled the screen. "Fee. Hang on, buddy. I got you."

Trip wanted to look away, to cover her ears and muffle the agonizing screams that bounced off the sterile white walls around her, but she couldn't. The young man, practically a boy, who had grinned as he escorted her to medical would die today. If he had to endure the pain, she could endure hearing his cries.

She squared her shoulders against the sound until it stopped. The gurgled breath and silence that replaced the cacophony crippled her. She imagined Nate and Carson taking their last breaths, dying quickly in the flash of flames. The broken pieces inside her could handle the sounds of battle, but the stillness of death proved too hard to bear.

"Excuse me." She turned and used every ounce of her remaining strength to walk, not run, from the room. McGuire called after her, but she continued walking, safe in the knowledge that he couldn't follow. He had men in the field waiting for guidance.

FORTY-FOUR

TRIP PUT THE CAR IN DRIVE AND HEADED for the guardhouse. They wouldn't stop her when exiting. The smart person guarded the entrance to keep the threat from entering. Who cared when the threat left?

Trip had no idea where to go. Her career ended the moment she left the base. No, it ended the moment she fell in love with Nathaniel Benz and opened her heart to Carson James. Somewhere in Crystal Beach, a baby waited to meet her father. Another little girl waited for her dad to take her away. Nate's parents waited for their son. No one waited for her.

A few miles down the road, Trip pulled into an industrial park and cut the engine. It occurred to her that she should cry, or scream, or something. Instead, she sat in the car and stared out the window. If any thoughts came, she didn't notice, nor did she notice the passing of time. They were gone.

How had she come to care so much for these men? Trip knew from the get go they were trouble, the kind of men she'd spent her career putting away. Fiorelli's last breath echoed through her memory, bringing a rush of tears.

Trip laughed. *I can cry over some wet-behind-the-ears Marine, but I can't conjure a single tear for Carson or Nate?*

She hadn't truly understood the depth of her feelings for Nate until he walked into that barn. It had taken every ounce of strength to keep up appearances and ignore his call.

His call! Why did I ignore him? I should have told him to run. Warned him. She turned the phone on and waited. It buzzed once, and the voicemail icon flashed on the screen.

"I can't do this." She tossed the phone onto the pavement and started the car. "Damn it."

What am I doing?

Trip cut the engine and scrambled out the door for the phone. Nate had left her a message. It could have to do with Izzy. She would honor her promise to take care of the baby, the only thing she had left. Izzy waited for her.

Nate's voice filled her ear. "Babe. It's after one. I'm at Tampa Harbor on Tyson Ave. I'll wait until four. I love you."

Trip checked the time of the call, then backtracked in her mind, trying to figure out what time he'd escorted Carson to the barn. It didn't add up. The marina sat on the south side of the city, easily an hour and a half drive from Crystal Beach.

Between her blurry vision and shaking hands, it took three tries to return the call.

"Hello?"

Her brain refused to make sense of the voice on the other end of the line. It couldn't be Nate. He never answered with anything but his last name or *yeah*. "Who is this?"

The voice chuckled. "Who did you call?"

Her throat tightened. "Ham-thaniel?"

"Trip? Where are you?"

"Nate? How? I saw you? I saw you at the barn."

"Babe, I've been waiting for you at the marina since noon. Are you coming?"

She nodded.

"Trip?"

"Yes, yes. I'm on my way. Have you spoken to Carson?"

"Earlier. He asked to see Izzy, but I didn't dare go back to Crystal Beach. Tom called, they found John."

"Nate." She drew an unsteady breath. "Someone who looked a lot like you drove Carson to the sit-down. No made it out of that building alive."

Nate made a noise that sounded like his heart broke.

"I'm sorry."

"Mack. He must have had Mack drive him. He knew the feds would be watching."

Trip's breath caught in her throat. Carson had followed through on his promise. He got Nate out free and clear. Unless forensics identified the body, the world would consider Nathaniel Benz deceased. "I'm on my way. Do you have the girls?"

"All present and accounted for. All we need is you."

To Trip, the seven-mile drive took hours. Every stoplight, every slow vehicle, kept her from Nate and the girls. She couldn't wrap her brain around what had happened.

Trip skidded into a parking spot and grabbed her bag. Row after row of shiny white boats filled her vision. The sun hung low, glaring off those rows of boats. She hadn't thought to ask which dock, let alone which vessel.

A mournful howl drew her attention. She'd know that sound anywhere—Mabelle. Trip turned and headed toward the calls of the Bassett Hound.

"Trip!" Sophie ran toward her on the wooden dock.

Oh, baby, don't run. You'll stumble and fall into the water. The thought tumbled through her head and made her smile. So, she did have a little maternal instinct after all.

Trip slung the bag over her shoulder and walked toward her family, two motherless daughters for a daughterless mother, and a man who knew her secrets and loved her anyway.

THE END

ABOUT THE AUTHOR

Kathryn M. Hearst is a southern girl with a love of the dark and strange. She has been a story teller her entire life, as a child she took people watching to new heights by creating back stories of complete strangers. Besides writing, she has a passion for shoes, vintage clothing, antique British cars, music, musicians and all things musical (including theatre). Kate lives in central Florida with her chocolate lab, Jolene; and two rescue pups, Jagger and Roxanne. She is a self-proclaimed nerd, raising a nerdling.

Find more books by Kathryn:

https://www.amazon.com/author/kathrynmhearst

https://www.kathrynmhearst.com

Newsletter:

http://eepurl.com/cmk6dv

People are sustained by eating food. Authors live on reviews. Please consider leaving a review for The Twelve Spirits of Christmas on Amazon, Goodreads, or social media.

Proof

Made in the USA
Charleston, SC
07 February 2017